Black

C000256719

S J Ricnards

BLACK MONEY

Published worldwide by Apple Loft Press

This edition published in 2023

Copyright © 2023 by S J Richards

S J Richards has asserted his right to be identified as the author of this work in accordance with the Copyright, Design and Patents Act 1988.

www.sjrichardsauthor.com

For Abby, Matt and Tommy

The Luke Sackville Crime Thriller Series

Taken to the Hills

Black Money

Fog of Silence

Chapter 1

Tania stifled a yawn. She had expected to be held up at the border, but not for so long, and it was now almost twenty-four hours since the bus had left Odessa. What was worse, she had been awake for most of the journey. The seat was stiff, the back upright and inflexible, but it was the snores of the woman next to her that had put paid to any decent sleep.

Her mother had been in tears when she waved her off at the station, unable to accept that what Tania was doing was sensible. Which was nonsense of course. It was only five nights and then she'd be back. She was a grown woman and Poland was a safe country. Besides, it wasn't as if she would be alone.

Ripples of excitement ran through her body as she thought of meeting Pavlo for the first time. She took out her phone to look for his photo, but it was the image on the home screen that grabbed her attention. She stared at it for a while, remembering what a wonderful spa day she and her mother had shared. They wore identical white dressing gowns and were both smiling as they held glasses of Prosecco up to the camera.

Tania realised her own eyes were becoming moist, took a tissue from her bag and dabbed at them. She had to admit making the decision to come to Krakow was hard for her too. It was the first time she and her mother had spent even a night apart since her diagnosis a decade earlier. The leukaemia was long gone, but those first two years had been devastating. She had been thirteen and wouldn't have been able to get through it without her mother's love and support.

The big positive, though, was the bond it had built

between them. They were unbelievably close.

Tania looked out of the window and realised that the fields had been replaced by warehouses. She turned to the woman in the aisle seat.

"Is this Krakow?" she asked.

"Of course, girl. Didn't you see the sign?"

A few minutes later they turned into a bus station and drew to a halt. Tania got off and walked to the side to wait for the driver to open the luggage compartment.

"That one," she said, pointing to it and speaking in Russian. He was Ukrainian so she knew he would understand. Just as well, she thought, because her Polish was very limited.

When he retrieved her backpack she put it over her shoulders and looked around. It wasn't what she had expected. She had heard Krakow was a delightful city and a big draw for tourists but the bus station was ultra-modern, all angles and sharp edges, and was surrounded by shops. It was ugly but she knew there was an old part, and that was where she had arranged to meet Pavlo. She was sure it was beautiful there, all she had to do was find it.

She pulled her city guide out of her bag and opened it to the transport section. It told her that the best way to the Old Town was by walking, using an underground route through the Krakow Glowny train and transit centre. She looked at her phone to find there was no reception. Never mind, she'd call her mum and dad when she was back above ground.

It was only a ten-minute walk and she emerged into an enormous square. The contrast with the bus station was incredible. In front of her was a beautiful old church, while on either side of it were elegant townhouses. There were many people milling around, a mixture of locals and tourists. She turned around to see she had emerged from an old market and recalled it being called the Cloth Hall. It too was stunning.

Tania looked at her watch. It was still only nine in the morning, and she wasn't due to meet Pavlo until eleven. She was hungry and decided to ring home then grab something to eat and have it on one of the many benches dotted around the square.

Her mother picked up on the first ring. "How was the journey, my love?" she said.

"Long but okay. I'm in the market square in Krakow now. It's very beautiful."

"Is it safe?"

"Please try not to worry about me, Mum. I'll be fine."

"Have you met Pavlo yet?"

"Not yet. We're meeting in two hours."

"Let me know what he's like, won't you?'

"Of course. I'll give you a call this evening. Give Dad my love."

"I will." Tania could hear a tremor in her mother's voice as she added, "Love you."

"Love you too, Mum."

She hung up, stared at the screen for a moment then put the phone into her back pocket. She sighed and turned back to face the Cloth Hall. Right, she thought, let's try those breaded cutlets that are supposed to be a Krakow speciality.

*

Tania took another sip of her Coca Cola Lite, taking care not to spill any. She was sitting at the cafe outside the Bonerowski Palace Hotel, directly in front of the market square. Drinks were ridiculously expensive but still, she would be meeting Pavlo for the first time and to do so at such an outstanding place would make it all the more memorable.

She had used the hotel bathroom to change into a deep

pink sleeveless dress that hugged her figure in all the right places. He was going to love it.

She felt butterflies in her stomach. Would he turn out to be as nice as he had been in all their conversations? Of course he would. They had talked on Viber endlessly, almost every day in the last few weeks, and he had proved himself to be a real romantic. Although he was originally from Lviv he now lived in Warsaw but had suggested they meet in Krakow because 'it is a beautiful city as befits a beautiful girl'. Who could resist flattery like that? He had sparkling eyes too and a cheeky sense of humour.

Yes, she knew a lot about Pavlo and she was unbelievably excited by the thought of meeting him. She wanted to look in his eyes, savour their first embrace, lose herself in their first kiss. She felt sure that she would know straight away whether he was right for her.

She looked at her watch. It was nearly eleven so he should arrive at any time.

There was a tap on her shoulder. She turned, already smiling, but it wasn't Pavlo. It was an older man, probably in his early thirties. He smiled back.

"Are you Tania?" he said in fluent Russian.

"Yes, but you're not…"

He laughed. "No, I'm not Pavlo. I am Sacha, Pavlo's friend. We've known each other for many years." He looked her up and down. "I must say you look lovely."

"Thank you. But where is Pavlo?"

"Aha." His smile grew even broader. "He wants to make your first meeting memorable and has arranged something rather special."

"Oh," she said, both confused and delighted at the same time. She looked around. "Is he here?"

"He and his…" he winked, "surprise are down the street." He put a fifty zloty banknote on the table. "Please come with me."

She followed him as he led her down the lane at the

side of the hotel. After a hundred metres or so he turned left then almost immediately right. "Don't worry," he said over his shoulder. "We're nearly there. The surprise will be worth the walk I assure you."

Suddenly he stopped and gestured to a narrow alley to the right. "Please go down there, Tania. You will love what Pavlo has prepared for you, I promise."

He gave way and she passed him and turned down the alley. She was smiling herself now, a bit nervous but with anticipation rather than fear.

No one was visible, and it looked like it was a dead end, but as she got twenty metres down she heard two people talking quietly to each other. She saw there was a door open a few metres ahead and realised the sounds were coming from there. She stepped up to the door and pulled it towards her, but there was no one behind it. She turned back to find Sacha standing immediately in front of her.

He was no longer smiling.

Tania started to say something but before she could speak someone grabbed her from behind, pinning her arms to her side. They dragged her back into the building, Sacha following. She tried to scream but he leaned forward and pressed his hand over her mouth.

He smiled again.

"Surprised?" he said.

Chapter 2

Once every two weeks, Monday if they could do it, ex-DCI Luke Sackville and DI Pete Gilmore met for breakfast before work. They were good friends, and had been for nearly a decade, but there was more to it than that. Luke found it useful to pick the brains of, and occasionally ask for advice from, his old number two. Pete, for his part, liked having someone he could run ideas by.

Luke checked his watch. It was just gone eight so he was running a few minutes late. Filcher had a meeting with his direct reports every Monday morning at 9:30 and much as he found them tedious he needed to be there on time.

He opened the door of The Good Bear Cafe and immediately spotted Pete in the far corner. To his surprise, he wasn't alone and was deep in conversation, although it seemed to be the woman with him who was doing most of the talking. She had brown hair tied back in a ponytail, strong features and an aura that signalled police with a capital 'P'.

Pete looked up as he approached. "Hi Luke," he said.

Before he could introduce her, his companion held her hand out. "Pleased to meet you," she said. "I'm Shirley Davenport. I've heard a lot about you."

Luke sat down. "From Pete?" he asked.

"From a lot of people." She smiled. "And I've only been here a week."

"Been here?"

"I've taken up the role of Deputy Chief Constable now that Alan Hudson has retired."

"Congratulations."

"Thanks."

Luke hesitated. "It's nice to meet you," he said, "but I

have to ask. Why are you here, Ma'am?"

"Please call me Shirley." She paused as a waiter came to their table. Luke confirmed he'd have his usual.

"We've already ordered," Pete said.

Shirley clasped her hands together, looked down at the table briefly, then lifted her eyes to Luke. "One of my responsibilities," she said, "is co-ordinating our response to organised crime, and it's clear that we haven't been making as much progress as we should. We've been pulling people in who we know are involved, drug dealers mainly, but they're at the bottom of the food chain and we're struggling to catch those in charge."

"The fact is, Luke…" she lowered her voice, "…they're scared. We ask them questions and they give us answers but they're inconsistent and our teams end up on wild goose chases. If I could use lie detectors I would, but since I can't I need someone on my team who is as effective as a polygraph." She let her words hang in the air.

"I'm not rejoining," Luke said.

Shirley held her hand up. "I'm not asking you to. I want you to work for us as a paid consultant."

Luke considered this for a few seconds. "My job at Filchers can be pretty full on. How much time would you require?"

Shirley smiled as she saw she'd got her man. "Not much," she said. "A few hours a week at most."

A waiter arrived and placed their plates in front of them: an English breakfast for Pete, a bacon roll for Shirley and steak, egg and chips for Luke. Shirley wrapped her roll in some tissue and stood. "Don't get up. I'll eat this on the way to my car." She gestured to Luke's meal and smiled. "Enjoy your little snack. It's been good to meet you. I'll get someone to draw the papers up and send them over."

Once she had left Luke reached for the English Mustard and put a spoonful next to his steak. "Thanks for that, Pete," he said as he began sawing into his sirloin. It was rare, just as he liked it. "You could have at least warned me."

"She asked me not to," Pete said. "Ordered me really. I didn't have any choice."

"I'll have to tell Filcher." The corners of his mouth turned up. "Actually, that'll be fun."

*

It was still only a couple of months since Luke had joined Filchers but he already felt comfortable as Head of Ethics and had had no hesitation in taking the role up on a permanent basis. Everything had calmed down since the first few weeks but that had given him a chance to build an understanding of how he and his team could best focus their efforts. In addition, he'd now met a lot of the key staff and had even been able to spend time with a couple of the account teams, one in Manchester and the other in Southampton.

As Luke walked into Head Office and nodded hello to the woman on reception he thought back to his interview and first meetings with his boss. It had been hard work initially because Edward Filcher was a pompous arsehole and it was clear he had reached his position through nepotism rather than skill. However, managing him had proven to be surprisingly easy. All he had to do was massage Filcher's ego and he became putty in his hands.

Glen Baxter, who Luke had worked with in the police and was now Head of Security, presented a different kind of challenge. Almost as tall as Luke, Glen had the body of Dwayne Johnson coupled with the brains of Daffy Duck. He was slow of mind and slow to action, a combination that could be frustrating to deal with.

Luke emerged from the stairs onto the Executive Floor and looked at his watch to see that it was just before 9:30.

"Good morning, Gloria," he said to Filcher's secretary. "Did you have a good weekend?"

"Lovely thanks, Luke. You can go in. The others are already there."

Luke opened the door to the office and walked in. Edward Filcher, Director of Internal Affairs, was at the end of his conference table and looked pointedly at his watch. "About time," he said. "I've got an important meeting at ten. Need to get on. Sit down, Luke."

To Filcher's left sat James McDonald who headed up Human Resources and next to him Glen Baxter. Fred Tanner, who had only recently taken up the role of Head of Marketing, sat opposite James and Luke took the remaining seat next to him.

Glen looked across at Luke as he sat down and smirked. "Nice of you to join us," he whispered.

"What was that?" Filcher said.

"I said it was nice of Luke to join us."

"Mmm." He seemed distracted. "Must be quick this morning. Have to go before ten. Need to hurry. Only one thing to cover. No time for Any Other Business."

"What's the one item on the agenda?" James asked.

"Oh, eh, what? The one item. Ah, yes, it's the Chairman, my Uncle Ambrose. He wants an Executive Conference, something about bonding, wanting to get to know the top team. The whole thing seems unnecessary to me. Bonding, pah." He snorted. "Let them eat cake, I say."

"That sort of thing can be very useful," James said. "I'd be happy to set it up and take on the planning and organisation."

Luke could see that James was keen for it to happen and decided to come to his rescue. "The visibility would be excellent for whichever section organised it," he said. "I'm sure the Sector Heads would like to pull it together. Shall I have a word with them Mr Filcher?"

"Visibility?"

"It would be a high-profile event."

"Mmm." Filcher paused for a moment, then nodded his head up and down, looking for all the world like a woodpecker digging for ants. "Perhaps you're right James. Visibility, eh?" He didn't wait for an answer. "And you would manage it, James? Under my remit, of course."

"I'd be happy to."

"Very well. As I say, these kind of events are the backbone of a company like ours. They foster teamwork, build camaraderie, enhance my, I mean everyone's, prospects."

James was about to reply when there was a knock at the door.

"What is it?" Filcher snapped as Gloria entered the room.

"Oliver Knight's here," she said.

"And?"

"He wants to speak to Luke."

Luke stood up and walked to the door before Filcher could say any more. "I'll be back as soon as I can," he said as he left the room.

The man sitting on the edge of Anna's desk was about Luke's age, early forties, with short neat swept-back hair, slightly greying. He sported an immaculate white shirt with a navy floral tie and looked every inch the business executive.

"Luke?" he said holding his hand out.

Luke shook his hand. "Nice to meet you, Oliver. How can I help?"

"What do you need, Oliver?" Filcher said, having followed them out of the room.

"I need to speak to Luke," Oliver said.

"About?"

"About eleven."

"Eh? I meant…"

"Eleven will be fine, Oliver," Luke said. "I'll come up to

your office."

"Great. I'll see you then."

"What?" Filcher said looking first at Luke and then at Oliver.

"We're meeting at eleven," Luke said. "Cheers, Oliver."

"See you later, Luke." Oliver said as he started to walk away.

Filcher looked at Oliver, gave a little harrumph and then turned his attention back to Luke. "I won't be able to join you. Important meeting at ten."

"Yes, you said."

"Keep me in the loop. Touch base."

"Yes, Mr Filcher."

"Right." He looked at his watch. "Need to finish."

"Before we go back in, Mr Filcher…"

"Yes. What? Very busy."

"I met the Deputy Chief Constable this morning."

"Really. Deputy Chief Constable, eh?" Filcher bent his head to one side. "What's his name?"

"Her name."

"My word. What is the world coming to?"

"Her name's Davenport. She told me how effective you've been."

Filcher thrust his chest out. "Did she indeed?"

"She was full of praise."

"I'm not surprised she's heard. I run a very tight ship."

"You do, Mr Filcher."

"Yes." Filcher nodded his head up and down.

"She wants to build a relationship."

"Does she? Does she indeed? And this is the Deputy Chief Constable?" He put emphasis on the last two words.

"Yes. She suggested I work as a part-time consultant for her. You and she would then both be my boss. You would be peers."

"Peers, eh?" Filcher savoured the word. "Yes, she and I should touch base regularly. Make sure we're on the same page. It needs executive management to take a helicopter view, keep the rudder straight and ensure we've got all our ducks in a row."

"Excuse me, Mr Filcher," Gloria said. "Your car's here."

"Ah right," Filcher said. "And do you have…?"

"I bought them on the way in." She passed him a box of six golf balls.

"Excellent, excellent." He started walking to the lift, and Luke could hear him mumbling three words over and over under his breath as he did so. "Deputy Chief Constable, Deputy Chief Constable, Deputy Chief Constable."

Chapter 3

The morning catch-up was going well, helped by the fact that there were only four of them and Josh's commentaries on each and every task, although sometimes illuminating and always entertaining, were missing.

Luke had to admit Josh was a valuable member of the Ethics Team though. He was young and inexperienced but keen to learn. The team's job was to ensure everything in the company was done ethically, and this often involved deep-diving into what was going on in the various delivery and support departments. In the police this would be called detective work, so it had seemed logical to send Josh on a detecting course. Unsurprisingly, Filcher had objected, but a quick reminder of the benefits and kudos it would bring him personally had soon won him around.

It had been a couple of months since the team had been formed and they had settled into a routine. It was new for all of them, Luke included, but he was soon able to get a handle on priorities and how they should use their time to best advantage. His experience as a Detective Chief Inspector at Avon and Somerset Police had been surprisingly valuable in getting to grips with what was needed.

"Helen," he said, "How's it going with Cartwrights?"

"All but finished, Luke," she said in her soft Edinburgh accent. "They'd missed out the clause on corporate social responsibility, but I've sorted it now." She smiled. "They tried to claim they didn't need one because they're in the public sector but I soon put paid to that wee argument."

"Good work," he said and meant it. Cartwrights supplied stationery to all government departments and were notoriously difficult to work with. They must have thought Helen would be easy to deal with but although she was fifty-nine, short of stature and everyone's image of a dear old granny, she was also tenacious as hell and loved it when she was drawn into a confrontation.

He turned to Maj. "What about you, Maj? Any luck with your review of Head Office security systems?"

"Still struggling, Luke. Girt great obstacles at every junction."

Luke smiled to himself. Maj was Somalian by birth and his use of Bristol idioms always came as a surprise. "Is it Glen?" he asked. Glen Baxter was Head of Security and he and Luke had history that preceded their time at Filchers.

Maj nodded. "Who else? He told me I was wasting my time."

"I'll have a word with him."

"Thanks."

Luke turned his attention to Sam who had been the biggest surprise of all. In his ignorance, he had always held the view that accountants were nothing more than bean counters, boring and good for nothing more than manipulating spreadsheets. Her skills and strength of personality had blown this view out of the water.

"I heard you had a run-in with the Head of the Communications Sector," he said.

"And some," Sam said. She brushed her hair off her shoulder before continuing, almost under her breath, "She's such a pompous ass."

"Filcher with tits," Helen said. She held her hand up. "Sorry, Luke, but it's true."

Sam laughed. "You've hit the nail on the head there, Helen. She told me our, and I quote, 'little section' needs to get its priorities straight."

"Do you need me to…" Luke started to say.

Sam broke in before he could finish the sentence. "It's sorted now," she said. "She's given me full access to their financial files."

Luke wanted to ask how she'd achieved such a breakthrough but decided to leave it. "That's great," he said and paused before continuing. "Right, I think that's everything covered. It seems like we've got a lot of work on."

"You can say that again," Maj said. "No Josh either."

"You're right. That should help."

"How's he getting on?" Sam asked.

"The course only started mid-morning yesterday," Luke said, "but he was on the phone to me as soon as the last lecture finished and he's full of it. He's learnt a lot more jargon so we can expect a whole bunch of that when he gets back."

"He'll think he's a right wee Sherlock Holmes," Helen said with a chuckle.

Luke looked at his watch and stood up. "I need to go," he said. "I've got to see Oliver Knight at eleven about the comms contract."

Sam reached for her crutches.

"When are they taking the plaster off?" Helen asked.

"Next Monday," Sam said. "I can't wait."

"Just a minute," Maj said. "In Josh's absence..."

Luke held his hand up. "Don't," he said.

Maj ignored him and smiled. "Be safe everyone," he said.

*

It was dot on eleven when Luke got to Oliver's office. Despite the brief nature of their earlier encounter, he had taken an immediate liking to the man. He exuded confidence but was friendly with it and exhibited none of the arrogance Luke had witnessed in some of the other Client Directors.

He knocked and entered without waiting for a reply.

Oliver was sitting down, two manila folders in his hand and papers over most of his desk, his suit jacket thrown over the left-hand side. The office was very small, with room for his desk a couple of chairs and nothing else. There were several cardboard boxes on the floor which were half-full, or in some cases full, of folders.

"Excuse the mess," he said. "I'm trying to get everything together before setting off for Oxford. Please take a seat. I'll be with you in a second." He stood up and put the two folders in his hand into one of the boxes on the floor, picked three other folders from his desk, looked briefly at them then added them to the same box before sitting back and sighing. "Sorry about this. I'm under the pump today. I want to make sure I get there by five if I can so that I can meet my direct reports and welcome them to Filchers."

Oliver took his glasses off and laid them on the desk. "Need them for reading," he said. "It's a recent thing. Sign of age I guess." He paused to collect his thoughts, then sat back and looked over at Luke. "Thanks for coming to see me. As you know, this is a big win for Filchers. It's worth thirty million over five years and we're taking on six hundred staff from Supracomm."

"Finance and call centre staff?"

"Yes, as well as IT development and operations. We're putting in sixty of our own people to improve business processes and help us reduce costs. Inevitably, there'll be job losses but, as you'll have no doubt gathered in your time here, that's the nature of what we do."

"I appreciate that," Luke said. "Is that where your issues lie? Are there some ethical considerations connected to redundancies?"

"No, it's nothing to do with the job losses. There are some financial anomalies. It's probably something and nothing but Robert Entwhistle thinks some of the existing processes look unwieldy."

"Robert Entwhistle?"

"He's one of our business process improvement consultants, our best probably. He specialises in finance, having been an accountant himself earlier in his career, and he's been insistent this needs looking into by someone independent."

"Isn't it normal for processes to be over-engineered though?" Luke asked. "Isn't that the reason functions are outsourced in the first place?"

"It is, but he felt these were particularly odd. It's all to do with the budgeting for some of the call centre functions. He feels they don't match up with the processes as he understands them, almost as if some numbers are being hidden."

"So he thinks someone is taking money and fiddling the accounts to hide it?"

"Possibly, but to be honest he didn't get much further. I kept him in there for a few more days but he met too much resistance from management. That's why I thought it would be best to get an accountant in as part of the team, rather than as an investigating consultant, and see if he or she can get a proper understanding of what's going on."

"I see," Luke said. "Would you happen to know the names of the people who were stopping Robert from finding out more?"

"Yes, he told me. Just a second." He picked his phone up from the desk, clicked a couple of buttons then read from the screen. "Audrey Manners, she's the Call Centre Manager, and the other one, wait a minute…" He clicked another button. "Ah, here it is. Mike Swithin, Lead Accountant."

"That's great. I'll pass those names on to Sam Chambers, the accountant on our team, and see if she can get up to Oxford as soon as possible." He stood up and walked to the door, then turned back. "I'll keep you up to date with progress. Good luck tonight."

"Thanks, Luke, and thanks for looking into this."
"No problem."

Chapter 4

Day two of the course and Josh was loving every minute. If he was honest a lot of it wasn't relevant to his role at Filchers, but golly it was fun! On Thursday he would be spending half a day on counter-espionage and counter-surveillance which he was really looking forward to. He doubted he would ever have to do stuff like find bugs hidden in light fittings but still.

Day One had definitely been relevant. The lecturer, an ex-Detective Inspector from the Met Police, had told them how to document and start an investigation. He'd covered assessment, dealing with the complainant, agreeing objectives and preparing an investigation plan. Josh had taken copious notes and Leanne had seemed impressed when he'd rung her to tell her all about it.

"I said bolognese or the chicken?" the lady serving the food asked impatiently.

"Pardon?" Josh said, his train of thought suddenly interrupted. "Oh, ah, sorry." He held his plate out. "Bolognese please." She doled out the food and he grabbed a spoon and fork and queued up to pay.

The girl in front of him turned around. "Are you enjoying the course?" she asked. She was about his age, maybe a couple of years older, and very pretty. Not as nicely made up as Leanne, hardly any make-up at all really, but with long brown hair that framed her face and emphasised her full lips and deep brown eyes.

He realised she was staring at him. "I, ah, what?" he said.

"You were in the front row this morning weren't you?"

Josh gulped. "Oh hi, yes."

"I'm Mandy."

"Fly me."

She raised one eyebrow. "What?"

"Sorry. It's a song. " He paused for a second. "By 10cc."

"I know."

"Right. Of course you do. Being called Mandy it must happen all the time."

"What must?"

"The song thing. 10cc or Barry Manilow."

"Barry Manilow?'

"You kissed me and stopped me from shaking."

"Ok-aaa-yyy." She drew the word out so that it became two long syllables and then turned away, paid for her meal and turned back to face him again.

"Do you want to join me at a table, Music Man?" she asked.

"Eh?"

"I don't know your name."

"Oh sorry. Josh. It's Josh. I'm Josh."

"Right, so do you…"

"What, uh, oh, the table. Yeah, sure. Gucci."

"Gucci?"

"Yes, ah, definito."

He paid and followed her to a table in the corner of the canteen, pulling out a chair opposite and plopping himself into it.

"Did you enjoy this morning's lecture?" Mandy asked.

"Absolutely. It was great learning how to use experts and inspect the scene of the crime."

"The crime?"

"Not the crime, ah, the incident, the event, whatever."

She bent to her food, the corners of her mouth turned up slightly, then looked back up at him. "You're new to all this, aren't you?"

His mouth was full of spaghetti and he chewed quickly so that he could answer.

Mandy held her hand up. "You don't need to say

anything." She tapped the side of her nose. "I'm a detective, so I know these things."

He swallowed quickly. "You are?"

"I was joking. I work for Integrity, have you heard of them?"

Josh shook his head, his mouth full of food again.

"It's one of the largest private investigation teams in England," she went on, "and I'm based in our London head office. I joined two years ago as a legal advisor after I graduated, but now they've said I can become an investigator and they put me on this course."

"That's exciting."

"Yes, it is. What about you? Are you planning to go it alone, or are you in a company like Integrity?"

"I ah…" He pointed at his mouth and then chewed and swallowed his latest mouthful before continuing. "I work for an ex-DCI."

"That's exciting."

"It is, but it's not a private investigation company. We're a small team within a large outsourcing business. I'm based here in Bath. We're responsible for Ethics."

"Ethics?"

She was staring at him now and he was struck again by how pretty she was. Her eyes shone and her smile was lovely.

"I've got a girlfriend," he blurted out, the pitch of his voice higher than normal.

She put her hand on his and he drew it back quickly. "I'm not chatting you up, Josh," she said. "You don't have to worry." She paused and a serious look came over her face. "I'm gay."

"You are?"

She laughed. "No, but really, you have to relax. Okay?"

"Okay."

"What do you think about this afternoon? I'm not sure how useful it's going to be. Missing persons investigations are pretty rare."

"I'm really looking forward to it. And to be honest, I could have done with that part of the course a month or two ago."

"Really, why?"

He told her about the women who had gone missing at Filchers, and how they had eventually tracked their abductor down. "I do have to make an admission though," he said when he'd finished.

"You made it all up?"

"No, but I, ah, well I told the team they were called whispers."

"Instead of mispers?"

He nodded.

"I've only known you thirty minutes, Josh," she said, smiling, "but somehow that doesn't surprise me at all."

Chapter 5

Eleanor was worried about John's deteriorating health. He was only forty-eight, a year older than her, but he'd suffered from Crohn's disease since his early twenties and the symptoms had been particularly bad in the last few weeks. Specialist consultants cost a lot, especially in the United States, but she kept telling him it was worth the money if it made him feel better. He resisted of course, that was the way he was, but when her husband had died he'd left her with a decent pot of money and she couldn't think of a better way to use it than to help the person she loved.

She looked up at the Welsh dresser, smiled and blew her husband a kiss. It was the photo she treasured the most, taken by a fellow guest when they visited Seville to celebrate Mandy's eighteenth birthday. Duncan and Eleanor stood on either side of their daughter on the terrace, arms around her shoulders, all three smiling and holding forward their glasses of rioja. It had been almost exactly a year later that Duncan was diagnosed with terminal bowel cancer. It had been a rough few years since he had died, but meeting John had done a lot for her mental well-being.

Eleanor took another sip of her tea and debated whether to ring him. She had spoken to him the previous evening but he hadn't messaged since and she was worried. What if his diarrhoea had come back? It was debilitating and caused him a lot of discomfort. On the other hand, she didn't want to bother him if he was napping or even just relaxing. The poor man had had to give up work because of his illness and she really felt for him.

She looked at her watch. It was eight, so that meant it was early afternoon in Florida. He probably was trying to catch forty winks. She'd leave it a few hours and ring him before she went to bed. She finished her tea, put the cup in the sink and went into the lounge.

Hers was a small bungalow with only two bedrooms, but plenty big enough for her and her cat Smoky. There was a spare room for Mandy when she came to stay and that was all she really needed. She sat down on the sofa and Smoky immediately leapt onto her lap. She stroked him absent-mindedly as he turned around two or three times before curling up in a ball.

She sighed. Her relationship with John had done wonders for her but she still felt lonely. She hoped they would be able to meet soon, that his wife would finally die. She hated wishing someone dead but the poor woman had been in a vegetative state since her accident. It would be a blessed relief for everyone when the doctors finally decided to turn her life support off. Eleanor fully understood that it would be inappropriate for her to visit John until that happened but it would be worth the wait. He really was a lovely man. She would never love him in the same way as Duncan of course, but she was growing fonder of him by the minute. He was so kind and caring, visiting his wife every day if his Crohn's allowed it.

Her phone rang and she grabbed it from the coffee table, hoping it was John. Mandy's photo came up and she felt a twinge of disappointment. She clicked the button.

"Hi Darling," she said. "How's the course?"

"It's great," Mandy said. "I met a really sweet guy today too. He's very funny."

"Boyfriend material?"

"Oh no, Mum. He's not my type. Already taken too. But he's amusing and it's great to have someone to talk to about the conference. What about you? How's John?"

"He wasn't feeling too bad when I spoke to him yesterday. I think the new drugs are helping."

"Poor man. It must cost him a lot too, especially given he's in Florida. How can he afford it?"

Eleanor hesitated before answering. She hadn't told her daughter she'd been helping John to pay for his treatment. It felt completely right to give him money, of course it did, but it was also Mandy's inheritance.

"Mum?" Mandy said.

"Sorry, Darling. I was miles away. The fact is, I've given John money towards his treatment."

Mandy hesitated before replying. "How much have you given him?"

For some reason, Eleanor didn't want to reveal the truth. "Not much," she said.

"And you're sure he's genuine?"

"Don't be silly, Mandy. Of course he's genuine. We talk every day and you should see how poorly he looks."

"Well if you're sure."

"I am, and he really appreciates my help. Keeps telling me not to, but it's the least I can do."

"How long have you known him now?"

"Almost five months." Eleanor thought back to when she'd first seen his profile on 'Plenty of Fish'. It was his honesty that had first attracted her to him, and she supposed she had felt sorry for him too, given everything that had happened to him and his wife.

"Any chance of meeting him? I know you can't go there because of his wife, but can he fly here for a quick visit?"

"His Crohn's is too bad, unfortunately, and he visits his wife almost every day. She's not going to recover and we'll get together when she's passed away..It's all right darling, I'm patient and I can wait. Tell me more though."

"About the course?"

"No, about this guy who's not your type."

"Mum, stop it!"

Chapter 6

Tania couldn't stop thinking about her mother and the agony she would be going through. She might at first have thought she had forgotten to ring, but as time went on…

She put her fingers to her eyes to wipe away the tears that were starting to form. How she wished she had never left home, lured to a foreign country by someone she now knew had been leading her on. Pavlo had seemed so genuine, so real, but Sacha had laughed when she had asked where he was. *Forget him*, he had said, *He is setting the bait for the next stupid bitch now.*

She shook her head. There was no point in moping about what had happened. Her situation might seem hopeless but she had to be strong and find a way to escape. She needed to remain alert so that she could take advantage of even the smallest opportunity.

But for now she had to be patient.

She looked around at the others. Several were asleep and they were split into two groups, she and four other women on one side while three men sat opposite. Crates were stacked from floor to ceiling at the rear of the lorry, and light came from a flickering fluorescent tube high up above the men. She had watched the crates being loaded in and they were clearly very heavy but there was no clue as to what they contained. It probably didn't matter anyway. It was the human cargo that was important.

For the first night she had been kept in the house Sacha had lured her to, her phone and bag taken from her so that all she had were the clothes she was wearing. She glanced down at her dress, dirty now and somehow tawdry, a sad reminder of what might have been.

The next day she was taken somewhere outside

Krakow, a blindfold tied tightly around her head for the journey. It was only removed when she and Izabella, the girl now asleep with her head on her shoulder, had been bundled roughly onto the lorry.

Izabella was Polish and spoke only a little English. She had fallen asleep with her head on Tania's shoulder within minutes of them setting off. The others had joined somewhere a long way from Krakow.

None of the other women spoke either Russian or Ukrainian and hadn't understood her English. The oldest of the three was about Tania's age, and smartly dressed as if for the office in a green belted dress, although her clothes were looking crumpled after the hours she had spent on the floor of the lorry. The other two girls were seventeen or eighteen. One was tall with short black hair in a bob and a black mini-skirt that showed off her long legs, while the other was of average height, but also dressed for an evening out in a short-sleeved jumpsuit with a low-cut v-neck.

Izabella nuzzled a little closer to Tania's neck but didn't wake up. Tania guessed she was only sixteen or so, a pretty young thing, with big blue eyes in a round face that was framed by blonde hair that was tied up in a bun.

With a start, Izabella raised her head and exclaimed something in Polish that Tania didn't catch. She looked wildly around and then at Tania.

"Where we are?" she asked.

Tania shrugged to indicate that she didn't know. She decided it would be prudent to pretend her English was as limited as Izabella's. "Many hours in lorry now," she said.

The three men looked up when they heard their exchange. It felt to Tania like they may have known each other before getting on board, even though she hadn't heard them say a word. Their poses were relaxed, despite the bumpiness of the ride, and they didn't share the haunted look that Tania was sure was on her own face and was certainly on Izabella's and the faces of the other three women.

"Where you live?" Izabella whispered.

"Odessa," Tania said, also keeping her voice low so the others couldn't hear. "In Ukrayeenah." She hesitated and then said her next words in broken Polish. "My mother is from Warsaw. Where are you from?"

"Krakow." Izabella's voice trembled as she said this.

"What happened to you?"

"I was with my two friends in the centre of Krakow. It was early evening and still light. A man brushed into me and apologised politely. He was very friendly and gestured for me to see something around the corner. When I followed him there were two other men and the three of them grabbed me and bundled me into the back of a van." Her lower lip shook as she added, "It was yesterday. My mother and my father will be really worried." She paused, put her hand to her head and pulled out the pin holding her bun in place. "My mother gave me this," she said, tears coming to her eyes.

"It's beautiful," Tania said, and it was indeed gorgeous. It was about ten centimetres long and U-shaped, but what made it stand out was the pearl that was set into twisted metal at the end. "Was it for a special occasion?"

"Yes, for my older sister's wedding. I was a bridesmaid." Izabella put the pin back in her hair. "It was only a week ago." She paused before continuing. "Do you know where they are taking us?"

Tania had wondered this herself. She was fairly certain they had picked the others up in Germany, which meant they were travelling west, but how far west she didn't know. Perhaps they would stop in Germany, or else drive on to the Netherlands, Belgium or France.

"I don't know," she said, and Izabella's next question seemed inevitable.

"Why?" Izabella asked.

This question had been burning Tania up. She was sure money wasn't the motive. She and her family and friends had very little and Izabella didn't look like she came from a wealthy background. She looked once more at Izabella's innocent face, then at the other three women. They all looked strained but were otherwise fit and well.

Tania shuddered. The answer was all too clear.

She looked over at the men. If she was right about why the women were there, then was the same true for the three men? Somehow she doubted it. Something about their poses suggested they felt in control, despite having been transported halfway across Europe in the back of a lorry.

The lorry came to a sudden stop and all eight occupants were thrown sideways. A few seconds later Tania heard the cab door opening and then closing again. Someone, presumably the driver, banged twice against the side of the lorry and the three men immediately stood up. Before she or the other women could do the same, the tallest of the men pulled a baton from his pocket and waved it threateningly. He was a big man, swarthy with ragged black hair.

"Bleib wo sie sind," he said, his tone aggressive.

This was gibberish to Tania and she continued to her feet. The man stood up and walked to within a metre of her, his top lip raised exposing his teeth. "Sit down," he hissed, "and stay quiet if you know what's good for you." His words were so clearly enunciated she felt certain he was English. He turned back to the German women. "Du auch."

Tania sat back down, put her arm around Izabella and looked over at the other two men, both of whom were looking at her and smirking. The one on the left nudged the other and whispered something in his ear. His companion chuckled and nodded.

"What is happening?" Tania asked.

"Border control," the man with the baton said.

"Welcome to the United Kingdom," he added. He smiled but it didn't reach his eyes. "Welcome to your future."

*

The lorry stopped about thirty minutes after they passed through Border Control. The men had been mumbling between themselves and Tania caught enough to know that the man with the baton, who seemed to be the leader, was called Greg.

Greg pulled the two crates off the top of the stack and sandwiches and bottles of water were passed through. He shared the food and Tania, who hadn't eaten for over twenty-four hours, tore into it, as did the other women. When she had finished she put the empty wrapper on the floor and took a glug of the water before looking over at him. "Where we are going?" she said.

"Never you mind," he sneered. "You'll find out soon enough."

The tallest, and probably youngest, of the three Germans suddenly stood up and advanced towards him. "Lass uns gehen!" she screeched. Greg stood up and shoved her hard in the chest with his left hand. She fell backwards awkwardly and her foot twisted as she landed. She immediately screamed and put her hand to her ankle. "Nein, nein," she said, now whispering, and Tania crawled over to her. She gently took the girl's hand off her foot and immediately saw that her injury was serious, her foot at an awkward angle.

Tania stood up and glared at Greg. "She is hurt," she said, her voice trembling.

Greg glared back, his eyes slits. He took a step forward and slapped her across the face. She recoiled and he punched her in the stomach causing her to buckle forward and put both hands on her belly. "Leave her," he said.

"We'll deal with her when we get there."

"Come," Izabella said behind her. "Sit down, Tania."

Tania backed up to Izabella and sat down. Her cheek burned and she was breathing heavily. Izabella put her arms around her. "We need to be quiet," she whispered.

"You all need to learn," Greg snarled, looking directly at Tania. "You're ours now and you do as I say. Do you understand?" Tania and Izabella nodded. He looked directly at the other three women. "Verstehen Sie?"

The German women nodded, though they couldn't bring themselves to look him in the eyes. The one who had fallen was sobbing, her hand back on her ankle. He bent over to her and lifted her face by the chin. "Verstehen Sie?" he said again, almost spitting the words out this time.

"Ja," she whispered.

He backed away and sat down with the other two men.

Chapter 7

Luke woke up early and decided a brisk walk with Wilkins would set him up for the day. He showered and dressed, then gave the cocker his morning bowl of kibble which, true to form, disappeared in a few seconds.

He let him off the lead as soon as they entered the field at the bottom of the back garden, and he set off immediately, darting this way and that way, familiar with the route and searching for new smells and experiences.

Luke looked back at the old stone farmhouse as he shut the gate. It had been left to him sixteen years ago by his favourite nanny when she died only a few weeks after a shock diagnosis of terminal cancer. She had been wonderful to him, his almost-Mum from the age of six until he was fourteen, caring, loving and understanding, the antithesis of his real mother.

It was a quirky building with many nooks and crannies, and he smiled as he recalled Chloe and Ben's games of hide and seek when they were seven or eight. They always seemed to find new places to squirrel themselves away, with the other twin eventually giving up and calling one of their parents for help.

Jess had loved it too. It was the perfect home for a growing family. Film nights were always special, he and his wife on the lounge sofa while the children sat on a rug on the floor feasting on pizza and chicken nuggets and taking in the latest Disney or Pixar film.

The memories flooded back: Jess laying out a picnic rug on the back lawn for the twins' birthday, her delight when he'd been promoted to Detective Chief Inspector, him opening a bottle of champagne when she sold her first painting.

What would Jess think of his new job? It was different, very different, from working in the police, but he knew she would be completely supportive, that was the way she was. He'd come home to tell her what had happened at work and she'd lap his anecdotes up, laughing at Josh's antics and expressing shock at Filcher's latest exhibition of bigotry.

God, he missed her. Time was a healer, they said, but how long did it take? The pain was still raw but it wasn't even nine months since she had died. Did it take two years, five years?

His thoughts were interrupted by barking and he looked around to see Wilkins running towards him clutching something in his mouth. *Not another dead bird*, he thought. As the spaniel grew closer he realised what it was.

"You stupid bugger," he said, as the dog dropped a rotting apple in front of him.

Wilkins sat back on his haunches and looked imploringly up at him, clearly proud of what he'd brought his master.

"Okay," Luke said as he fished a doggie treat out of his pocket. "Just one, boy." He held his hand out and Wilkins snaffled it, then turned and ran off again. Luke shook his head and set off to follow him around the field.

*

Luke was in the Ethics office when his phone rang. It was Gloria, Filcher's secretary.

"Can you come up, Luke?" she said. "Now? He told me it's urgent."

It always is. He closed his laptop and took the stairs to the Executive Floor.

"You can go straight in," Gloria said when she saw him.

He pushed the door open to see Filcher sitting at his desk, a broad smile across his face. He was mid-sentence and the man opposite him was leaning back in his chair looking relaxed and comfortable.

"…most important contract," Filcher concluded and looked up. He was wearing his usual navy waistcoat over a white shirt, and sporting what Luke guessed was an Old Etonian tie. Filcher saw him looking at it, lifted it with his right hand and waggled the end of it in the air. He looked over at the man opposite. "MCC. I'm a member you know." He smiled and sat back in his seat, before looking back at Luke, and saying in his most patronising tone, "Marylebone Cricket Club." He paused for a moment, evidently pleased with himself. "Sit down, Luke."

Luke ignored the instruction and held his hand out. "I don't think we've met have we?"

The other man stood up, smiled and shook his hand, his grip strong. He was in his late thirties, Luke guessed, a touch short of six foot with brown hair and a tightly clipped boxed beard. He was smartly dressed but in casual clothes, with brown chinos and a pale blue shirt unbuttoned at the top.

"Evan Underwood," he said. "Pleased to meet you."

"Luke Sackville."

They both sat down.

"As you know, Luke," Filcher said, "we're close to winning Project Iceberg." He smiled smugly. "It will be yet another government string in our bow. Evan has something hush-hush to tell us about it."

"Luke," Evan said.

"Eh, what?" Filcher bent his head forward, his beaked nose making him look like a pelican reaching for a fish.

"I can only share this information with Luke, Mr Filcher. I'm sure you understand."

Filcher's eyebrows narrowed and he gave out a little harrumph before sitting forward in his chair. "Luke works for me, Evan," he said. "I need to know what he's working on. The Board expects me to have a handle on everything he…"

Evan interrupted him. "No," he said.

"I beg your pardon."

"This is 'need to know', Mr Filcher. Would you mind leaving us for a few minutes?"

"But this is my…" He harrumphed again, before adding, almost under his breath, "I mean really."

"I would greatly appreciate it. We'll only be a few minutes."

Filcher stood up, took his suit jacket from the coat rack and pulled it on. He opened the door and then turned around again, "Please inform Gloria when I can have *my* office back."

Evan waited until Filcher had closed the door. "Is he always like that?" he said.

"Always," Luke said. "Are you police?"

"Not quite, but a good guess. MI6. You're ex-police aren't you?"

Luke laughed. "Evan, I know you'll have done your research so please don't pretend you don't know exactly what my background is."

It was Evan's turn to laugh. He held his hand up. "Okay, you got me there." He paused, collecting his thoughts, before reaching down and pulling a sheet of paper from his briefcase. He passed it to Luke. "I'm sure you've seen one of these before."

Luke nodded as he skim-read the document. "Once," he said. Evan held out a pen and Luke took it and filled in his details before signing the declaration and passing it back. "This must be sensitive stuff if you're asking me to sign the Official Secrets Act."

Evan nodded. "Very. Have you heard of U-N-O-D-C, the United Nations Office on Drugs and Crime?" Luke shook his head. "I'm not surprised, they keep their profile pretty low. The Office was set up by member states to help combat drugs, crime, corruption and terrorism. I and colleagues across Europe and the Middle East have been working closely with them for the past six months looking at terrorist financing."

"And you're telling me this because?"

Evan took a deep breath. "I believe Filchers is carrying out money laundering for Al Ummah."

"Al Ummah?"

"It means 'The Community' in Arabic. They're what you might call a start-up." Evan laughed but it was humourless. "Their leader has stated that Al Qaeda has gone soft and more action is needed. We believe they are trying to amass funds ahead of a major operation against the West."

"My God," Luke said. "And you think Filchers is involved?"

"I do. Are you aware of the Supracomm contract?"

"Of course. The staff transferred to us yesterday. As it happens, one of my staff has joined the Finance Team."

"May I ask why?"

"A Filchers consultant spotted some anomalies, and the Client Director wants us to look at what's going on to make sure everything's ethical and above board."

"Mmm." Evan mused on this for a moment. "Do you know the nature of these anomalies?"

"I gather some of the numbers didn't seem to add up." He paused for a second. "If there's money laundering going on then that might explain it."

"It might indeed. Tell me, do people in Supracomm know that your man is from the Ethics team?

"It's a woman actually, her name's Sam Chambers, but to answer your question, no, only the Client Director knows."

"We need to keep it that way, Luke. Is she ex-police as well?"

Luke smiled. "No, she's an accountant. But she's already demonstrated a lot of other skills. She's a sharp cookie too."

Evan came to a decision. "I need to meet Sam as soon as possible to give her a full briefing," he said, "and I want you there. In fact, I want you closely involved until we crack this. Your police experience is going to be invaluable." He hesitated. "I need to warn her as well. We're dealing with an organisation that is absolutely ruthless and she needs to keep her investigations as subtle as possible so that she's under the radar. If she doesn't, she could be in great danger."

Luke looked at his watch. "She's in Oxford now. Do you want to meet her today?"

"Definitely. I'll book us a couple of rooms and let's see her this evening."

"Fine. I'll set it up."

"Thanks. You'll need my phone number." They exchanged contact details. "Are you okay to deal with Filcher?"

"No problem," Luke said. "Leave that pleasure with me."

They said their goodbyes and Luke opened the door. Filcher stood facing them next to his secretary's desk, his arms folded across his chest. Evan walked over to him.

"Nice meeting you," he said offering his hand.

Filcher shook it peremptorily. "Mmm," he said, then turned his attention to Luke as Evan made his way to the lift. "Luke, in my office."

Luke went back into the office and sat down. Filcher followed him in, hung his suit jacket up then descended slowly into his chair. He glared across the desk. "Spill the beans," he said. "What does the fellow want?"

"You understand I can't tell you everything?" Luke said.

"Of course not. Understand. Very secret. Has to be." Filcher sat back in his seat.

Luke paused. "I'm not sure I should really be telling you anything at all…"

"Don't be silly man, I need to know. You work for me."

"Yes, and I guess in your senior role…"

"Very much so. Senior role. I need to know," he repeated. He lowered his voice to a whisper. "Won't tell others, obviously, but important I understand. Help you get control. After all, you haven't been here long."

"You're right, Mr Filcher. I'm going to need your help and guidance."

"Indeed, indeed." Luke didn't say anything. "Well?"

"It's about Project Iceberg."

"I thought so!" Filcher said triumphantly. He clasped his hands together and lowered his voice again. "Have we won it?"

"It seems likely."

"Excellent, excellent. My hard work has paid off."

Luke wasn't aware Filcher had had any role in the bid but let it pass. "But there are a few people concerns," he said and Filcher's eyes widened. "Not you of course."

"No, of course not. Others then?"

"Yes, but I can't say who."

"Obviously." Filcher thought for a few seconds. "Magnus? " he prompted. "Or David perhaps?"

"I can't tell you the names, Mr Filcher."

"No, of course not. Need to know." He put his finger over his lips.

"I have to go to GCHQ today."

"Really. GCHQ, eh? Should I…'

"Just me, Mr Filcher."

"Of course. Understood. But keep me in the loop, won't you? Secretly, of course. Make sure we're on the same page."

"Naturally. You're my manager."

"Good, good."

Chapter 8

Josh and Mandy took their trays to the table they had used at lunchtime the day before. He had chosen the steak pie and had smiled nicely at the lady which bought him an extra serving of chips. He looked across at Mandy's plate. "What's that?" he said. "It looks very healthy."

"Caesar salad."

"Interesting. I usually love Italian food but that's a bit different." He paused. "Very salady."

"Well, it is a salad." She grabbed a piece of chicken, raised it to her mouth then stopped and looked over at him, her eyebrows raised. "It's not Italian though. Why would you think it was Italian?"

"Because…" he felt colour coming to his cheeks and bent to his plate again. "Ah, nothing."

"You thought it was named after the Roman Emperor didn't you?"

"Might have done."

She resumed eating, but found it hard to stop smiling. She looked up at him again. "I bet you think a waldorf salad contains waldorfs don't you?"

"Never heard of it," he said, "but I guess so." He decided to change the subject. "What did you think of this morning?"

"I thought it was great. Fascinating to learn how a criminal psychologist builds up a profile of someone, and how they use it to narrow the suspect list down."

"Seemed straightforward," he said. "I bet I could build a profile of someone. Go on, try me."

"How?"

"Well, imagine someone broke in, say to your parents' house."

"My Mum lives on her own."

"Right, no problem. So someone breaks into your Mum's house and they, uh, they take jewellery but leave her iPhone." She started to speak but he held his hand up. "No, I know your Mum probably hasn't got an iPhone but let's say she had and he left it. And say he also left some nice food for her cat."

"She's got a cat."

"Yeah, good. So he leaves food for the cat. That gives us information to build a profile, doesn't it?"

"We're looking for someone who likes cats and jewellery but not iPhones?"

"Ah, I guess it doesn't help much." He thought for a second. "Perhaps he looked on her laptop and found her financial details, and then the next day money gets taken from her account."

Mandy went quiet and bent her head to her plate.

"What is it?" Josh said.

"It's nothing."

She looked up and he could see there were tears in her eyes.

"What's wrong? Was it something I said?"

"It's the idea of money being taken from my Mum's account." She told him about John and his Crohn's disease.

"It's important she helps him," she went on, "but she hasn't got an infinite pot of money, about twenty thousand pounds. I'm worried about her mental well-being if it runs out and he can't afford any more medicine and treatment. She's on anti-depressants anyway, has been since Dad died, so heaven knows how she'll feel if she can't help him any more." She hesitated. "There's also a niggling worry that he might be fake. You hear about people being conned out of their life savings, don't you? I'm sure he's genuine though. My mum's no fool."

"Do you know how much she's spent so far?"

"No. When I rang her a couple of days ago she said not

much, but I'm not sure I believe her. Although John's British he lives in Florida and I know how expensive hospitals and doctors are in the States."

"I think you ought to ask again and try to get it out of her. Better to prepare her rather than have to cope with the aftermath if she does run out of money."

"Thanks, Josh, that's a good idea. I'll give her a call this evening."

*

The afternoon lectures covered matrimonial and domestic disputes. While Josh knew it would never be relevant to his role at Filchers he found it riveting, especially the bits around child care and custody. When the last session ended he said goodbye to Mandy, wished her luck with the call to her mother, then set out for Filchers. It was about fifteen minutes if he walked quickly, and he wanted to get there as soon as possible because he was seeing Leanne. He was growing very fond of her and hoped it was reciprocated. It would be fun telling her all the stuff he'd learned too, and she'd love hearing about the friend he'd made.

It was just after five-thirty when he arrived at Filchers and Leanne was already waiting outside looking as gorgeous as ever. She'd only just finished work but looked set for a posh night out. She wore a tight black dress with wide white lapels. It really showed off her curves. Her makeup was immaculate too, eyebrows neatly sculpted and lips a vivid red.

"Wow," he said as she pecked him on the cheek, "You look scrummy." He took her hand. "How long have we got?"

"Not long. I've got a lesson tonight and it starts at seven."

She was learning Russian because, she had told him, her

great-grandparents had been from Moscow. Josh was very proud of her industriousness. She was a hard worker and intent on improving herself having not gone to University because she'd been, in her words, 'a bit wild' in her teens and failed all her exams. She was intent on getting somewhere now though.

Like him, Leanne lived at home with her parents. Josh hadn't met them yet, but they'd talked about it. His heart fluttered a little when he thought about the prospect. It would be a distinct step up in their relationship.

He took Leanne's hand and they walked the short distance to Costa Coffee where Josh insisted on buying the drinks. Leanne asked for a cappuccino, and he ordered himself a luxury hot chocolate.

"Cream and marshmallows?" the girl behind the counter said.

He looked at her as if he couldn't believe what she had just asked. "Naturallo," he said.

They found a table with a couple of comfy armchairs and dropped into them. "Come on then, tell me all about it," Leanne said, wriggling still further into her seat.

"About what?" Josh said, pretending not to know what she was talking about. She tilted her head to one side and smiled. "Oh, okay then," he added. He launched into a description of every session, telling her how 'wowzy' this lecturer was or how 'incredibilo' he found a particular bit of information. The only break in his monologue was when the drinks arrived.

Leanne gazed at his hot chocolate in mock horror. "Are there enough marshmallows on that for you?" she asked.

"No," he said, eyes focused on the cup and his teaspoon already diving in, "but I'll cope."

It took him twenty minutes to bring her up to date. To Leanne's surprise, she found it interesting, though the real enjoyment came from Josh's savouring of every moment.

"I'm glad you're enjoying it," she said when he'd

finished describing that day's lectures.

"I made a friend too," Josh said.

"That's great. What's his name?"

"It's a girl. Her name's Mandy. She works for a detective agency in London."

"Really?"

"Yeah. She's great. We've had quite a laugh, talking about the lecturers and stuff."

"Really?"

"She's about a year older than me I think. She's on the legal side at the moment but they've offered her a job as an investigator. That's why they've sent her on the course."

"Really?"

"You'd like her a lot."

"Mmm."

Josh sat back in his armchair and smiled across at her. It wasn't returned.

"Is Mandy pretty?" she asked.

"Oh yes, very pretty." He continued smiling for a second or two before something clicked in his head. "Not as pretty as you," he added hastily. "She doesn't wear as much make-up and…"

"Is that because she doesn't need it?"

"No, uh, yes, but you don't, uh, you just do…wear more that is…and it suits you. You look lovely."

"And she doesn't?"

"Uh…" Josh put his hand to his throat and started rubbing it. "Do you want another cappuccino?"

"No thanks."

"Right, uh, I'll have another hot chocolate I think, uh, yes…" He got up, looked across at Leanne who was now staring fixedly out of the window, and then walked back to the girl at the counter.

She smiled across at him. "Same again?" she said.

"Just the luxury hot chocolate, please. My girlfriend's okay."

"That'll be four pounds eighty." She lowered her voice to a whisper as he retrieved his iPhone from his pocket to pay. "She's not though, is she?"

"What?"

"Your girlfriend's not okay."

He held his phone to the reader and then turned around to see Leanne still staring out of the window. "No. I, uh, I kind of put my foot in it."

"I heard. My advice is to change the subject and don't talk about this other girl again." He nodded, and she raised her voice back to its normal level. "Okay sir, I'll bring it over in a few minutes."

He swallowed. "Thanks," he said. He fell back into his chair, which no longer felt as comfortable as it had earlier, squirmed around, sat forwards and then back again.

"How are your parents?" he asked, trying to keep his tone natural.

She turned and looked him in the eyes, then shook her head as if shaking a fly away. "Not so good," she said.

"Why?"

"They're worried about my Aunty Pam. She's got herself into a financial mess." Leanne sat back in her chair again and curled her legs up in front of her.

Josh could sense he was returning to safer ground and had to fight to stop himself from smiling. He pursed his lips together and frowned. "Oh dear. What's happened?"

"She's been conned out of all her savings. Eight thousand pounds."

"That's awful." He was sincere now. "How did it happen?"

"She met this guy online and they got close. He's British but he lives in Florida and he started asking for money because he was ill and medical treatment was so expensive. Then he withdrew contact when the money ran out."

"Buggery-boo!" Josh exclaimed. "That's exactly like..." He caught himself just in time.

"Like what?"

Josh stared at Leanne, his mouth open, then past her to the girl at the counter who was shaking her head from side to side and mouthing 'Stop talking' at him.

"Josh, are you okay?" Leanne asked.

"Sure." He swallowed.

"Exactly like what?"

"Uh, like her."

"Like who?"

He gave a little laugh. "Like it. Not her, it." She raised an eyebrow. "The article," he went on. "I read an article. That's the 'it'. What happened to her, in the article, she's the 'her', yes, she's definitely the 'her', well it was exactly like..." He gestured vaguely with his hands.

"Josh, you're not making sense."

He swallowed, looked down at his mug and then back at her. "What's happening now? Is there any way your Aunty Pam can get her money back?"

"It doesn't seem that way. His phone's not connecting and he's not replying to her emails. She's in a right state. It's only three years since my uncle died so she's had a rough time and now this."

"How terrible," Josh said, his mind whirring.

Chapter 9

Luke had texted Sam but he was almost at his hotel when she rang.

"Sorry, Luke," she said. "It's not very easy to ring from work."

"Can you meet me this evening?" There was a pause at the other end, and he realised she was confused. "I've got important news to share with you and I'm in Oxford."

"I see. Yes, of course. I'm staying at the Leonardo."

"Is there a coffee shop nearby where I can pick you up?"

"Sure, the Wild Bean Cafe's almost next door."

"Anything a little further from the hotel?"

"Why, Luke?"

"I'll explain when we meet."

"There's a Starbucks. I can be there in fifteen minutes."

Luke looked at the car's sat nav. "That's about right for me."

Sam was waiting outside when he arrived. She threw her crutches in the back and then manoeuvred her way into the front passenger seat.

"I'll be glad when this thing is off," she said, gesturing to the plaster encasing her right leg from the knee to her ankle. She put her seat belt on and he set off. "Where are we going?"

"My hotel. It's the Manor and it's between Oxford and Bicester. I'll drop you back afterwards."

"Why not meet in the centre, or at my hotel? What's going on Luke?"

He snuck a sideways look at her. "There's someone we need to meet. His name's Evan Underwood and he's staying at The Manor as well."

"Is this connected to Supracomm?"

"Yes." He swallowed. "It turns out the anomalies you're looking into could be part of something much bigger."

"Is Evan from the police then?"

"Not quite, Sam. He's MI6."

Neither of them spoke for the rest of the journey, both deep in their thoughts. After fifteen minutes or so they pulled up at The Manor which, to Luke's surprise, turned out to be a rather grand Country House Hotel.

"I see there are different hotel grades for senior staff," Sam said, but there was a smile on her face.

Evan was sitting in reception when they walked in. He stood up, smiled and came over to shake their hands. "Hi again, Luke," he said, then turned to Sam. "And you must be Sam?" He looked down at her leg. "Been in the wars?"

"The perils of being an accountant," she said. "Dangerous occupation."

"Yes." He hesitated. "We'll go to my room if that's okay. We can order food from room service. I think it's best we don't talk in the main restaurant where we might be overheard."

Sam opened her mouth slightly and then turned to Luke. "What on earth is going on?" she said.

"You'll find out in a minute," Luke said. "Please, Evan, lead on. We'll use the lift if that's okay."

"Thanks," Sam said. She looked at Evan. "As you might have guessed, I'm none too wonderful with stairs at the moment."

They took the lift to the first floor where Evan led them to room 103. It was spacious, decorated in a modern style but retaining original features including a large Georgian sashed window that overlooked the lawns to the rear of the hotel. As well as the king bed, dressing table and wardrobe it had a seating area with an elegant pale pink sofa and matching armchair as well as a dining table around which were four chairs.

"Shall we order food straight away?" Evan said.

"I'd like to know what this is about first," Sam said.

"Yes," Evan said. "I understand. But at least let me make you a drink." He gestured to the sofa. "Please make yourselves comfortable."

Luke took the armchair while Sam sat at the end of the sofa. Evan took the kettle into the bathroom and filled it. He flicked it on. "Coffee or tea?" he asked.

"Strong black coffee for me please," Luke said.

"I'm okay," Sam said. "I'd prefer to get on with it."

"All in good time," Evan said. "No biscuits I'm afraid."

Sam looked at Luke, impatience written on her face. He lifted his hand then lowered it a couple of times, palm down, in an effort to calm her. Evan was putting coffee in the cups, oblivious.

"Ah, here goes," he said when the kettle had boiled. He brought the drinks over and placed Luke's on the coffee table before sitting on the sofa at the opposite end to Sam. He raised his own mug to his lips and let out a little sigh in appreciation. "Lemon tea is my tipple of choice," he said, before taking a second sip.

Sam gritted her teeth. "So what's this all about?" she asked, fighting hard to keep the irritation out of her voice.

Evan put his mug on the table, leaned down and pulled an OSA declaration and pen from his briefcase. Sam picked it up, read it and looked across at Evan and then at Luke before completing the form and returning it.

"This is in strict confidence," Evan said, his tone serious now. Sam nodded her understanding. He paused for a second. "I take it Luke's told you I'm from MI6?"

"Yes."

He took a deep breath. "We believe that Supracomm is being used to launder money for an international terrorist organisation called Al Ummah. They've only been established for a couple of years but their intentions are clear." He paused. "Think Al Qaeda but more hard-line."

"What!" Sam said.

"Calm down, Sam," he said. "I'm sure you'll be fine."

"You're sure I'll be fine?" She stared at Evan, then at Luke, then back at Evan again. "What the hell does that mean?"

Evan ignored her question. "I need to give you some background," he said, and took a sip of his tea as he collected his thoughts. "Al Ummah was founded by Amir Bashar, one of Al Qaeda's operational directors who became disenchanted with their inaction. In two years he's built up a significant multinational operation with its finger in a lot of pies. It's not just the obvious places, like Syria and Afghanistan. They've also been involved in Ukraine, where they've supported Russia and Belarus, and in Sudan. We've even seen evidence of their activities in South America. The extent of their work requires funds, a lot of funds, and that's what my colleagues and I have been looking into. Some of the money is obtained through legal entities, for example charities, but the majority is through crime."

"What sort of crime?" Sam asked.

"A wide variety. Drugs naturally, but also the sex trade and that's how we linked them to Supracomm. A few months ago the Dutch police raided a brothel in Rotterdam at our request."

Sam was surprised. "At the request of MI6?"

"Evan's seconded to the United Nations Office on Drugs and Crime," Luke said.

She looked at him. "Of course he is," she said, thinking that only two months earlier the biggest challenges in her day-to-day work had been preparing a profit and loss account.

"We already knew Al Ummah was behind the brothel," Evan continued, "but the Dutch police found a financial statement that had fallen behind a desk in the manager's office. It showed funds being transferred to an offshore account. Our guys at the United Nations managed to trace it from there to one of Supracomm's wholesale customers, only it turns out that the customer doesn't really exist."

"Money laundering," Sam said.

"Exactly. We believe the money is channelled through Supracomm's legitimate activities so that it comes out clean the other side, at which point it's transferred to some other account and ultimately to Al Ummah."

"I presume you want me to find out how it's manipulated within Supracomm?"

"Got it in one." He hesitated. "If you hadn't already been in the team we'd have tried to place one of our own, but with you there, someone who's been with Filchers a long time, well it's manna from heaven."

Luke tried to speak but Evan held his hand up. "I know what you're going to say, Luke, and I'm with you." He turned back to Sam. "There's a certain amount of risk involved…"

"A lot of risk," Luke said.

"A certain amount," Evan repeated. "I have to admit they're a nasty outfit, Sam, ruthless as hell. If you want to pull out, I totally understand. This is hardly the kind of thing you're used to."

Sam thought back to being abducted twice, having her leg broken by a metal bar, and being stabbed in the arm. "You're right," she said drily and looked over at Luke. "It's very different from a normal accountant's job."

"I'll find someone in my team," Evan said.

"Don't you dare," Sam said. "Count me in."

"Just a minute, Sam," Luke said. "There's one condition."

"Let's hear it," Evan said.

"I need the other members of my team in on what's going on." Evan started to speak, but Luke held his hand up. "It isn't an option, Evan. There's no way we can do this without them finding out. In any case, there'll be a lot of background digging to do after Sam starts to unravel things and they'll be invaluable."

"Very well." Evan sighed. "It's against my better judgement, but if you trust them…"

"I certainly do."

"How many of them are there?"

"Three."

Evan passed three more forms to Luke. "I'm going to stay out of the picture," he said, "but I want regular updates. Can you ring or text me every day, Luke? I think it's safer than Sam doing it since she'll be in Supracomm's office most of the time."

"Sure."

"And Sam," Evan said. "You need to be able to signal immediately if you've found anything highly significant or if you've been compromised."

"Okay," Sam said. She pondered for a few seconds then turned to Luke. "I'll text you about my mother. If I say she's feeling better I've found something and if she's fallen ill I've been sussed."

God forbid I ever hear her mother's ill, Luke thought. "Fine," he said. "Good idea."

Chapter 10

Many hours had passed since the German girl had broken her ankle and she was in a lot of pain. Tania had thought about speaking to Greg again but she knew after her last experience that she would get nowhere. The other Germans were comforting their injured companion as best they could while Izabella hadn't left Tania's side. They had talked some more, but Izabella's limited English and Tania's limited Polish made it difficult.

Greg had kept himself to himself, occasionally scowling across at her but otherwise saying little. The other two men, however, had talked to each other almost continually. They'd kept their voices low but the lorry wasn't huge and she was able to pick up bits of what they said. Tania was thankful she hadn't revealed how well she spoke and understood English.

Laurie, who had a Scottish accent, was the older of the two. He was above average height and looked trim, not over muscly but clearly kept himself in good shape. His black hair was receding slightly and she put him at forty or so, perhaps a little older. He wore faded jeans and a navy blue polo neck.

The other man, Danny, was English, slightly shorter than Laurie and perhaps five years younger. He wore grey denim jeans with a red Metallica t-shirt and had short brown hair neatly styled and trimmed to about an inch above his ears.

It was soon clear that Laurie and Danny, unlike the five women, were there voluntarily. It was also evident that they had known each other before this journey. At one point they seemed to be telling each other jokes, and then for a while they talked about major illnesses before this turned to money talk and investments. The flow of their conversation struck Tania as odd and at first she wasn't sure why. Then it hit her. It was the way the discussion about cancer and the like seemed to lead seamlessly into them talking about savings accounts and interest payments.

She was conscious that they looked in her direction every now and then, but she was careful to keep her eyes down.

When Laurie moaned about the journey time, Danny commented that at least they didn't have far to go at the other end.

"Yeah," Laurie said, "but Cheppy's a dosshole state. Wales is nice but too far to walk for lunch."

It sounded like nonsense. She had never heard of the expression 'dosshole', and wasn't Wales a country? Tania had never heard of anywhere called Cheppy either. She filed the information away though, just in case.

Her ears pricked up when they started talking about people they called 'clients' and the phases they were in, using terms like 'push' and 'promote' and 'drift'. She concentrated hard. Laurie's accent wasn't overly strong and his voice, even at a whisper, carried better than Danny's. She heard Christian names, mainly women, and thought she caught a full name but it sounded like Herbie Hawson which didn't sound real to her. Perhaps they gave their clients codenames.

Danny was expanding on the challenges of 'the push' when the lorry stopped. A moment later Tania heard the whining of an electric door being raised. After twenty seconds or so the noise stopped and the lorry was driven forward a few metres. Then the whining came again and there was a clunk as the door hit the floor.

"Stay where you are," Greg ordered before repeating the instruction in German.

The doors were opened and she heard the sound of people climbing onto the rear of the lorry. The top crates were removed then the next layer and Tania saw that there were four men lifting them off and placing them to one side. Standing to the other side and watching was a short man in his late forties. He was pale-skinned and completely bald, with a paunch, a large bulbous nose and a permanent sneer. She almost screamed when she saw he had a pistol in his right hand.

When all the crates had been removed Laurie and Danny climbed down from the lorry.

"Your car's outside," the bald man said in a cockney accent, gesturing behind him but not looking at them. He kept his focus on the women, eyes flitting between them, the sneer ever-present. Laurie and Danny didn't say anything, didn't even look at him, but walked quickly to the door and out. He looked at Greg. "Everything okay?"

"I'd watch this one, Mr Anderson," Greg said gesturing at Tania. "She could be trouble."

"And the rest? Make 'em stand up. I wanna look 'em over."

Greg passed on the instruction in English and then in German. The four who were able to stand did so, while the injured girl remained on the floor. "This one can't," Greg said, gesturing to her. "She's done something to her leg."

"That's no fucking use." Anderson climbed into the lorry and walked up to Izabella. Tania could see her lips trembling as he put his hand under her chin and lifted her face. He looked her up and down then stood back and looked down at her legs then up to her breasts. He nodded to himself before doing the same with Tania and the two Germans beside her. He backed away and looked down at the injured girl. "What have you done?" he said. She shook her head, eyes wet with tears.

"She only speaks German," Greg said.

"She's broken ankle," Tania said. "Need doctor."

Anderson turned to look at her, grunted then raised his arm.

"No!" Tania howled.

The noise of the gunshot was deafening. Tania put her hands to her mouth, vaguely aware of the other women screaming. She looked down at the girl, now motionless, eyes staring and a hole in her temple. Blood was already pooling beneath her head.

Anderson backed away and gestured to the men who had removed the crates.

"Take these four to the van," he said. He gestured to the dead girl. "And get rid of that."

Chapter 11

It was already warm and the sun was shining as Sam approached Supracomm's Head Office, but after what she had heard the evening before she was in no mood to appreciate it. Unsurprisingly, her night had been a rough one. It had taken her several hours to get to sleep and she was sure it showed on her face. She'd tried to take care with her make-up, and had worn one of her favourite dresses, but still felt ragged. She decided to go to the bathroom before she went into the office to freshen up and make sure her hair looked okay.

She walked in to find another woman applying mascara at the middle of the three sinks. She was a few years older, maybe thirty-five or thirty-six, petite, with a neat black bob. She saw Sam approach and smiled at her in the mirror.

"Good morning," she said. "Late night for you too?"

"I didn't sleep well," Sam said. She filled the left-hand sink and decided she ought to explain herself. "I'm staying in a hotel, rang my boyfriend after dinner and we had a massive argument."

"Tell me about it." The woman put the cap on her mascara and started rummaging in her handbag. "Lipstick's here somewhere." More rummaging. "I'm Audrey, by the way, Audrey Manners. Ah, here it is."

So this was Audrey Manners, the call centre manager and one of the two who had blocked the Filchers consultant.

"Pleased to meet you," Sam said. "I'm Sam Chambers. I only started yesterday."

"Welcome to the madhouse." Audrey applied some lipstick, then said, "What happened?"

It took a moment for Sam to realise she was talking

about her boyfriend trouble. "He proposed," she said, drawing on what had happened a couple of months earlier, "and I said no, which kind of upset him. Upset him a lot actually. He told me I was a prick-tease among other things."

"Bastard," Audrey said, then a few seconds later said, "Nice hotel?"

Sam's heart skipped a beat, thinking for a split second she was referring to The Manor. "The Leonardo's okay," she said. "Typical business hotel. Wouldn't want to holiday there though." She paused and decided she ought to take advantage of this encounter, find out a bit more about the other woman. "Are you having problems with your boyfriend as well?"

"Have been for a few weeks." She looked at her lips in the mirror and applied a little more lipstick. "He works here which doesn't help."

"What's he done?"

"Decided to have his cake and eat it, that's what." Audrey put her lipstick down and turned to face Sam. "He told me it was all over with his wife and that they were living separate lives and now the bastard says he's going to stay with her."

"That must be hard."

Audrey nodded. "It's unbelievably hard." She put her lipstick in her bag and stepped back, checking her hair before turning to leave. "Nice meeting you, Sam. And good luck with your boyfriend."

"You too, Audrey."

Sam gave her hair a last brush. This was intriguing. She made a mental note to try to find out who Audrey was in a relationship with.

She headed for the large open-plan office used by Supracomm's finance department and glanced up at the clock. It was almost ten to nine and most of the seventy or so staff were in. She was one of eight people seconded from Filchers, but the only one from Head Office and fortunately she'd never met any of the other seven before. The only person in the building who knew she was from the Ethics Team was the Client Director, Oliver Knight.

She nodded hello to a couple of people and sat down at her cubicle. Although it was open plan, all the accountants, but not the clerical staff, had their own small alcoves separated from neighbouring workspaces by partitions about five feet tall. She was grateful for the privacy.

Her desk had a computer, monitor, keyboard, mouse, phone and three blue letter trays stacked on top of each other. The top one was her in-box and there were three paper-clipped sets of documents in it that hadn't been there the day before. She sat down and took the top document out of the tray. There was a post-it stuck to the top with a handwritten message saying 'Latest accounts - Omniphone. Please check. Ron". Ron Young was her team leader, a short overweight man in his fifties. He had a permanent smug look on his face and she had taken an instant dislike to him.

She put the Omniphone stack to one side and picked up the second. It had an almost identical message stuck to it, also from Ron, but for a company called Robintree. The third was the same, this time for Haverford Green.

The challenge was dealing with this routine work while also investigating the anomalies. Sam was relieved she was a quick worker and decided to process these three requests straight away. With any luck she could do them in half a day whereas others might be expected to take a lot longer, which would free time up to do some prying around. She could then send her replies back at the end of the day.

It was nearly noon when Sam finished the Robintree analysis, which left only Haverford Green to go. Satisfied with her progress, she finished typing an email to Ron but left it in her drafts folder.

She stood up and made her way to the water dispenser.

The other cubicles were full of people beavering away and it was surreal to think there was any connection to an international terrorist organisation. A ripple of anxiety ran through her body and she shook her head. Stop it Sam, be cool.

She reached the dispenser and waited patiently. A man in his late twenties was filling a cup and smiling to himself.

"Penny for them," Sam said.

"What?" He jumped in shock and the paper tumbler fell to one side spilling water over the side of the dispenser.

"Sorry," Sam said.

"No problem. I was miles away." He righted his cup, refilled it and then turned and held his hand out. "Hi, I'm Chris, Chris Nevin."

"Hi. Sam Chambers. Pleased to meet you."

She shook his hand, pleased to find he had a firm grip but didn't overdo it. Some men seemed to think it was super-masculine to break your bones, but not this one thankfully. As she looked at him again she revised her view of his age. He was early thirties, she thought, but clean cut, with slightly chiselled features and deep blue eyes.

"You're new aren't you?" he asked.

"Yes, shipped in from Filchers to help prepare the annual report. I've joined the supplier team."

"Mmm," he said. "Bit of a challenge there then."

"It seems straightforward so far.'

"It's not the work." He dropped his voice. "It's Ron."

"What's wrong with him? He's a bit abrupt but as long as he lets me get on with things I don't have a problem with that."

"He's a bit hands-on, if you get my meaning. "

"Oh."

"I've arranged to meet a couple of women from the central accounts team for lunch today. Anne used to be in the supplier team and can tell you how to deal with him if he tries anything. Do you want to join us?"

"That would be lovely thanks."

"Is one o-clock okay?" She nodded. "Great, I'll come by and get you."

*

Sam grabbed a sandwich and followed Chris to a table where two women deep in conversation were sitting facing each other. The younger of the two looked up as they approached. She was around her own age, with short hair in a pixie cut, a nose ring and tattoos on both arms.

"Hi Chris," she said.

"Hi Anne," Chris said. The other woman turned when she heard this and smiled. She reminded Sam of her mother: around the same age and slimly built. Her hair was very different though: long, blonde and straight with black showing at the roots. "Hi Mary," he added before gesturing to Sam. "This is Sam. She's from Filchers and joined us this week."

"An alien," Anne said, but the corners of her mouth turned up as she said it. Sam went around to the other side of the table to sit next to her. Chris sat next to Mary.

"Yes indeed," Sam said, "but without the antennae."

"What are you working on?" Mary asked.

"Supplier analyses."

"You work for Ron then," Anne said. "Good luck with that."

"Chris warned me about him. Did he give you any trouble?"

"He patted my bottom soon after I joined his team but I gave him a right earful. I suggest you do the same if you need to."

"Will do." She peeled the cellophane from her sandwich. "So where are you working now?"

"I'm working with Mary in Mike Swithin's office. With

the annual report due out at the end of next month we're really up against it." She shook her head. "Some departments are okay but there are a few that are useless at meeting our deadlines."

"I'm having a big struggle with IT," Mary said, "and Sales Support are almost as bad."

"Any others?" Sam prompted.

"The call centre team are particularly useless. The manager's Audrey Manners and she's forever claiming they're too busy, can it wait another week, blah blah blah. She really screws us around."

Anne gave a little chuckle. "She screws with Mike more," she said.

Sam was confused. "What do you mean?"

"It's an open secret," Anne said and a broad smile spread across her face. "Mike and Audrey have been playing hide the sausage for months."

"Anne!" Mary said.

"He's married too," Anne added.

So Mike Swithin was Audrey's paramour. That was interesting.

Sam decided a little white lie was in order. "I used to work with a call centre department for another Filchers' client, so I could help you."

"Shouldn't you be working on supplier analyses?" Anne asked.

"Yes, but I've already completed the three in my in-tray this morning, and in any case my remit is wider than just the supplier team. If I can do something to help I'd be delighted to."

"That would be great. If you come with me after lunch I'll show you what we've got so far and what we still need."

"I'll do that," Sam said before taking a bite of her BLT sandwich.

Chapter 12

Luke enjoyed the journey back to Bath. He found himself chuckling out loud as he listened to the latest JD Kirk audiobook.

Or at least he enjoyed the journey until the phone rang.

"Hi," he said.

"Luke?"

He recognised his father's voice immediately. "Is this about the Tatler article?" he asked, struggling to keep the anger from his voice. "Has it been published?"

"No." There was a pause at the other end. "You must come to see your mother. She asked for you in one of her more lucid moments."

"What do you mean 'more lucid moments'?"

"It's accelerated." There was a tremble in Hugo's voice and Luke sensed his father, normally a strong resilient figure, was struggling to hold himself together. "Mark's already here," he went on. "He flew in this morning."

"What's accelerated?"

"You need to come today." There was a pleading in Hugo's voice that Luke had never heard before. "I'll have Amy prepare your room."

There was a click as his father ended the call.

The audiobook resumed playing and Luke paused it. He needed time to think. His mother was clearly ill and she had to be in a bad way if Mark had travelled over from Canada. But that didn't explain why she had asked to see her eldest son.

The phone rang again and he clicked the button on the steering wheel to accept the call.

"I'll see her tonight," he said without waiting for the voice at the other end.

There was a short pause before the reply came.

"Cool."

"Josh?"

"Ace detective work, guv," Josh said. "I say nothing and yet you know I want you to see her. Is that your Truth Wizard thingamabob at work?"

"What?"

"Mandy's mum and Leanne's aunt."

"Eh?"

"You need to see them. They don't know about each other of course. Mandy's mum and Leanne's aunt that is. Mandy and Leanne know about each other, not that Leanne wants to know about Mandy. I learned my lesson there…"

"What on earth are you wittering on about?"

"I've put two and two together…"

"And made seven?"

"And made four, guv. They're linked and it's unethical and we're from ethics, not from ethics, we are ethics, well the ethics team. Obviously, we can't be ethics…"

Luke couldn't take this any more. "Where are you Josh?"

"Between sessions. We finish at five."

"I'll meet you at Costa Coffee, the one near Filchers, straight after you finish."

"Funny that, guv. That's where Leanne and Mandy fell out, not that they've met, and it's kind of a one-sided falling out because…"

It was Luke's turn to end a call abruptly.

He resumed listening to his audiobook. Josh was making Bob Hoon look balanced and rational.

Maj was at the whiteboard when Luke walked into the Ethics Room. It was covered in symbols and diagrams connected to each other by arrows and dotted lines. It looked like the random doodlings of a physics lecturer.

Maj saw him looking. "Firewalls and servers, Luke," he said by way of explanation. "I've mapped them out to understand how the Wagstaff leak could have happened."

"Interesting," Luke lied.

"I don't understand it either, Luke," Helen said, swivelling around on her chair. "Me, I'm much more comfortable with these wee babies." She gestured to the pile of contracts on her desk.

"Mmm," he said. "Could you two spare me a couple of minutes?

"What is it?" Maj said as he and Helen pulled up chairs opposite him at the table.

"This is top secret," Luke said. "And I mean that in the literal sense. It's to do with Sam's work at Supracomm."

He got them to fill in the Official Secrets Act declarations and then told them all about Evan Underwood and the suspected money laundering for Al Ummah. When he finished Maj had his mouth half open while Helen was shaking her head from side to side.

"Unbelievable," she said, then smiled.

"Why are you smiling?" Luke asked.

"Josh is going to be so excited when he hears this. When are you telling him?"

"Later."

"I'd love to be a fly on the wall."

"You can be. I'm meeting him at Costa Coffee but I can't tell him there - I'll bring him back here afterwards."

*

Luke took a sip of his double espresso. He considered ringing his brother to find out more about their mother and looked at his watch. It was quarter past five. If he got away at six-ish he could still be at Borrowham Hall between eight and eight thirty. Yes, better to wait until he could talk to Mark face to face.

"Okay, guv?"

He looked up to see Josh cradling a large mug covered in marshmallows.

"Are you having a drink or supper?" he asked.

"Just a drink," Josh said. "My mum's cooking a meal later."

Luke shook his head as Josh took a seat opposite him. "How's the course?"

"Wowza. On Monday we started with…"

Luke held his hand up. "That was a polite enquiry, Josh. 'Wowza' is enough."

"But we…"

"Sorry, but I haven't got enough time. I'd love to hear about the course," he lied, "but I have to visit my parents this evening."

"Do they live in Bath?"

"No, Dorset?"

"Bournemouth?"

"They live in the country." Luke wasn't embarrassed by his heritage, but neither did he feel like absorbing the gushing noises if Josh discovered his parents were the Duke and Duchess of Dorset. "So tell me about Leanne's Mum and…"

"Leanne's aunt and Mandy's mum."

"Right. You said I need to see them. Why?"

"Well…"

Luke tapped his watch. "I'll give you ten minutes then we stop. I have to leave by six, and there's something I need to tell you, but it has to be at the office not here." He saw Josh's face drop. "I'm not going to tell you off." The smile returned. "It's about another project."

"Right, guv." For some extraordinary reason, Josh saluted.

"Don't do that again," Luke said.

"Right, uh, okay."

"Go on then."

"What?"

"Leanne's aunt…"

"Oh, uh, yeah."

Josh proceeded to share everything he knew about the romance scams that he suspected the two women had fallen for. To Luke's surprise and delight he did so clearly and concisely, referring every now and then to a notebook he pulled out of his backpack. When he finished he sat back in his seat.

"That was very clear," Luke said. He cocked his head to one side and lowered his eyebrows. "Surprisingly so in fact. Are you taking something, Josh?"

"Day two session three," Josh said, and tapped his left temple. "Recording and sharing information."

"This course is already paying dividends. And I think you're right."

"You do?"

"Definitely."

Josh punched the air with his fist.

"And you're saying," Luke went on, "that Mandy's mum Eleanor won't countenance the idea that she's being scammed?"

"Not at all, guv."

"But Leanne's Aunty Pam has accepted the fact?"

"Eventually, yes."

"Then I agree it would be a good idea for me to talk to them. Do you think you can find a tactful way of arranging it? If I could meet both at the same time I think that will help no end."

"Good idea."

"Thank you, Josh, your praise means a lot."

"No problem guv," Josh said, oblivious to the sarcasm.

"Right, we need to go to the office."

"Just need a second." Josh wiped his spoon around the bottom of his mug, capturing two pink marshmallows that had evaded his previous attempts. He put them into his mouth and nodded. "Done."

*

Maj was back at the whiteboard and Helen was on the phone when Luke and Josh returned to the Ethics Room.

"Got to go," Helen said, then ended the call. She beamed across at Luke. "Mind if I join?"

"I don't want to miss this either," Maj said, putting his marker down and walking to the table.

Josh looked from one to the other as they sat down. "What is it?" he said.

"It's big," Helen said.

"Massive," Maj added.

"What is? What is?" Josh said, almost bouncing up and down in his excitement.

Luke decided he had to bring him down to earth. "I need to share some information about a project with you, that's all it is."

"Top secret information," Helen said.

"Top secret?" Josh said. "Like on 'Mission Impossible', that kind of thing."

"More like 'Zero Dark Thirty'," Maj said.

"I've seen that. Great film. Are we hunting Obama?"

"Obama?" Luke said.

"Yeah, guv. Obama Bin Laden?"

"It's *Osama* Bin Laden."

"Right."

"And no, we're not hunting him. He's dead. That's what the film was about."

"Oh yeah, of course he is." Josh tapped the side of his nose, then leant forward. "So who are we hunting?"

There was a snort from Helen. "Sorry," she said and bent to retrieve a tissue from her handbag.

"We're not hunting anyone," Luke said.

"So why did you mention Obama Bin Laden?"

"I didn't…" Luke sighed. "Forget Bin Laden okay. Just forget him." He placed a blank OSA declaration in front of

Josh. "Sign this please, Josh."

Josh looked down at the form. "For real?"

"For real."

Josh completed the form.

Luke took a deep intake of breath. "We are looking into the activities of Al Ummah."

Josh looked at him blankly. "Al Ummah?"

Luke didn't want to hear his guess as to what Al Ummah was. "They're a terrorist organisation," he said.

"Right guv, gotcha." He nodded for a moment, then the cogs turned and his voice went up an octave. "A terrorist organisation?"

"Yes."

Josh stared at Luke for a second, his mouth open. "Wowza!"

"Indeed. We think they're in Supracomm."

"How many?"

"Not physically in Supracomm." Luke sighed. "God, give me the will…" He paused for a second. "They're using Supracomm to launder money."

"Making illegally gained money appear clean…" Josh said.

"Finally some sense," Luke said.

"…by putting it through a washing machine." Josh held his hand up. "Only joking."

"Right," Luke said, addressing all three of them. "This is what we're going to do…"

Chapter 13

It was almost nine when Luke reached Borrowham Hall. It was the second time he'd been there in three months. Before that, it had been almost twenty years.

It hadn't changed, but then it probably hadn't changed for centuries. He stepped out of the BMW and looked up at the facade. It stretched a hundred feet or so on either side of a massive oak door within a taller midsection. Mullioned sash windows were spaced across the length of the upper storey with larger ones directly beneath them at ground level. It had been in the Sackville family for five hundred years and he had to admit it was stunning and totally Tudor.

He pulled the bell chain and heard the familiar resounding 'boing' from within. A few seconds later the door was pulled open to reveal his brother. It felt for an instant like he was looking in a mirror, but the illusion was shattered when he took in Mark's all too neat hair, his crystal smooth complexion - no scar for him - and his designer clothes. He sported a grey and white striped Hugo Boss shirt over pale grey slacks.

"Hi Luke," he said. "It's been a long time."

Luke held out his hand.

"Come on," Mark said, his voice as plummy as it had ever been. He held out his arms and they embraced awkwardly for a few seconds.

Luke took a step back. "You're happy to move on?"

"I think it's best."

"Is Erica here?"

"Yes. Come on in and say hello."

Luke wasn't looking forward to seeing Mark's wife, but he put on his best smile and walked past his brother into the spacious entrance hall where she sat at the bottom of the stairs, resplendent in an elegant blue dress that wouldn't have looked out of place in a ballroom. She wasn't far from being classically beautiful, and Luke had no doubt that in her own mind she was, but her face was slightly too angular and her lips turned down at either side making her look permanently displeased.

"Hi Erica," he said.

"Hi Luke," she said, unsmiling and without getting up. Her voice was exactly as he remembered it: New York trying to be Hollywood, deeper than most women with a slight drawl that made her accent settle somewhere in the deep south.

Luke turned back to Mark. "What's wrong with mother?"

It was his father Hugo who answered, emerging from the Grand Salon and closing the door behind him.

"Alzheimer's," he said abruptly. "Come into the conservatory. We can't talk here."

He led the way. As they passed Erica she stood up.

"Just the three of us," Hugo said. There was an exchange of looks between Mark and Erica, then she turned and went upstairs.

When they reached the conservatory Hugo walked to the window and stared out at the neatly terraced gardens. "Sit down both of you," he said. Luke and Mark looked at each other, shrugged and sat in the two armchairs facing the window.

Hugo waited a few seconds and then turned and looked at each of them in turn. "Your mother's illness has progressed significantly these past few weeks," he said, "and this week…" He hesitated and swallowed. "This week has been bloody awful. I know neither of you likes her." Mark started to object but he stilled him with a glance. "I think it's time to be honest, Mark. The fact is that despite her faults she loves you both. I wanted her to have the chance to see you again before she…"

He stopped and moved to the sofa facing his sons, grabbing the arm and bending over before righting himself and sitting down. He had aged even more since Luke's previous visit, and every month of his seventy-six years was showing on his face and in his movements.

"Of course, Father," Mark said.

"And you, Luke?" Hugo said.

Luke thought of everything his mother had done over the years. She had been cruel on many occasions when he had been young, but it was the way she had treated Jess that hurt the most. She was ill now, extremely ill, but did that make her a better person? Of course not, but still.

"Yes, I'll see her," he said.

"She's in the Great Library," Hugo said. "I'll stay here."

Luke and Mark made their way back to the Hall and then into the Salon. At the far end, Mark approached the door and Luke put his hand on his arm before he opened it.

"I appreciate she's ill," he said, "but if she asks us to change our minds, don't automatically say yes. We need to discuss it first."

"Understood," Mark said. He pushed the door open.

Daphne, their mother, the Duchess of Dorset, was sitting upright on the pale green chaise longue. She held a framed photo in her hand and was looking at it curiously.

"Hugo," she said, without looking up. "Is this Martha?"

"Hello, Mother," Luke said.

She looked up, but her eyes seemed somehow out of focus. "Who are you?" she said. "Get out of here. Hugo!" She almost shouted the last word.

"It's us, Mother," Mark said. "Mark and Luke."

She calmed down immediately. "Oh yes," she said. She held the photo up for them both to see. "Is this Martha?"

Luke walked over to her. The photo was of his maternal grandmother. "No, Mother," he said. "That's grandmother."

"Of course it is. Martha's dead."

Martha was her younger sister and very much still alive, living in a Scottish castle with her husband of forty years.

"Martha's not dead," Luke said.

"No," she said. "Martha's not dead." She put the photo back on her lap, still face up.

"How are you feeling?" Mark said.

"I'm fine." She raised her voice again. "Why wouldn't I be fine?" She shook her head and then looked at each of them in turn as if recognising them for the first time. "You need to agree."

"Agree to what?" Luke said, though he knew the answer.

"This," she said, waving her arm to indicate everything around her. "The two of you need to agree, sign and confirm. Will you, Lucas?" He'd almost forgotten that she used their full names. She turned to his brother. "Will you, Marcus?"

Luke held his hand up before Mark could answer. "We'll talk about it, Mother."

"Good." She nodded, and then held the photo up again. "Martha's dead," she said.

Chapter 14

Tania lay in her bunk staring at the single bulb that hung from the centre of the ceiling. The other women were still asleep but she had been awake for over an hour.

She was on the top bunk above Izabella. The poor girl was struggling more than the rest of them and Tania had had to hold her for a long time before she eventually drifted off. The Germans had talked to each other for a while before they too had fallen asleep. She looked across at the girl in the top bunk who looked at peace, the horrors of what had happened and might yet happen mercifully absent from her dreams.

The bulb was turned off but the sun had risen and light was streaming through the small window high up on the wall opposite the door. It was a small room and there was barely enough space for the two sets of bunk beds. A curtain had been erected in the corner next to the door and behind it was a portable toilet which she had had to use in the night. Aside from that the room was empty. It was clearly temporary before they were moved to somewhere more permanent. She shivered as she thought about what that might mean.

She sat up as she heard the sound of footsteps outside the door. It was thrown open and Greg walked in, followed by the four men who had unloaded the crates from the lorry.

"Wake up, all of you," Greg shouted, not bothering to repeat his words in German. Izabella screamed and he walked over to her bunk. "Calm the fuck down," he said. She lay back, pulling her duvet tightly above her neck.

He stood back and two of the other four men moved forwards, one grabbing hold of Izabella's arm and yanking her out of her bed.

"You two, down," Greg said, gesturing to the top bunks.

They climbed down and the third and fourth men went to their sides. The man beside Tania wasn't much older than her and she caught wafts of garlic coming off him as he leant into her ear. "Off to earn your keep," he whispered.

"Shut it, Jed," Greg said. He stood back and the four women were unceremoniously bundled through the door, down the corridor and into the back of the van they had arrived in. Tania tried hard to see anything that might identify where they were but there was nothing.

The van had a partition between the cab and the passenger area with five seats along either side. Three of the men climbed in and sat facing the women and then Greg and Jed closed the doors. After a few seconds the van started up and they drove off.

"Where we going?" Tania said.

It was the man on the left who answered. "To work," he said. His voice was flat and he sounded almost bored.

"Where?"

He ignored her and the rest of the journey was spent in silence.

When the van stopped there was a bang on the partition, and the man who had spoken stood up. He pulled a short knife from his pocket and held it up.

"You will be quiet. Understand?"

His meaning was clear to all the women and they nodded. The rear doors opened revealing Greg and Jed. Tania could see that they were in a city and were parked on a minor road off a main thoroughfare. She saw a shop behind the two men on the far side of the avenue selling clothes for women, and next to it a bookstore. There were a lot of people walking along the street, going about their normal daily lives, looking as if they didn't have a care in the world. She thought of running, or of shouting out, but the look on Greg's face told her it would be fruitless.

As they clambered out Tania caught the eyes of a young girl of eight or nine who nodded hello. She tried to express her distress and her need for help in her facial expression but after a moment the girl turned away, ran to her mother and grabbed her hand.

The men hustled the women through a gate and across a short path to a large Georgian terraced house. A slate sign to one side of the door said '42' but there was no house name.

Greg unlocked the door and stood back for the women to enter first. The entrance hall had high ceilings and was decorated in dark blue below a dado rail at waist height and then pale cream above. A corridor led to the back, beside which stairs rose to the next floor. There was a single door to either side of the corridor and the one on the left was open. Through it, Tania saw two chintzy armchairs facing a large open fire. It was all very elegant.

"You have a room each," Greg said. "You must keep it clean." He repeated this in German, and then indicated for them to go upstairs. Once there he showed them their rooms which were all large and recently decorated. Inside each was a large ornate double bed, a dressing table and a wardrobe. Tania had been allocated room two which was decorated in a soft pink with dark mahogany furniture.

"I sleep here?" she asked.

Greg laughed. "No," he said. "This is for work. You sleep upstairs."

Chapter 15

Maj was looking forward to his day's work, and that had never been the case when he had worked in Security. He had a better boss now, which undoubtedly helped, but it was also the variety that made every moment interesting.

He didn't know how, but Luke had managed to persuade Glen Baxter, Head of Security, to give the Ethics Team access to their systems. This included 'Otto', which recorded people going in and out of the main buildings and high-security areas, and 'Cassy', Filchers' Camera Security System.

He settled down at the desk, opened his notebook and logged into Cassy. He had planned his approach carefully. First, he would look at what the senior members of Filchers' Supracomm team had been up to, then he would work his way through each of their teams. He would make a note of anything even slightly unusual, and use Otto and a deeper dive into Cassy to follow up. It was, he had to admit, a bit nerdy, but it was fun nerdy.

Maj unwrapped a Double Decker, took a bite and started.

After a couple of hours, he had nearly finished with the senior team, and had made a few notes, but hadn't seen anything significant. The HR consultant had passed a note to one of the consultants that he thought at first was suspicious, but it turned out to be nothing more than an expenses form.

He moved on to the Supracomm invoicing team. There were eleven of them of varying ages from mid-twenties to mid-fifties, seven men and four women. He used the cameras to flick between them, watching out for anything that seemed in any way unusual. At one point he saw Sam walk through and a couple of the men's eyes follow her. No surprise there. She was an attractive woman.

As she disappeared out of camera view one of the men stood up from his desk, and there was something in the way he did it that drew Maj's attention. It was cautious, almost furtive. Maj switched cameras so that he could follow his progress and saw him look over his shoulders a couple of times as if afraid someone might be following.

He reached a cubicle and stepped inside before bending down and opening a notebook on the desk next to the keyboard. He flicked through a couple of the pages then closed it again and moved the book slightly in what looked like an attempt to make sure it was in its original position. He stood upright and headed back the way he had come.

Maj kept the camera focused on the cubicle, keen to see whose it was. After a few minutes, Sam walked into view, sat down and opened the notebook before signing into her computer.

Maj took a screenshot of the man who had visited Sam's cubicle and called over to Helen who had spent the morning going through a massive pile of Supracomm contracts and other documents.

"Helen," he said. "Could you come here a moment?"

"Sure."

She walked behind him and he pointed to the man on the screen. "Do you know who that is?"

"I recognise him from somewhere." She thought for a moment. "I think I saw his photo in a Supracomm staff magazine. Hang on, it's here somewhere."

She returned to her desk, opened the top drawer and lifted up the top few documents.

"Got it," she said and brought the magazine over to Maj's desk. She opened it to the centre where there was a double-page spread. 'Meet our High-Flyers', it said in bold black letters above a photo of three men and three women.

"There," she said, pointing to the man on the left.

Maj looked at the photo. Sure enough, that was him. He looked at the caption underneath which revealed that the man's name was Chris Nevin.

"Of course, it could be something and nothing," Maj said.

"What did he do?"

Maj showed her the footage from the point where Sam passed in front of the camera.

"It's certainly suspicious," Helen mused. "The trouble is that we can't ask him what he was up to."

"No, but we could follow his movements more closely to see if he does anything else out of the ordinary."

"True. Let's raise it in our catchup with Luke."

Chapter 16

Josh led Mandy to a table in the corner.

"Are you going to say something you don't want overheard?" she said. "Like you love me or something?"

"Yes," Josh said.

"What?"

"Uh…" Josh looked blank for a few seconds then realised what he'd said. "I meant yes to the first bit, uh, of what I said. Not to the second."

"You really know how to hurt a girl." She was smiling from ear to ear.

"Shut up, Mandy."

"Out with it then." She dropped her voice to a whisper. "What is it that you don't want overheard if it's not your undying love for me?"

"Did you speak to your Mum about her friend John?"

The smile vanished from Mandy's face. She bent to her plate and absent-mindedly put together a forkful of her salmon salad.

"Are you okay?" he asked.

She looked up and he could see tears in her eyes. "Mum's given him almost £17,000, and now he needs another £5,000 for a new form of treatment and it's breaking her heart that she hasn't got enough. She asked me if I knew anyone who could help."

Josh swallowed. It was time to tell her.

"Mandy," he said, "I think you were right when you suggested that John might not be telling the truth."

"What do you mean?"

"I don't think he's ill. In fact, I don't believe his real name is John or he lives in Florida."

"That can't be the case. Mum's known him for ages and

they FaceTime almost every day."

Josh told her about Leanne's aunt. When he finished, she looked at him slack-jawed. After a few seconds, he could see that realisation had dawned.

"It's almost exactly the same," she said, her face a picture of horror. "Poor Mum. She's besotted with him, and she's loved helping him but I think, no I'm sure, that you're right."

"It's a romance scam," Josh said.

"Is there anything we can do?"

"At the very least we need to stop her giving him any more money."

"The trouble is that she's not going to believe it's a con." She hesitated for a second. "He's groomed her, hasn't he?"

Josh nodded. "From the beginning. My boss has offered to help and suggested a meeting. If your Mum hears directly from Leanne's aunt she's bound to see the similarities."

"Is there any chance we can get back the money she's lost so far?"

"From talking to the guv, I'd say there's very little chance unless we can track him down and confront him."

"Who needs to be at the meeting then? Obviously your boss and my Mum and Leanne's Aunt. I guess you, me and Leanne as well?"

"No, uh, no," Josh stuttered. "I, perhaps, I mean, maybe that's too many. I suggest we keep you and Leanne apart…"

"Apart?"

"I mean out of it." he said hastily. "Leave you and Leanne out of it. Too many eggs spoil the broth as they say."

"Chefs."

"What?"

"Never mind. I guess it makes sense to keep the

numbers down. But will you go, Josh, and tell me how it went afterwards?"

"Of course."

"And I guess I'll meet Leanne another time."

"Oh yes, some other time, definito." He nodded his head to give his words extra emphasis. "Yes, you must meet, uh, some other time."

*

Leanne was surprised to see Luke standing next to Josh when she emerged from Filchers later that afternoon. She nodded to him before pecking Josh on the cheek and putting her hand in his.

"Coffee?" she asked.

"The guv's going to join us if that's okay," Josh said.

She raised one of her perfectly sculpted eyebrows. "Why?"

"I told him about your Aunty Pam and he's offered to help."

"That's nice of him. What does he think he can do?"

"He's thinking of a meeting to start with, but says there might be a way of tracking the con man down."

"You do know I'm standing right here?" Luke said.

They turned and looked up at him.

"Sorry, guv," Josh said.

Luke shook his head. "It doesn't matter. Come on, let's get that coffee."

Once they were seated, Luke told them his idea. "It's straight out of the manual," he concluded, "but it's the obvious ploys that often work the best."

"There's a manual?" Josh asked.

"No Josh, it's just an expression."

"Right, yes. Obvious really."

Luke turned his attention to Leanne. "Do you think

your aunt would go along with my idea?"

"Definitely."

"And she'll be all right with Mandy's Mum joining our meeting?"

Leanne flicked her gaze to Josh who shrank back into the folds of his chair. "Mandy's Mum?" she said.

"Yes, didn't Josh tell you?"

She kept her eyes fixed on Josh. "No, he didn't."

Luke sensed the tension in the air and fought to keep the smile from his face. He looked at his watch. "Gosh, look at the time. I have to drive to Dorset tonight. Why don't you tell her, Josh?"

"Can't you tell her, guv?" came a weak voice from the depths of the armchair.

Luke stood up. "No, it's okay, Josh. I'll let you deal with it. I'm free Sunday if that works for the meeting, or else we can do it during the week. Let me know what suits everyone."

"Bye Luke," Leanne said, without turning her attention away from Josh.

"It was that news item I mentioned," Josh said. "Only it wasn't a news item."

"It was Mandy."

"Yes."

"And you didn't tell me because…"

"Uh, because, uh, help…"

Chapter 17

Eleanor shook Luke's hand then Josh's.

"Please take a seat, Mrs Jones," Luke said.

"Eleanor, please."

Josh was struck by how much she looked like her daughter. She was much the same height and build, and it was only the lines around her mouth and eyes that marked her out as a quarter of a century older. From what Mandy had told him they were lines founded on sadness rather than laughter.

Eleanor looked across at Luke. "Mandy told me it was really important I meet you," she said, "but I'm not quite sure why. I understand you're a financial adviser?"

"Not quite," Luke said. "Ah," he added, looking up. "Here's our other guest."

The waiter was leading another woman to their table and this time the differences were more apparent than the similarities. Pam didn't look or act like her niece. While Leanne was curvaceous, below average height and confident, her aunt was slim, tall and looked very much on edge.

"I have to be honest with you, Eleanor," Luke said once they'd all introduced themselves. "I'm not a financial advisor."

She frowned. "What are you then?"

"I work with Josh and I'm ex-police, but I'm not here in a strictly professional capacity. I think you'll understand more when you hear what Pam has to say." He turned to the other woman. "Pam, I know this is hard, but would you mind telling us what happened to you?"

"I'll give it a go," Pam said. "I'm ashamed of what I let that man do, but if I can help Eleanor by sharing my story then sure."

"What is this all about?" Eleanor asked.

"It'll all become clear in a minute," Luke said. He turned back to the other woman. "In your own time, Pam."

Pam took a deep breath. "I met Seb online about six months ago," she said, "and we hit it off straight away. He's got a great sense of humour and we found we had a lot in common." Tears started coming and Josh passed her a tissue.

"Has he died?" Eleanor asked.

Pam half-laughed at this. "I wish," she said. "Sorry, I know I shouldn't say that but, well, I feel such a fool."

"Please continue," Luke said.

She dabbed at her eyes. "At first Seb didn't mention his cancer, but a few weeks in it kind of slipped out. He was upset because he was in a lot of pain and couldn't afford the physio his consultant said he needed. And of course, it being America you can't get physiotherapy for free."

Luke noticed that Eleanor was listening intently.

"So I gave him money," Pam went on. "He tried to resist, and said he was sure he could raise it himself somehow, but I could see he was in pain, and my husband left me a little nest egg, so I thought, why not?"

"And then…" Luke prompted.

"It was fine for another few weeks until the physio was complete, which was when the pain returned and…"

"You gave him more money?"

"Yes, and again a third time which drained my savings completely. So when he asked a fourth time I had to say no."

"What happened?"

"He withdrew contact. This was about three weeks ago and I haven't heard a word since."

"And you believe now that this was a con?"

Pam sighed again. "As I said, I've been a fool." She turned to Eleanor. "Is that why you're here? Is something similar happening with you?"

Eleanor sat upright. "Not at all," she said.

"Please tell us about John," Luke said.

"It's completely different," Eleanor said, a note of anger in her voice. "I feel really sorry for you, Pam, but my John's very genuine, a lovely man." She scowled at Josh. "What has Mandy been telling you? My relationship with John is personal."

"Uh, ah." Josh looked at Eleanor, then at Luke then back to Eleanor. "She's worried, and, uh, she mentioned John and, well, it sounded similar to me."

"Nonsense."

Luke decided to help Josh out. "Does John have cancer, Eleanor?" he asked.

"Crohn's."

"And he's British but lives in the States?"

"Yes, in Florida."

"That's where Seb lives," Pam said.

"Well that hardly proves anything," Eleanor snapped. "There are millions of ex-pats in Florida."

Luke realised they weren't getting anywhere. One last try, he thought. "Pam," he said. "What finally made you realise you were being scammed?"

"It was his photos," she said.

"His photos?"

"Yes." She swallowed. "Seb never answered straight away when I FaceTime'd him. He'd always ring me back, and always from the same place in front of a bookcase. It was his study, he said. Fucking bastard!" She paused. "Sorry, I don't swear normally, but…" She dabbed her eyes again before continuing. "Anyway, the bookcase has two photos on the top shelf. One showing him holding a big fish on a boat and one of him and his wife in Thailand taken a decade or so ago."

Eleanor was now sitting forward in her chair.

"The photos were always there," Pam went on, "but a

couple of weeks ago I noticed they'd been replaced. The new photos showed a man on a motorbike and the same man with his arm around a woman's waist. I asked why and Seb told me they were pictures of his brother which he'd put up because he'd recently passed away. I thought nothing of it, but when I talked everything through with my sister it soon became obvious what was going on. The so-called study was a set, and it was being used by more than one person."

Eleanor now had her hand over her mouth.

"What is it, Eleanor?" Luke asked.

She took her hand away and he could see that her lower lip was trembling. "Oh my god," she said. "That's John, the man on the motorbike. Has to be." She turned to look at Pam. "Has the bookcase got painted grey shelves?"

Pam put her hand over Eleanor's. "Yes," she said.

Eleanor shook her head and they all gave her time to compose herself. After a few seconds, she turned to Luke. "If I get my hands on him…" she said.

"I have an idea," Luke said. "It may bring these men to justice, and it may even enable one or both of you to get some of your money back, but it's a long shot."

"Anything's worth a try," Pam said. "If only to stop them doing the same to someone else."

Luke's phone rang and he looked down to see Pete Gilmore's name on the screen. "Hi Pete," he said. "Can I ring you back in a couple of minutes?" He hung up. "Pam and Eleanor, I think it would be useful if you share all the details of your communications with each other. It might highlight anything else odd which might help us to track them down." He held his phone up. "I'll leave you now if that's okay. I need to call my colleague back."

"I'll stay and take notes, shall I, guv?" Josh said.

"Yes please, Josh."

Luke stepped outside and hit redial. "What is it, Pete?"

"Your first paid consultancy work. We've pulled

someone in and can't get anything out of him. Can you come down to the station?"

"Sure. I should be there in ten."

Chapter 18

Pete was waiting for him when Luke walked into the reception area in Manvers Street.

"He's in Interview Room 1," he said. "Name's Jeremy Scott, he's twenty-four and he's got previous for low-level dealing. We pulled him in after a spot-check and found cocaine on him."

"So what's the deal?" Luke asked. "Why do you want a second opinion?"

"He wasn't dealing, so normally we'd just give him a warning and let him go, but I thought I'd probe a bit, just in case." Pete gave a humourless chuckle. "He's a cocky sod and there was a lot of to-ing and fro-ing and he made a throwaway comment about a brothel. I pushed him on it and he tried to make out it was a joke, but the way he reacted was just, well, weird. Almost as if he was frightened. It got my insides twitching. And then he started clamming up. I'm hoping you can get more out of him."

"Did he ask for a solicitor?"

"No. I told him he was entitled to one and that seemed to shake him up even more."

"I trust your instinct, Pete, but it still sounds like something and nothing. How did you persuade the powers that be that it was worth paying money to get me in?"

"It could be that Jed's involved in a lot more than drug-dealing. I had a call from a DI at the Met last week after one of her informants told her a gang had expanded into Bath. Her source said that they were already running drugs and other activities here and that they were also planning to set up a brothel using women they'd trafficked in from Eastern Europe. As you know, Bath and organised crime have never been close bedfellows so this got the wind right up the Chief Constable's sails."

"I bet."

"He set up a Project to look into it and put DCC Davenport in charge to give it impetus." Pete grimaced. "It's Operation Porkchop. The Chief's got one of those Kune Kune things. You know, a miniature pig."

"For Christ's sake!" Luke shook his head. "Right then, I'll give it a go. Anything else I should know?"

"He's been cautioned, but it's a voluntary interview. We're not going to press charges for the cocaine, unless you turn something up that is."

"Okay. Just you and me?"

Pete nodded and Luke followed him into the meeting room, where a sullen-faced young man sat at a table cradling a cup of tea in both hands. He had greasy shoulder-length brown hair and wore a stained white polo shirt. He looked up when they entered and scowled but didn't say anything.

"We'll take it from here," Pete said to the officer who was sitting opposite Scott. The constable left and Luke took his chair, while Pete took the one nearest the room's recording device and clicked one of its buttons.

"Interview with Jeremy Scott continued," he said. "The time is 14:51. Police Constable Jefferson has left the room. Present are Detective Inspector Pete Gilmore and ex-Detective Chief Inspector Luke Sackville."

"What's he doing here," Scott said, "if he's not in the police no more?"

He was attempting to sound disinterested, but Luke could sense nervousness in his tone. Something to get behind.

"Mr Sackville works for us as a consultant," Pete said.

"Why? Is he some kind of expert?"

"I help occasionally," Luke said, smiling. "No need to worry. It's good to get a second opinion on things, that's all."

Scott grunted and lifted his plastic cup to his mouth. "Get on with it then," he said. "I got things to do."

"It shouldn't take long, Jeremy," Luke said, "and then you'll be on your way. Is it all right if I call you Jeremy?"

"Don't care. Whatever." He paused. "Prefer Jed though."

"Okay, Jed. Please call me Luke."

Scott shrugged.

"I gather you had drugs on you," Luke went on. "Cocaine."

"Had a bit, yeah. Personal use though innit."

"Yes, DI Gilmore told me that. Tell me, are you from Bath? Your accent seems more London than West Country."

"Yeah. I'm from Brixton."

"Ah right. So have you been in Bath long?"

"A few months."

"Right, and where do you live?"

Scott hesitated for a second. "Mates' sofas. Just while I find somewhere permanent.'

There was a subtle tensing of Scott's fingers around the plastic cup as he said this, and Luke immediately knew he was lying. The tells on this guy were going to be easy. He decided to move to some easier questions so that he could get a clear picture of Scott's body language and facial expressions when he was telling the truth.

"How old are you, Jed?"

"Twenty-four.'

"Were you born in Brixton?"

"Camberwell. Moved to Brixton when I was little."

"Always London until recently then?"

"Yeah."

"And DI Gilmore tells me you were found guilty of dealing drugs a few years ago."

"Two years ago, yeah. Got a community order and a fine. Don't do it no more though." He smirked. "Bad for you, innit?"

Luke could see he was still telling the truth, which in itself was interesting. If he wasn't involved in drugs any more what was the little scrote up to? Time to challenge him.

"So what made you move to Bath, Jed? It's a big move given you've lived in London all your life."

"Got the offer of a labouring job. Mate set it up. Helping out at that new development by Avon Street."

All lies, Luke was sure of it. Well rehearsed though, and he was sure that Scott would be able to back up what he was saying with paperwork of some sort. No point in probing there. Time to shift topics.

"That's great, Jed," he said. "I'm pleased to see you've found an honest job."

"Yeah right. Can I go now?"

"One thing I'm intrigued by, then you can leave."

Scott folded his arms across his chest and sat back. "Go on then."

Luke leaned forward across the desk. "Who is it you're so frightened of?"

Jed remained leaning back, his arms still folded, but his knuckles clenched and his pupils widened slightly.

"Ain't frightened of no-one."

"That's not true, is it Jed? Who do you work for?"

"His name's…"

Luke slammed his fist on the table and leaned forwards. "I'm not talking about your cock-and-bull labouring job, Jed. Who do you really work for? And what do you do for him?"

"Mr Grant," Jed said defiantly, but there was nervousness in the way he said it.

"That's not true, is it?" Luke asked, and his voice was more assertive now. "Here's what I think." He paused, watching the other man carefully. "I think you've been fed a story because you're involved in something that makes your drug dealing look like a five-year-old's white lie. You're up to your eyes in some proper nasty stuff, aren't you, Jed? You're helping out at this brothel you told DI Gilmore about. Come on, admit it."

Scott stood up. "You're talking shit. You don't know nothing. I'm leaving."

Luke sat back. "Fine." He smiled and turned to Pete. "I think we've finished, DI Gilmore. Do you agree?"

"Interview finished at 15:03," Pete said, and clicked the stop button on the recording system. "You're free to go, Mr Scott."

"Nice to meet you, Jed," Luke said but there was no response as Scott disappeared through the door.

Pete closed it after him and turned around. "Why did you let him off so lightly?" he asked

"No point in asking more, Pete. He's been well-briefed and wasn't going to steer off the script. I'm convinced you're right though and he's involved in some really heavy stuff."

"What makes you say that?"

"He's scared, but not by the police. No, he's working for someone who's put the fear of God into him. I suspect he's taken something on because the money's good but is now regretting it." Luke paused for a second. "Is there any way you could put a tail on him?"

"Not on the basis of that. Even though Project…" Pete hesitated, unable to bring himself to give the project its name. "Even though the Project's seen as important, as you well know a tail costs the earth."

"Well at least circulate his photos to all the officers in Bath. Ask them to keep an eye open, and if they spot him make a note of where and when and also who he was with.'

"Good idea. I'll do that. Thanks for coming in."

"No problem, Pete."

Chapter 19

Sam decided she would approach Audrey Manners face to face rather than by email or phone.

The call centre was at basement level, a faceless area with over two hundred staff, an abundance of fluorescent lights and no windows. When she got there it was mid-afternoon, a relatively quiet period but the place was buzzing, almost every desk occupied by a man or woman wearing a wired headset while tapping away on their keyboard. There were several whiteboards along one wall, each bearing the name of the team at the top, below which were the statistics that mattered: call volumes, time to respond, sales made and so on.

Audrey had her own glassed office at the far end and Sam could see she was in discussion with two men and one woman. As she approached Audrey saw her, smiled and mouthed 'two minutes' before resuming her conversation.

After five minutes her visitors left and Audrey gestured for Sam to come in.

"Sorry to keep you waiting," Audrey said. "There was a new router release last week and it's caused all sorts of problems. I'm in firefighting mode today." She sighed. "But I'd like to help if I can. Have you got a supplier problem?"

"It's something else actually."

"If it's about your boyfriend I'm not best qualified to help."

Sam laughed. "No, it's about work. I've been asked to help pull information together for the annual report."

"For Mike?"

Sam nodded. "And he's really on my back because I haven't pulled together the call centre data yet."

"He can be like that."

"I've found the emails requesting the info, but I can't see your replies. I think I must be looking in the wrong place, but I don't want to admit it to Mike and look like a fool. I wondered if you had a copy of the emails you sent."

Audrey smiled. "The truth is I ignored the emails. Mike and I…" She paused for a second. "Well, we've had differences and to be honest the last thing I felt like doing was helping him with his blessed annual report."

"I see. I can't tell him that though."

"I'd love to help but now's not a good time. There's a whole load of data consolidation needed and I'm up to my eyes in it."

"I don't mind pulling the information together from the raw data if that helps." Sam tried not to sound too eager.

"It certainly would, but there's a lot of it. Are you sure? I don't want to put too much pressure on you."

"I'm sure. How do I access it?"

"It's all in our management information database, CCMI. I'll give you access."

Audrey logged back into her computer, hit a few buttons, then grabbed a post-it, wrote the file address down and passed it over.

"There you go, but as I said, there's a lot of it. Any problems let me know."

"Thanks, Audrey, you're a lifesaver."

*

Sam retrieved the draft emails to Ron Young and hit send.

Audrey had been right, there was a lot of information to trawl through. Sam knew from Supracomm's intranet that Audrey had five direct reports, each with about forty staff though teams were flexed depending on demand. That many people generated a lot of data.

She spent an hour learning how everything was stored then worked her way through the database chronologically, using one notebook to jot down information she needed for the annual report and a second for anything that looked odd. She was determined that the second notebook would never leave her sight.

She was working her way through October, reconciling staff numbers with expenses and overheads, when she found the first discrepancy. She flicked back in her notebook. Sure enough, there had been four fewer staff in September after allowing for leavers and joiners. She dived into November's data then December. The four extra staff were still there, but as with October there were no associated overheads.

This could be human error. Perhaps someone had miscounted staff and the mistake had never been spotted. But that didn't make sense. And if it was deliberate then why? How would artificially upping staff numbers help with laundering money? Sam decided to park it for the time being and come back to it later.

After finishing with staff she turned her attention to income. The call centre was internal and didn't make a profit, but Filchers' projects did have to 'pay' for the use of the call centre.

The income made sense and Sam started looking at costs. It pleased her accountant's mind to see that the total costs for the year matched the income. Costs comprised 'real' payments to outside organisations and also internal payments for services like IT, cleaning and security. Sam went through the external costs first, because that was where it was most likely monies might be hidden. She started with office supplies, then moved on to headsets and lastly to communications suppliers.

"Bingo!" she said.

Kevin, a short bespectacled accountant occupying the next cubicle, popped his head up at this. "Made a breakthrough?"

She looked up. "Yes," she said, closing her notebook as subtly as she could.

"With…?"

"The annual report." She beamed up at him. "I've been looking for a document for a while and I've finally found it."

"Good for you," he said, and disappeared beneath the partition again.

Sam opened her notebook, made a note and smiled to herself. This final anomaly was definitely suspicious and she felt in her gut she had found something crucial. The problem was with payments to Ventyx, a company described on its website as 'a global supplier of communications expertise'. Supracomm spent between £5,000 and £10,000 each month on their services. This made it one of their less significant suppliers, just making it to the top fifty.

What didn't make sense was that the money for their services seemed to be coming from nowhere. It wasn't part of the total costs that had matched the total income.

She flinched when she felt a hand on her shoulder and turned her head to see her team leader, Ron Young, a grin plastered over his face.

"Thanks for doing those reports so quickly," he said, his voice raspy, his hand still pressed lightly down.

She looked at him, then pointedly at her shoulder, and he lifted his hand away.

"You did a great job," he went on, flicking his eyes around as he spoke. He really was an unattractive man, she thought, and revised her opinion on his age from fifties to sixties. His face was heavily lined, but what was really weird was his hairstyle. He was completely bald from forehead to crown, but had blonde-grey hair running from the centre at the top to both shoulders. It was an attempt to be cool, but accentuated his creepiness. He reminded her of Argus

Filch, the school caretaker at Hogwarts.

"I'll have some more reports for you to do next week," he said. "It's great having you on my team." He put his hand back on her shoulder and she pulled away and shrugged it off.

"Keep your hand where it belongs," she said.

"I'm only being friendly."

"Don't ever touch me again."

He grunted. "I'll see you on Monday." He was still smirking. "Have a good weekend."

"I intend to."

He walked away and Sam looked at her watch. Time had flown by and she had to leave in half an hour to ensure she caught her train back to Bath. She looked at a few more files, made further notes then left for the station.

She was pleased to find the carriage almost empty when she climbed on board the 6:10 to Bath. Making sure no one was watching, she removed her notebook from her bag and re-read her notes. It looked like someone had taken great care to ensure costs matched income, and it was only her deep dive into individual payments to Ventyx that had revealed the anomaly.

She flicked back to where she had made notes about the four extra staff, the ones counted in staff numbers but with no associated overheads. Were they linked to the mysterious Ventyx payments in some way? Or could one or other of these anomalies be nothing more than a simple mistake? She needed to delve deeper but it would have to wait until after the weekend.

Sam looked up to see the train was now crowded and decided to read rather than risk someone seeing what was written in her notebook. She opened her Kindle app but was no more than a page into her book when her phone rang. She recognised the number immediately even though she'd deleted him from her contacts. With a sigh, she accepted the call.

"Hi, Tony," she said.

"Hi, Sammy." He was the only one who had ever called her that and she hated it. No point in telling him now though. This was the first time he had tried to contact her in over a month. She had worried he would stalk her after he took her dumping him so badly, but he seemed to have accepted they were finished.

"I've met someone else," he said.

"Good for you." But why was he telling her?

"I want you to meet her."

"Why?"

"You're going to think this is odd, Sammy." She already thought it was odd. Could it get any odder? "She wants advice on karate classes. She's thinking of taking it up."

"Can't she just google them?"

"But you're a Dan or something and know your stuff. I said you'd know the best ones to go for."

"I know a couple. Why don't I message you with them."

"I suppose you could, but I thought you'd like to meet her."

"Why would I want to meet her?" There was a pause at the other end. "Has she asked to meet me, Tony?"

"No, but I…" He let it hang there.

Sam sighed. "I'll text you some details, but I don't want to meet her, okay?"

"If you're sure?"

"Yes, I'm sure. Bye, Tony."

"Bye Sammy."

Sam stared at her phone for a few seconds after she ended the call. That was plain weird. What on earth reason did Tony have for wanting her to meet his new fling? She was damned sure it wasn't to exchange details of karate classes.

Chapter 20

Luke invited the MI6 man to sit down and introduced him to Helen, Josh and Maj.

Evan smiled. "It's really good to meet you all," he said. "Thanks for your help with this."

"I invited Evan," Luke said, "so that he can meet you all and hear what we've found out so far. By the way, I'm going to ask Security to put a fingerprint-controlled lock on our door so that only the five of us can get in."

"Cool," Josh said.

"Helen," Luke went on, "can you talk us through the board please?"

Helen stood up and walked to the whiteboard. "It's early days," she said, "but thanks to Sam and Maj we've already got a couple of leads." She pointed to the centre of the board where she had written 'Supracomm'. "As instructed, everything we're doing revolves around Supracomm. Our focus has been here and here," she indicated arrows pointing off to 'Personnel' and 'Accounts', "with Sam trying to unpick financial transactions while Maj has looked at individuals across the project teams to see if they're up to anything unusual."

"I see you've written '4 staff' and 'Ventyx' on those post-its," Evan said, pointing at the board. "What do those mean?"

"Probably best if I explain," Sam said. "I found four unaccounted-for staff. They first appeared in the call centre numbers last October and have been there ever since but there are no associated overheads."

"That's interesting," Evan said. "It ties up with something I've found out. Let's come back to it later."

Sam indicated the second post-it. "Ventyx is a

communications supplier. They're paid five to ten thousand pounds each month but the figures don't make it to the balance sheet. There's no matching income. I need to do a lot more digging but it certainly seems suspicious."

"Maj," Luke said, "can you update us on what you've discovered?"

"Sure," Maj said. He pointed to the board. "As you can see I've identified three people so far who've acted suspiciously. I've still got to follow through on the top two, but the one at the bottom, Chris Nevin, is definitely up to something."

"I've met Chris," Sam said. "He seems a really nice guy. I find it hard to believe he could be mixed up in financing Al Ummah."

"One of the things I learned early on in the police," Luke said, "is not to trust anyone. Criminals are very good at hiding in plain sight."

"What did he do?" Evan asked.

"He waited until Sam was away from her desk," Maj said, "and then went into her cubicle and leafed through her notebook. Of course, he could have had another motive, but it struck me as very odd. I'm watching him closely now to see if he does anything else."

"Do we know anything about him?"

"Not a lot. We know he's viewed as a high-flyer, but that's about it."

Evan produced a small notebook from the inside of his jacket. "I'll get my guys to do some research into Ventyx," he said. "Given you've got access to Supracomm's systems it's probably best you look into this guy Chris Nevin."

"Fair enough," Luke said. "You were saying you had information that might link to the four spurious members of staff that Sam identified."

"I do indeed. As you know, we're ninety-nine per cent certain Supracomm is being used for money laundering." He took in a deep breath. "However, what we've uncovered over the past few days makes us think we're actually looking at black money."

"What's that?" Josh asked.

"It's money gained from illegal trade or criminal activity."

"So they're not just passing money through Supracomm's books?" Luke said.

"No, we believe they're using Supracomm to fund some of their illegal activities and then to pass the income through to clean the money. Last week Border Force foiled a delivery of 2 kilograms of Class A drugs, heroin and cocaine. It's not a massive haul, but what was curious was that it was hidden in a package of routers addressed to a company that is a Supracomm subsidiary. It could be a coincidence of course, but I think it unlikely."

"So they're earning money through drugs?" Helen asked.

"And almost certainly other illegal activities such as prostitution and human trafficking. Perhaps even kidnapping."

"Hold on a second," Luke said. "Did you say prostitution and human trafficking?"

"Yes," Evan said. "Why?"

"The Supracomm subsidiary the drugs were addressed to wasn't in Bath by any chance?"

Evan raised an eyebrow.. "How on earth did you know that?"

"Operation Porkchop," Luke said. He lifted his hand. "Sorry, everyone. It's the Chief Constable's name not mine. He likes to name projects after his pets."

Josh looked up at him, his mouth open. "Who'd have thought the Chief Constable would keep a pork chop as a pet?"

"He doesn't, he… Look, it doesn't matter." Luke turned his attention back to Evan. "The police believe a gang is moving into Bath and one of the things they're thought to be doing is setting up a brothel using trafficked women."

Evan thought about this for a moment. "Of course, this could be a coincidence." Luke raised an eyebrow and Evan smiled. "No, you're right. There has to be a link."

There was silence for a few seconds while they all thought about this and then Josh put his hand up.

"Do you need the toilet?" Luke asked.

"No, guv." Josh pulled his hand down. "But I was wondering if you were thinking what I was thinking?"

"I very much doubt it."

"About…" Josh jerked his head to one side and Luke looked in the direction he was indicating.

"Am I thinking about the door?" he asked.

"No, not the door, the…" Josh nodded his head to one side again."

"For Christ's sake, Josh."

"About…" He lowered his voice to a whisper. "…the man who's been diddling Leanne's Aunty."

Helen gave a little snort. "Sorry," she said, and put her hand over her mouth.

"Conning, I meant," Josh said. "Diddling sounds like, well, like…"

"We all know what it sounds like, Josh," Luke said.

"Perhaps I'm being idiotic."

"Heaven forbid."

"But I was wondering," Josh went on, "if the men who scammed Leanne's Aunty Pam and Mandy's mother could be part of this as well?"

"You mean linked to Supracomm and this gang who have moved into Bath?" Luke asked.

"Sorry, guv. Stupid suggestion."

"Not at all." Luke paused. "Their operation could be anywhere in the country or even abroad and it's a long shot but it's definitely possible."

Josh smiled. "So I'm not being stupid, guv?"

"No. We should keep our eyes and ears open for

anything that links their operation to Bath or the surrounding area just in case you're right."

"What's this all about?" Evan asked

Luke told him about the money Pam and Eleanor had been conned out of, and what he had decided to do next.

"There's always the possibility that could well be one of their enterprises," Evan said when he'd finished. "Good work, Josh."

Josh beamed with pride.

"I'll add it to the board," Helen said.

"Right, thanks everyone," Evan said. "I'd best be off."

Luke showed him out while the others got back to their work. On his return he took his phone out and placed a call.

"Glen Baxter, Head of Security."

"Hi Glen, it's Luke."

"Call me later. I'm in a disciplinary meeting."

"I'm sorry to hear that."

"Not me. It's one of my large team. I'm giving him a seeing-to."

"A seeing-to?"

"Yes, a seeing-to."

"I don't think you know what that means do you, Glen?"

"What?"

"You mean a talking-to."

"As I said, I'm busy. Ring me later."

Luke smiled as he ended the call and decided a face-to-face meeting would be more productive. He gave it five minutes, then made his way to the Executive Floor where Glen's new office was. There was a shiny bronze sign outside saying 'Glen Baxter - Head of Security'.

He knocked and went straight in. There were boxes crammed with folders on the floor on either side of a mahogany desk. Glen sat behind the desk and was rocking backwards and forwards on his chair staring at a single photo of himself in a tuxedo on the bookcase against the wall.

"Nice sign," Luke said, indicating the door with his thumb as he sat on the chair opposite. "I see you're still Head of Security. No promotion yet?"

"Not yet, no."

"And you've given your guy a good seeing-to?"

"Yes, he won't screw me again."

"I bet he won't." Luke tried to keep a straight face, but it was hard.

"What do you want?" Glen said. "I've got a lot on my plate."

"You must have with forty staff."

"Forty-one."

"Forty-one! A growing empire. You must feel very important."

"And busy. Get on with it."

"I need a security lock on the Ethics Room door."

Glen shook his head "No need to bother me with something so trivial. You know the drill. Submit a request through the normal channels."

"It's urgent."

Glen gave a low laugh. "Urgent! For the Ethics Team? I don't think so."

Luke leaned forward over the desk and looked into the other man's eyes. "I need it fitted today."

After a few seconds, Glen turned his face away. "Can't be done," he said, his eyes back on the photo. "It needs proper authorisation."

"You mean you're not senior enough to approve it yourself?"

"Of course I am. I'm a senior manager."

"A Head of Department."

"Yes," Glen said, turning back to face Luke, his chest puffing out. "A Head of Department."

"Which was what they asked for at the Annual Security

Awards, and the reason you asked me to stand in for you."

Glen nodded. "Yes," he said.

"Incidentally, how is the acting going?"

"Fine." Glen wiped his hand across the top of his number 1 buzz cut. "Now, I need…"

"You said you had a small part."

"A big part, actually. I was one of the main performers, ah, actors. I mean actors."

Luke took the photo Maj had given him from his pocket and placed it on the desk. "It doesn't look like a big part to me,' he said.

Glen stared down in horror. "Where did you get that?"

"Don't worry, Glen," Luke said. "It can be our little secret. You can keep the photo."

Glen snatched it up and thrust it into the top drawer of his desk.

"The Chippenmales, is that right? " Luke asked. "Clever name."

"The name was my idea."

"Why am I not surprised?"

"Eh?"

"So, the security lock?

"Ah yes, uh, I think we might be able to get it sorted this week."

Luke stared at him intently.

"Okay," Glen said. "I'll get one of my guys on it today."

"Thanks," Luke said as he stood up. "You be sure and give him a good seeing-to."

Chapter 21

Laurie brought the tray in and held it down for the other three to take their coffees. He had a sip of his own then sat down in front of his computer, clicked on refresh and was pleased to see four new messages in his email inboxes.

Two of them were from Alison and he made an instant decision to leave those for the time being. She was in hot pursuit and he needed to make her sweat. She was almost there but it was very much a case of softly-softly-catchee-monkey. Too fast and she'd pull back. He'd read her emails this afternoon but wouldn't reply for at least a couple of days.

The other two were from Monica and Herbie, which was good news. He had almost given up on Monica but perhaps there was still a chance. As for Herbie, he found it interesting with a man. It was more of a challenge for obvious reasons.

"Herbie's replied," he said.

"That's good," Danny said absent-mindedly. They had their backs to each other and had been working solidly for four hours. "Fancy a break in a bit? Maybe grab some lunch."

"Sure thing," Laurie said. "Couple of things to do then I'll be free."

He decided to start with Monica's email.

Hi Sweetie,

I thought about what you said last week. You were right, I was being unfair. Please forgive me. I've been thinking about you a lot.

You're not thinking of ending our relationship are you? I couldn't bear it if you did that. I know I'm not a great catch but we've got so much in common. I miss our chats too. I always feel better after we've FaceTime'd.

Your loving M

There was a stack of hardcover notebooks lined up against each other on his desk. He pulled out the one with 'Monica Fairbanks' on the side and opened it to his last entry which was dated almost a week earlier. He added today's date, re-read her email then made a few bulleted notes.

He thought for a moment. The big question was whether it was time for the push or whether he should wait, perhaps be distant for a little longer and make her really want him. The push usually only worked once, and he had learned from experience that timing was everything.

He put Monica's file back in the stack and pulled out the notebook labelled Herbie Cutler. He opened it, studied the last couple of entries then clicked on the email.

Hello Cherry,

I was shocked to hear your news. It must be awful for you and I think you're amazingly brave the way you cope and keep your head held high. It's truly awe-inspiring. The fact that you are able to hold down such a high-pressure job with everything you're up against is nothing short of a miracle.

As for me, it's the same old same old here. My son and daughter-in-law invited me over for a Sunday roast which was great. Brilliant to see the grandchildren too. They grow up so fast, don't they? It felt lonely when I got home though. Ever since Lynda died it's felt like that.

But my problems are so minor compared to yours. If you want to pour your heart out please do. I would like nothing more than to feel I give you words of encouragement to help you through this frightening time.

All the best

Herbie

Laurie jotted a couple of notes down under today's date. Still at phase one but there was some promise there. He re-read the email. Yes, those last couple of sentences were definitely encouraging. He'd leave it a day before replying to the old fart. He didn't want to appear over-eager.

He was about to say he was ready for lunch when his laptop pinged. It was from Pam. What a pain. She'd been emailing him every day for the last couple of weeks and he was getting sick and tired of it. Still, he had to read each email, just to be on the safe side.

Hello Gorgeous

I'm sorry I've been bombarding you with emails lately. I've been really worried that you'd gone off me, or even worse that your cancer has come back. I couldn't bear it if you were suffering and I wasn't able to help, and I know how much better physiotherapy makes you feel.

I've got some good news though. I sold some old stamps that my grandfather left me in his will, and would you believe they made over four thousand pounds! Which means you can have that next course of treatment you were so keen on.

Please please please get back to me as soon as you can. I need to know you're well.

Pammy

xxx

This was an interesting development. The last time they had talked he had started 'the drift' but perhaps there might be mileage in Pam yet. She wasn't one of his most profitable clients, but she'd brought in getting on ten thousand so no slouch either. He'd leave it for now though, perhaps discuss it with the others over lunch and see what they thought.

He smiled to himself. Job satisfaction was what motivated him and sucking money from these rich bitches gave him just that.

"Ready for lunch, guys?" he said. "I could murder a burger."

*

Danny and the others had said he should play it slow and carefully with Pam otherwise she would smell a rat. On reflection, Laurie thought they were probably right. He re-read her email and smiled to himself. A subtle approach and it would be easy pickings. The woman was desperate.

He pulled down the notebook labelled 'Pam Greening', leafed through to the most recent page and checked his name and terms of endearment. Right, here goes. He looked down at the laptop and held both hands above the keyboard twiddling his thumbs while he pulled his thoughts together. After a moment or two, he started typing.

> Hi Babe
>
> I feel embarrassed that I haven't replied to your emails. I'm truly truly sorry. I haven't had a good couple of weeks to be honest, but I don't want to worry you with my problems.

Yes, that was good. He deliberately hadn't responded to her whining about his illness. Let the bitch ask again.

Now he needed to decline her offer of money. It was a risky strategy but the guys had felt strongly that it was the correct approach. They were right. She was hooked and Laurie was sure that in her next email she would insist he accept it.

> Thanks for the offer to help with my physio - it means a lot. I couldn't possibly say yes though. You've already done so much to help me.

And finally, he needed to ask about her. He didn't want to

appear self-centred.

> That's awful news about your grandfather. Were you close
> to him? I hope you and the rest of your family are keeping
> well.
>
> Seb
>
> xxx

He read the draft email back to himself. Was it too short?
He debated adding more questions about her family but no,
he didn't want to detract from the main message. He
changed the sign-off so that it read 'Your darling Seb' and
added two more x's.

He sat back and hit the send button.

Done.

Laurie made a note in the notebook, smiling as he did
so. The bait was dangled and all he had to do was wait,
though he was pretty certain she'd get back to him pretty
quickly.

Chapter 22

Tania knew what she and the others were going to be forced to do, and she almost wished they would get on with it. The waiting was horrendous and Izabella, in particular, was struggling. She had hardly said a word since they had been locked into their dormitory. Even when Greg had brought them food she had barely raised her head from her lap.

The room they were supposed to sleep in couldn't have been more different from those downstairs that they had been told would be used for their 'work'. It was large, with 5 single beds, a sink, a large wardrobe and a chest of drawers. Peeling pink wallpaper covered the walls and there was no carpet, just aged and dirty floorboards. A single ceiling bulb hung within an ancient pink-tasselled shade.

She looked over at the two German women. They were deep in conversation, but she knew none of their language and hadn't the faintest idea what they were talking about. Their faces, she was sure, reflected her own, fear etched into their expressions as they awaited their fate.

With a start, she realised there were footsteps on the landing outside the room. The Germans immediately stopped talking and turned to look at the door. Only Izabella failed to react.

A key turned in the lock and Greg pushed the door open. He left it ajar and stepped to one side, allowing another man to enter. Tania's heart gave a leap as she saw who it was. This was the man who had killed the German girl, the man Greg had called Mr Anderson.

"Get 'em all to stand up," Anderson said. Greg did so, pulling Izabella roughly to her feet when she didn't react immediately. "I'm going to explain how everything works,"

Anderson went on, "and you had better fucking listen." He turned to Greg. "Repeat what I say in German so the Krauts understand."

"Will do," Greg said, and translated what Anderson had already said.

Anderson gestured to Tania and Izabella. "I'm gonna assume you two understand enough English. Savvy?"

Tania didn't know this last word but got the gist. She nodded.

"What's the matter with her?" Anderson said, indicating Izabella who was standing but still had her face down.

Greg went over to Izabella, put his hand under her chin and jerked her head up. She had tears in her eyes. "Keep your head up," he hissed.

"Right," said Anderson. He started pacing left and right, looking forcefully at each of the women in turn. "It cost a lot to bring you here and you need to repay me. When you've earned enough you'll be allowed to leave."

Tania didn't believe this for a moment.

"Until then," he went on, "you need to do exactly as you are told, whether it's by me or Greg or any of your customers." He waited while Greg translated before continuing. "Men pay a lot to come here and you need to be nice to them. And I mean really nice." He smirked as he said this.

"When are customers?" Tania said.

Anderson walked to her until his face was almost touching hers. "Shut it! I'm talking." He stepped back a pace before continuing. "You will be allowed out separately for ninety minutes every day, but if you fail to come back one of the others will suffer for it." He paused and shook his head. "I'm not so sure it's a good idea but this is Greg's place and he's convinced me."

Tania kept her face blank while Greg translated what Anderson had said but her mind was working overtime. If they could leave the building she could find out where they were, ask to borrow someone's phone and ring home. This was her opportunity.

"And don't even fucking think about calling home or contacting the police," Anderson said, almost as if he had read her mind. "We have your phones and we know where you live."

He stepped back towards Tania. "You're a gobby cow and I bet you're thinking how to take advantage of Greg's idea of free time." He gave a mirthless chuckle. "But believe me, you don't wanna do nuffin."

He moved back and looked her up and down. "Is your Mum as pretty as you, darlin'? My guys would have an awful nice time with her if I asked them to pay her a visit."

Tania's eyes widened and she felt her bottom lip start to tremble.

Anderson stepped forward again and spat his next words into her face. "Don't fucking cross me. Understand?"

Tania nodded. "I understand."

"And don't you worry darlin'," he said, the smirk back. "Your customers will be here soon enough."

Anderson turned and left. Greg followed, locking the door after him. All four women sat back on their beds, lost in their thoughts.

A few minutes passed and then the key turned again. This time Greg was alone.

"You heard Mr Anderson," he said. "You saw what he did to that other one."

"Do you even know her name?" Tania asked.

Greg glared at her and ignored the question. "He'll do it again if he needs to, so you all better do as I say. If you do it'll be a lot easier for you."

"When customers?" Tania said.

"First ones are tomorrow evening at 8."

"Which of us?"

Greg shrugged his shoulders. "Who knows? They'll

choose." He paused. "From here on I'm not going to lock the door. You need to cook your own meals and keep your rooms clean and tidy. You're free to move around the house, but you're not to leave the building unless it's your time to go out. I'll decide when that is but, as Mr Anderson said, you better not be longer than ninety minutes. And don't even think of trying anything. You speak to the police or contact your family and you'll pay for it."

Anderson was waiting near the front door when Greg came downstairs. "You sure you can trust 'em?" he asked.

"Yeah, don't worry Mr Anderson," Greg said. "They're not going to give any trouble."

"You watch that mouthy one. If she puts a foot out of line let me know. The punters are gonna love her, but she can be replaced." He paused. "Any of 'em can."

Greg hesitated. "I've got an issue with one of my men," he said. "I think we need to have a word with him."

Anderson sneered. "What's he done?"

"One of the others saw him getting into a police car. He said it looked like a routine stop, but we need to make sure he didn't say anything."

"Fucking right we do. Where is he?"

"He's out back having a fag."

"Right." He indicated the door to the lounge. "Bring him in here."

Greg went out to the back where Jed and two others were sitting on a low wall smoking and talking quietly.

"Jed," he said, "come with me."

"Sure Greg," Jed said. He stubbed his cigarette out on the top of the wall and stood up. "What is it?"

"We'll talk about it in the front room." He led Jed to the front of the house and pushed the lounge door open. Jed walked in and Greg followed, shutting the door behind him. Anderson was standing with his back to the fireplace.

"Hi, Mr Anderson," Jed said, a slight tremor in his voice.

Anderson walked forward and Jed instinctively took a step back. Anderson kept coming until he was only a few inches away.

"What's your name?" he snarled.

"Jed."

"I hear you been talking to the police."

"No, I…"

Anderson punched him hard in the stomach and Jed bent double and gasped.

"Don't you fucking lie to me," Anderson said.

"I - didn't - say - nothing," Jed said as he took deep intakes of air.

Anderson turned to look at Greg. "Where'd you get him?"

"One of the others said he'd be good."

"Has he got previous?"

"Drug-dealing. A few years ago though, and minor stuff."

"Didn't I say clean records only?"

"I didn't say nothing," Jed repeated. He was still bent over, but he was breathing more regularly now.

"We're going for a drive," Anderson said.

"No, Mr Anderson, I…"

Anderson turned and patted Jed on the shoulder. "Don't you worry, Jed. I want you to show me where the police picked you up, that's all." He smiled, but it was a distant cousin of the real thing. "'I need to make sure everyone avoids the area, that's all."

Jed looked at Anderson, his eyes wide, then at Greg who stared back stoney-faced.

"Want me to come?" Greg asked.

"Yeah, that'd be good," Anderson said. He turned and led the way out of the house, Jed behind him and Greg at the rear.

When they got to the car, Anderson threw Greg the keys. "You drive," he said. "I'll keep Jed company in the back."

They got in the back, Jed behind Greg and Anderson next to him.

"They picked me up outside the Guildhall," Jed said.

"Shall I head there?" Greg asked.

"Nah, it's a nice day," Anderson said. "I fancy a trip out of town. Ever been to Bathampton, Jed?"

Chapter 23

"Mum, please can I go to the mall this evening?" Sabrina's tone was pleading

"I said no," Asha said.

Maj took a bite of his flatbread, keeping his eyes down. This was not a conversation he wanted to be involved in.

"But Mu-u-um, all the other girls are going. It's cool."

"All the other girls? Is Susan going, or Fatima, or Idil?"

"Idil said she'd go."

"What about Susan?"

Asha ignored the question. "Come on, Mum. I'll be back by ten."

"Ten! You're thirteen, Sabrina. I'm not letting you stay out at a shopping centre until ten in the evening."

Maj took another bite, his head still down. It was only a matter of time before...

"Dad, what do you think?"

Blast it. Maj looked up from his breakfast and across at his daughter. She was giving him her puppy dog look. He had to be strong.

"I think your mother's right," he said, and winced slightly at the hurt look from Sabrina.

"Thank you," Asha said.

Sabrina stood up and looked at her mother. "You don't understand." She turned to her father. "Neither of you do." She left the table and flounced to the bottom of the stairs.

"We're leaving in twenty minutes," Maj said.

"Huh," Sabrina said as she stomped upstairs.

Asha called after her. "Don't forget your gym kit."

Maj buried himself in his flatbread again. He knew what was coming next.

"You should support me more," Asha said.

"I did. I said you were right, didn't I?"

"I suppose so."

Maj decided to change the subject. "I'm working on some secret stuff at the moment. Girt good fun it is."

"What is it?"

He smiled. "If I told you it wouldn't be secret any more would it?" He paused. "I even had to sign the Official Secrets Act."

"Really?" The pride was evident in his wife's voice.

"Really."

Asha's eyebrows furrowed. "It's not dangerous is it?"

"Of course not."

"I worry, that's all." She put her hand over Maj's. "After what happened to your colleague Sam, I worry a lot."

"No need to. That was a one-off."

Sabrina had calmed down considerably by the time she came downstairs, and seemed her normal self when she climbed into the passenger seat next to Maj.

"You okay about the shopping centre?" Maj said.

She shrugged. "Sure."

He looked across at his daughter, marvelling at how quickly his baby had grown into this beautiful girl. She was in those difficult teenage years, half adult and half child but wanting to be one hundred percent a grown-up. It seemed no time at all since he had been carrying her in a sling around his chest, and now she was her mother's height and already attracting looks from the boys.

He dropped her off at school, waved goodbye then drove the short distance to Filchers. He logged in to Otto and Cassy, using the latter to look for anything suspicious and then following up by looking at footage on Otto.

After he had been working for a while his phone rang and he looked at the screen, surprised to see it was already gone eleven and also to see his wife's photo appear. It wasn't like her to ring him when she was at work.

"Hi, Asha," he said. "Is everything okay?"

"Not really."

"What is it?"

"It's Sabrina."

"Is she all right?"

"She's fine, but she got into a fight at school and she's cut herself. The school nurse said it's nothing to worry about, and probably won't even need stitches, but that she ought to go to A&E to check it out."

"You want me to take her?'

"Please, Maj. We've got a backlog of orders to send out and I'm up to my eyes in it."

Helen had got the gist of what had happened and mouthed 'Just go'.

"I'll leave now," Maj said.

"Thanks. Let me know how she is, won't you? And find out what this fight was about."

"Of course."

He hung up. "Are you sure you don't mind, Helen?"

She shook her head. "Don't be silly. Family always comes first."

As Maj drove to the school he wondered what it was that had caused his daughter to get into a fight. She wasn't an aggressive child, never had been, so it was very out of character.

The school receptionist greeted him with a smile. "Sabrina's fine, Mr Osman," she said, then gestured to a door further down the corridor. "She's in there with Mrs Parkin."

Maj knocked on the door, heard 'Enter,' and walked in. Sabrina turned and he saw she had a nasty cut on her left hand at the bottom of her thumb.

"Sorry, Dad," she said.

"What happened?"

"It wasn't Sabrina's fault," Mrs Parkin said, a smile on her face. "In fact she's been a star and the other girl is most likely going to be suspended. Look, why don't you take her to A&E and get this patched up? I think it might need a few stitches. Sabrina can tell you exactly what happened on the way."

They walked out to the car and Maj could see that his daughter's hand was hurting. She sat in the front passenger seat and he had to help her buckle her seat belt.

"What happened?" he asked as he pulled out of the school car park.

"It was Millie Sanders," Sabrina said. "She's an ugly cow."

"Sabrina!"

"Well she is, Dad. She's 15 and a bully."

"Did she bully you?"

"No chance."

Maj felt stupidly proud of his daughter just for that.

"I was talking to Susan in the playground at break," Sabrina went on, "and I saw Millie in the road outside arguing with another girl."

"Another girl from your school?"

"No. I don't know what school she goes to. She didn't have a uniform and she looked about fifteen to me, though she wasn't as big as Millie. About as tall but much slimmer."

"Why did you get involved?"

"The other girl looked terrified, and I could see Millie was giving her a hard time, showing off to her nasty little friends. Then she grabbed the other girl's hair and pulled her to the ground and, well, I rushed out and…"

"And what?"

"I whacked her on the side of the head."

"Is that how you injured yourself?" Maj gestured to Sabrina's hand.

"Yes. I caught my hand on her earring."

"What happened then?"

"Millie started screaming." A grin smeared itself across Sabrina's face, "And I saw the earring had torn through the bottom of her ear."

"Ooh, nasty." Maj was smiling too now.

"Yes," Sabrina said, still grinning.

"What happened to the girl?"

"She muttered something, but it wasn't in English, and then she ran away. Mr Weston came out and it didn't take long for him to find out what had happened."

"Why had Millie gone for her?"

"Apparently because she was standing across the road watching the school. She's like that is Millie."

"She sounds like a cow."

"Yes, Dad," Sabrina said. "An ugly cow."

Chapter 24

Luke returned from lunch to find Glen Baxter standing at the Ethics Room door and cursing under his breath.

"Are you okay?" Luke said.

"Fine," Glen said without looking around, his tone suggesting anything but. He was trying to fix something to the door but his screwdriver kept sliding off. "I'm fitting this bloody lock you wanted so urgently."

"I thought you were going to get one of your large team to fit it."

"I decided to do it myself and leave them to more important work. You know the saying, 'If you want a job done properly, do it'."

Luke waited for a moment but it was apparent Glen wasn't going to say anything else. "Yourself," he said.

"Eh?"

"The saying is 'If you want a job done properly, do it yourself.'"

Glen looked up at him, confusion etched on his face. "Right, well I am doing it myself, aren't I?" The screwdriver slid off again. "Shit!" he said.

"It looks like you're struggling."

Glen stood up and turned around. "It's a new model, the Norton FS-433, and needs adjustment. I'm not struggling, I'm calibrating."

"So why were you swearing?"

Glen grunted and turned back to the door.

"I'll let you get on," Luke continued. "Let me know when you need to register our fingerprints."

He walked into the Ethics Room and Josh immediately called over.

"I've arranged to go to Leanne's aunt this afternoon,

guv," he said. "Is that okay?"

"Yes, that's fine," Luke said.

"Don't we need to wait for…" Josh nodded his head to one side indicating Glen who was bent over the door and still cussing.

"I think he might take a while," Luke said. "No, let's head off now."

"I'll have to pop home for my MacBook," Josh said. "I'll see you there."

They had agreed that it was important that Pam Greening FaceTime'd the man calling himself Seb from her house otherwise he would smell a rat. Luke hoped she could pull it off and that the scammer would let something slip that would help them track him down.

Luke left a few minutes after Josh and drove the short distance to Pam's house.

"Are you sure you're happy to do this?" he asked when she had shown him into her lounge.

"Definitely," she said. "I want to get him as much as you do."

The doorbell rang and Pam left to open the front door.

"Here's my baby," Josh said as he entered the room ahead of her and removed a slim gold laptop from his backpack.

"Why can't I call Seb on my iPad as usual?" Pam asked.

"We need something with more features and this is a MacBook. Christmas present from my parents and it's got loads more goodies. I won't be a second."

Josh placed the laptop on the dining table, raised the lid and clicked his way through a few screens. "I've set Quicktime up so that it'll record the whole call, both audio and video," he said. "Pam, can you log into FaceTime please?"

She entered her sign-in details.

Josh clicked a couple more buttons and then stood back. "All set," he said.

"Well done, Josh," Luke said. He turned to Pam. "Are you ready?"

"Yes, sure. I'll try to stick to what you suggested."

"Great. Good luck. We'll go in the kitchen and let you get on with it."

"Right," she said, and Luke could see she was nervous.

"Try not to worry, Pam," he said. "You can only do your best."

She nodded and sat at the dining table. Once Luke and Josh had shut the kitchen door behind them she took a deep breath and clicked on the MacBook to start the call.

She let it ring for a while then hung up and clicked the button again. He had never answered on the first call in the past and she knew why now. He needed time to prepare himself.

At the second time of asking there were only a few rings before Seb's face appeared on the screen. As usual, he was in his so-called study, the bookcase behind him.

"Hi Pammy," he said. "It's lovely to hear from you."

"How are you, Seb?"

She could see that he looked pale, and for the first time wondered if it was make-up.

"I've not been well," he said and sighed. "I hate to tell you this, but my consultant told me it's come back."

"Oh no," she said, secretly proud of her acting ability. "In the same place?"

"He thinks so. He wants me to start chemo again next Monday."

"That's awful. So you don't need the physio any more?"

"Just as well you couldn't afford it, Babe." His use of the term of endearment made her feel a little sick inside. "Not much use doing physio," he went on, "when the big C is eating me up again."

"Can I help pay for the chemotherapy?"

She thought she saw the corners of his mouth turn up slightly when she said this, but it was gone as soon as it came.

"I couldn't possibly ask you for more money," he said. "Medical costs are so high here in Florida. It's going to cost £6,000 and you've given me enough. My brother's got a bit."

Let me guess, she thought, *he's got £2,000.*

"He can only manage £2,000," Seb went on, "but I'm sure I can raise the rest somehow."

"Nonsense," Pam said. "I know how hard it is for you. Let me give you the other £4,000."

"If you're sure, Babe?"

"Of course I am." She swallowed. She'd laid the bait. Now was the time to try to reel him in. "There's a complication though?"

"What's that?"

"I can't transfer it to the account I put the other money in. My bank has told me they've changed their policy on offshore accounts. I have to transfer it to one of the main UK banks."

Seb only hesitated for a second. "That's no problem," he said. "I've got an account with NatWest."

"Oh great. I've got a pen here. What's the sort code and account number?"

"I, uh, I can't remember it offhand. Tell you what, I'll email the details to you as soon as we finish the call."

"Great. I'll transfer the money this afternoon."

He had an even harder time concealing his smile this time. "Thanks, Babe," he said. "So how are your family?"

Ten minutes later Pam ended the call and sat back in her chair. Boy, that had been tiring. She hoped she had done everything Luke had suggested.

"Guys," she called. "I've finished the call."

Luke and Josh came into the room. Josh went straight to the MacBook and Luke walked over to Pam and put his hand on her shoulder.

"Well done," he said. "How was it?"

"Bloody awful," she said, and gave a little shiver.

"It's worked," Josh said. He clicked a few more times and a man's face came up on the screen, with Pam's face confined to a small rectangular window in the top right. He pressed pause.

"Do you mind if we watch this through now?" Luke asked."

"Not at all," Pam said. "I hope I did all right."

Luke and Josh watched the entire FaceTime call, Josh pressing pause and making notes when Luke asked him to.

"Well?" Pam said.

"I can see why you fell into his trap," Luke said. "He's a smooth so-and-so." He paused before continuing. "For most of the time he did well. He certainly does a good job of looking ill, but I'm pretty sure there's a whole bunch of makeup helping there. There were two occasions when he gave himself away though. First off, when you offered to help pay for the chemo he was practically beaming from ear to ear."

"I spotted that, guv," Josh said.

"The biggest tell of all though," Luke went on, "was when he lied about having a NatWest account."

"He lied?' Pam said.

"Definitely."

"He's a Truth Wizard," Josh said, pointing his thumb at Luke.

"I can guarantee he's opening an account right now," Luke said, ignoring Josh's comment. "The big question is whether, when he opens the account, he provides any information that can help us to identify him or his location."

"But surely the bank will keep that confidential," Josh said.

"From us," Luke said, "but I know someone who might be able to do us a favour and try to extract it from them."

"Gotcha, guv." Josh flicked his fingers together. "Evan.

Easy-peasy."

"I'll let you know when he sends me the details," Pam said.

"Thanks," Luke said. "I'll call my contact now and ask him if he'll help. What will the name be on the account?"

"Sebastian Crown.'

"Great." Luke turned to Josh. "I want to look through the call again. Let's do it back in the office."

Once they had returned to the Ethics Room Luke opened the MacBook, started the recording and immediately paused it so that he could look carefully at what was behind Seb.

Most of the background was filled by what looked like the right two-thirds of a tall bookcase. Three shelves were visible, each with a number of books and ornaments, and the middle shelf also had 2 photos. The photos were of no help. They were the ones Pam had described, one showing Seb on a fishing boat, the other with his arm around a woman's waist.

The ornaments weren't useful either, a few small vases and a couple of china figurines.

The books, though, were intriguing. On the bottom shelf were twelve or so Agatha Christie paperbacks while the top shelf had hardbacks, also fiction though more recent, plus a couple of autobiographies. He could just make out Schwarzenegger's name on the spine of one and he thought he could see David Jason printed on the other.

On the middle shelf were travel books, and this was where it got interesting. He counted nine, six thick Lonely Planet Guides and three slimmer titles, the print too small to read the words on their spines.

"Josh," he said, without looking around "Can we enlarge this image?" Josh came to stand behind him and Luke pointed to the books. "I want to read what those say."

"Sure, guv. Just a sec." Josh used the mouse bar to encircle the area Luke was interested in, then clicked a couple of times. "There you go."

"Well, that's interesting," Luke said, as he bent his head to one side to read what was on the spines. "One book about the Glastonbury Tor, a second on Bath in the Blitz, and a third on the building of Wells Cathedral. For someone with a Scottish accent who now lives in Florida, I'd say that was somewhat odd, wouldn't you Josh?"

"You think it proves he's somewhere local, guv?"

Luke nodded. "Highly likely, I would say. Highly likely." He thought for a moment and then said, half to himself. "I know someone who might know more about those books."

What's more, he could kill two birds with one stone. He took out his phone and clicked on his brother's name. It was picked up straight away.

"Hi Mark," Luke said. "I think we need to talk about what Mother said."

"I agree," Mark said.

"Not there though. Any chance you could come up here? The spare room's made up so you can stay over."

"I'll need to check with Erica."

Of course you do, Luke thought but said, "Okay, I'll hang on."

Mark came back after a couple of minutes. "Fine," he said. I'll be there about seven."

Chapter 25

It was almost eight-thirty when Mark turned up.

"Friday evening traffic problems?" Luke asked as he let him in.

"Erica problems," Mark said, shaking his head. "She changed her mind, and I had to do some serious persuading."

"Have you eaten?"

"I had a big lunch. Why?"

"They don't serve food where we're going. You can leave the car keys. We're walking."

Mark dropped his keys on the hall table. "Where are we going?"

"Tucker's Grave."

"A cemetery?"

Luke laughed. "No. You'll see." He gestured to the boot rack. "Put my spare wellies on. You're going to need them."

It was a cloudless evening as they set off from Norton St Philip towards the smaller village of Faulkland. Luke led them first onto a bridleway then through a field. It was starting to get dark and he used the torch on his phone to guide them over a couple of stiles.

"This grave had better be worth it," Mark said at one point as he swerved to avoid a sheep that had suddenly loomed out of the darkness. "How far now?"

"Another ten minutes," Luke said. "Worth the wait, believe me."

True to his word, within a few minutes an old stone building materialised out of the twilight, a couple of Victorian lamps highlighting the sign above the entrance door which read 'Tucker's Grave Inn'. There were dimmer lights in the field to the right, and the sound of people talking.

"The camping is a relatively new venture," Luke said, "but Tucker's Grave has been a cider house for a couple of centuries or more. Watch yourself," he added as he ducked through the door and led his brother into a room that had changed little over those two hundred years. To the left was a line of barrels on and underneath a deep shelf, and to the right a large, battered pine table in an alcove around which sat a group of seven. Luke nodded hello. "Room for a couple of small ones?" he said to universal laughter.

"I'm sure we can squeeze you two titches in," one of the men said in a strong Somerset accent. He was a large man himself, though horizontally rather than vertically, with a florid face and a beaming smile.

A middle-aged woman sporting a grey apron came through from the room next door. "Evening," she said. "What can I get you?"

"Mother Tuckers for me," Luke said.

"Good choice." She grabbed a pint glass and bent to one of the barrels.

There was a hand-written board on one of the walls with 'Tuckers Tipples' at the top and drinks listed underneath.

"Is it only cider?" Mark asked, before spotting San Miguel at the bottom of the board. "Ah," he said, pointing, but Luke interrupted before he could finish.

"He'll have the same as me," he said.

"Coming up," the barmaid said as she grabbed another glass.

Mark shrugged. "I guess, when in Rome…"

"Exactly," Luke said. He turned back to the florid man at their table. "I don't suppose you know if Stan's in tonight, do you?"

"He definitely is. Saw him earlier. In the snug I reckons."

"Thanks."

"Who's Stan?" Mark said.

"He's someone I want to speak to about a work issue. I'll catch him later."

Their drinks were placed in front of them and Luke handed over a twenty.

"Back in a mo, my luvver," the barmaid said, and disappeared out for his change.

"What did she say?" Mark said.

Luke smiled. "Don't worry about it. It's just an expression."

Mark shook his head. "So," he said, "what do you think about Mother?" He took a sip of his cider and immediately threw his head back. "Wow, that's got some bite."

"Lovely stuff," Luke said as he glugged a mouthful. "Much as I don't like her," he went on, "it was sad to see her like that."

Mark nodded. "It's an awful disease."

Luke sighed. "We need to do something, Mark. And not just because she's asked. Father's not getting any younger, and someone's got to take Borrowham on. With Mother being the way she is I think he'll want to transfer responsibility sooner rather than later. He's looking very tired."

"I expect you're right, but you're the oldest. By rights, it should be you."

"It's not my cup of tea, and you know it. Whereas Erica would relish it."

Mark half-smiled. "She mentions it all the time. Sometimes I wonder if it's the only reason she married me."

Luke had wondered this more often than he could remember. "What about you though?" he asked. "You were adamant you never wanted to take it on once you'd settled in Toronto."

"I've mellowed, I guess. Toronto was fun for a bit. It's got great nightlife, and I made lots of new pals, but Dorset appeals again now. Being a merchant banker isn't all I thought it would be. There's an awful amount of office politics and it would be nice to be my own boss."

Luke stifled a laugh. With Erica in tow, Mark was never going to be his own boss. "You're up for it then?"

Mark nodded. "I'll tell Father when I get back tomorrow."

"Great." Luke tapped Mark's glass. "Another?"

"Okay." He drained the rest of his pint. "This stuff is definitely growing on me."

Luke ordered two more pints and then asked about Mark's last holiday, in the Bahamas it turned out, and they spent a pleasant hour talking about lighter subjects and getting to know each other again. Underneath his poshboy exterior Mark wasn't much different from him, and it was nice to be properly in touch again.

Mark was about to order a third round of drinks when a thin man in his late sixties with a white comb-over came into the room from the snug.

"Stan," Luke called. "Have you got a minute?"

"Course I have," Stan said, his accent even stronger than their florid table-mate, and his voice unusually deep for a man so slight of build.

"Black Rat?"

"Lush."

"Can you get Stan a Black Rat please, Mark?" He saw his brother's expression of disbelief and added, "It's a cider."

Stan laughed as he squeezed in beside Luke. "He's not a local then?"

"No." Luke paused. "Stan, I recall you've got a fair bit of knowledge about Somerset books."

"A fair bit, yes. Wrote a couple of 'em."

"I remember. So if I said someone had three books on the Glastonbury Tor, Wells Cathedral and Bath in the Blitz where could they have got them?"

"Depends on which books. There are lots on the Tor. Do you know the author?"

"Bob Pritchard."

"That's a rare one. Been out of print a few years."

"So he wouldn't be able to buy it online."

"No, you'd have to go to a specialist. Sadler's Books in Wells, they'd likely have it. Not sure where else would actually."

"Thanks, Stan. That's really helpful."

"No problem, Luke." He looked up as Mark handed him his cider and proceeded to down half of it in one swallow. "That's the badger," he said as he wiped his sleeve across his mouth. "Tell me now, are you two brothers? 'Cause you look awful alike."

"Yes we are," Luke said.

"So how come…"

Luke laughed. "How come we sound so different?"

"Yes. I mean you sound kind of normal Luke, but you, Mark, well it's like you've got a whole apple stuck in your mouth and your tongue's struggling to get past it."

It was Mark's turn to laugh. "Shall I let you into a little secret, Stan?"

"Go on then."

Mark lowered his voice to a whisper. "Mine is a true Dorset accent," he said. "Our family have lived there hundreds of years but my brother ditched the brogue when he came to Somerset."

"Well, I never." Stan threw back the rest of his Black Rat. "I knew they was proper weird down there but I didn't know they spoke like that. You learn something new every day."

Mark looked at Stan in shock. His glass was still almost full and Stan's was now completely empty. "Do you want another?" he asked.

"It's all right," Stan said, indicating the snug with his thumb. "I ought to get back to my Winnie."

"I didn't know your wife was here," Luke said.

"She's in the snug. Brought her out for a romantic drink or three." Stan stood up. "Anyway, best I take the missus home 'fore it gets dimpsey. See you around, my kidders."

Chapter 26

Maj hated shopping.

He could just about bear Amazon. Buying things online in your PJs was quick and painless but traipsing into Bath on a Saturday morning shopping for, of all things, a suit, was anathema to him. And when you coupled it with buying clothes for his daughter well, he'd rather have his eyes gouged out with a toothpick.

Asha had insisted. "You've got a new job, Maj. You need to dress well. And Sabrina's growing up fast. She needs something a bit more grown-up."

He'd tried to insist his old suit was good enough, but she wasn't having any of it. True, he'd had it since their wedding fifteen years ago, but still.

At least he was quick. They'd been in and out of Moss Bros in less than thirty minutes. Now, two hours later, they had been to Next, Urban Outfitters, Apricot Clothing, Flock and he was currently sitting on a sofa in a shop called, of all things, FatFace.

And what had Sabrina bought so far? Nothing, that was what, big fat zero. Not that she or her mother seemed to mind. Oh no, they were having a great time.

He sighed and looked at his watch. Nearly 3 pm - his day was evaporating fast.

"Dad, I've bought a skirt." He looked up to see Sabrina marching towards him, smiling from ear to ear. "It's lovely," she said. "Thanks."

Asha was behind her, also smiling.

"That's great, Sabrina," he said, pleased for more reasons than one. "Let's head home and you can show me properly when we get there."

"Don't be silly," she said. "I've got to get a top to

match, haven't I, Mum?"

"Yes, darling," Asha said.

"There were some nice ones in Apricot. I liked the turquoise one in Flock too."

"Yes, that was nice. Let's start with that one."

"We haven't tried H&M yet though, Mum. And isn't New Look almost next door?

"Good idea," Asha said. "Let's start with H&M. It's just this side of Milsom Street."

Maj found himself flicking his head from side to side, unable to believe what he was hearing. "You mean we're going back to start again?" he said.

"Duh,' Sabrina said. "We have to get one to match."

Maj stood up and gestured to the door, resigned to his fate. "After you then, ladies."

He followed them up Stall Street and then onto Union Street. They were a few yards ahead of him and he found himself smiling. Yes, this was hard work, but it was lovely to see them enjoying themselves. They were arm in arm, smiling as they chatted to each other and, goodness, there was only an inch in height between them. My, how his little girl had grown up.

Sabrina suddenly stopped, looking at something over her mother's shoulder. Maj was up with them in a couple of seconds.

"What is it?" He asked.

"Can you wait here a second, Dad? Mum?"

They both nodded, and Sabrina walked briskly away from them along Upper Borough Walls.

"What did she see?" Maj asked.

Asha shook her head. "I don't know," she said. "Perhaps it's one of her schoolfriends."

Maj watched as Sabrina got closer to a slim blonde girl. The girl turned as she heard Sabrina approaching and a scared look came over her face. She started to move away but Sabrina grabbed her by the arm, said something and the other girl appeared to calm down. They exchanged a few words then the girl turned and walked in the direction of Queen Square. Sabrina watched her go for a few seconds then turned and gestured for her parents to come to her.

"What is it?" Maj said, as they drew close to their daughter. "Is that one of your friends?"

"She's that girl from outside the school, Dad. You know, the one that Millie attacked."

"Is she okay?"

"No, I don't think so. She seems really, really scared."

"Did you ask her what was wrong?"

"I tried to, but she doesn't speak much English. I think she's from Poland or somewhere like that."

"There's not much that we can do then, Darling," Asha said. "Come on, let's go to H&M."

"She kept saying 'Wait', Mum. I think she wants me to wait for her to come back. Perhaps she went to get someone who speaks English." She paused and then turned to her father. "I'm worried about her Dad. I think she's frightened for some reason. Can we wait and see if she returns?"

"Of course, Sabrina," Maj said. "There's a bench over there. Let's sit down and you can show me your skirt."

They sat down and admired the skirt which, if he was honest, looked no different from any other he'd seen, then Sabrina and Asha resumed their discussion of tops and where was worth visiting.

After twenty minutes the girl still hadn't returned.

"I don't think she's coming back," Asha said.

As they stood up an attractive woman in her early twenties stopped in her tracks about fifteen yards away. Maj could see that she had been zeroing in on Sabrina, but had stood still when she saw that she was with two other people. When she spotted him looking at her she immediately turned around and in that split second he saw that she too, like the blonde girl before her, was scared, unbelievably scared.

He raced towards her, ignoring his wife and daughter as they asked him where he was going. She started to walk away but he was too quick and grabbed her by the shoulder.

"Are you okay?" he said.

"Leave me, or I scream," she said, and he could tell that she too was from Eastern Europe.

"I'm not going to hurt you," he said. "I want to help."

"No, you cannot help." She tried to shake herself free, and he could see they were drawing the attention of people walking by. It was only a matter of time before someone intervened, thinking he was trying to mug her or worse.

"Please," he said. "What's wrong? At least tell me your name."

She swallowed. "My name is Tania."

"I'm Maj. You can trust me."

She looked him in the eyes and seemed to come to a decision. "I know a little," she said. "Perhaps you can track Laurie and Danny then perhaps us, we can be okay. It may fall then, like pack of cards."

He didn't know what she was talking about.

"Laurie, Danny," she repeated, talking quickly now, looking around from side to side as she spoke. "They talk about Cheppy. They say too far to walk to Wales from there."

"What do you mean? Where is Cheppy?"

"It's a state." She looked around, as scared as anyone he had ever seen.

"Come with me," he said. "I'll take you to the police station. They'll help you."

"No!" She yelled. "They will kill me. No police. Please, no police." She shook her head. "I should not have said anything. Please forget. I must go."

She turned and ran away.

Maj stood and stared, thinking for a moment that he should run after her. A couple of people had stopped but moved on now that she had left, the excitement over.

"Was she with the other girl?" Sabrina asked when he returned.

Maj looked from his wife to his daughter and then back again. "Yes, I think she must have been. She was very scared."

"Should we go to the police?" Asha asked.

"She was adamant I mustn't say anything to the police. No, I think I'll talk to Luke first. See if he has any ideas as to what we should do."

Chapter 27

Josh handed everyone their drinks and sat down.

"Thanks," Luke said. "Sam, what time have you got to leave?"

She looked at her watch. "About forty minutes. My plaster's being removed at 10:30."

"Right. We'd better get on then. Maj, has Chris Nevin done anything else suspicious?"

"Not that I've seen," Maj said.

"How's he been with you, Sam?"

"Okay," she said. "Very friendly in fact."

"Just be careful. I rang Evan this morning on the way in. He's convinced, as am I, that they've got at least one person working for them on the inside. Is there anyone else who's acting oddly?"

Sam shook her head. "Not that I've noticed, no."

Luke looked at Maj. "Have you seen anything else on CCTV?"

Maj pointed up at the board. "There's her."

Sam looked up and was shocked to see Audrey Manners' name on the board. "What did Audrey do?"

"She's the call centre manager, right?" Maj said.

Sam nodded.

"I saw her looking furtively around," he went on, "then she took some papers from her desk. I managed to follow her progress through a series of cameras and she went to one of the storerooms. Not the call centre storeroom though, she went to the one on your floor, Sam. There isn't a camera inside unfortunately, but she was in there for a good fifteen minutes. And when she finally emerged she didn't have the papers any more. She looked mighty flustered though."

"Good work," Luke said. "Sam, could you have a look at that storeroom and see if there's anything unusual in there? There might be a phone, say."

"Burner phone," Josh said.

Luke sighed. "Thank you for that, Josh." He turned his attention back to Sam. "Also, Sam, Evan gave me an update on Ventyx and they're definitely part of this. Their only UK address is a PO Box in London, and they're owned by an offshore company, which in itself is owned by another. His guys are still investigating. Did you get anything else on the headcount anomaly?"

"Not really, no," she said. "It had been really well hidden. A normal audit of the accounts wouldn't have spotted it in a million years."

"It reinforces my belief that they've got one or more insiders. But so far the only suspects we've identified are Chris Nevin and Audrey Manners, and we've got very little on them. The other question is why four invisible staff are being put through the books." He looked at Josh. "Josh, please can you bring everyone up to speed on the romance scamming operation."

"Sure, guv," Josh said. He flicked through his notebook, looked down at it briefly then began. "Pam Greening, who's Leanne's aunt, and Eleanor Jones, who's the mother of a friend of mine, have been conned out of money by two men who groomed them online. Both men are supposedly suffering from a serious illness, and both have said they live in Florida. They're different men but the guv and I have discovered that they're part of the same operation." He stopped, pleased with himself.

"The bank account, Josh," Luke prompted.

"Oh, yes." Josh looked at his notes again. "We got Pam to tell the man who calls himself Seb, short for Sebastian Crown, that she had extra money but could only transfer it to a UK account. He said he would send her his NatWest account details and we're hoping Evan can work his magic to get information from NatWest when he does that." He stopped, clicked his fingers together and smiled. "Guv," he said. "I bet they're two out of a team of four."

"Hell Josh, you could be right," Luke said. "Well done."

Josh's smile broadened.

"Sorry," Helen said. "I've lost you."

"There's a chance," Luke said, "an outside chance admittedly, that this romance grooming team is being funded through Supracomm."

"I see what you're getting at,' Sam said. "These con men could be making money for Al Ummah while their staff costs are also being covered by Supracomm."

"Exactly," Luke said, "It would be a win-win for them."

"The other thing was the bookshelf, guv," Josh said.

Luke explained about the Somerset books they had seen behind the scammer. "I spoke to someone over the weekend," he went on, "who's an expert on local books. He told me they had to have been bought at a specialist bookshop in Wells. It doesn't tell us where they're based but my bet is they're no more than a short drive away."

"It's likely set up as a mini call centre," Maj said, "but they'll need one or more extra rooms to use for their video calls. Rooms that are set up to look like their homes."

"Yes, that's true. With the technology they need, it's unlikely to be in someone's house. It's more likely they're renting premises in a business park or an industrial estate. Could you make a list of those within a ten-mile radius of Wells please, Helen?"

"Sure, Luke." Helen made a note on her pad.

Luke's phone rang and he looked down to see Pete Gilmore's name. "Excuse me, guys," he said and stood up.

He clicked on the icon. "What is it, Pete?"

"Jeremy Scott's dead."

"The guy we interviewed last week?"

"That's him. A couple on a narrowboat spotted his body in the canal early this morning."

"Where was that?"

"About 200 yards from the George at Bathampton under the road bridge. It proves you were right, Luke. He must have been mixed up with some seriously dangerous people."

"Any idea of the cause of death yet?"

"Nothing obvious. Sally Croft's doing the post-mortem later."

"I'd be interested to know what she says."

"I'll let you know."

He ended the call and returned to the meeting table.

"I think we're just about done," he said. "Sam, give me regular updates won't you?"

"Will do, Luke." She said goodbye to the others, grabbed her crutches and hobbled out.

Luke sat at one of the desks and thought about what Pete had just told him. It was highly unlikely that Jeremy Scott's death was accidental, and he was sure the post-mortem would confirm it. Was there any chance it was linked to the 'call centre' Supracomm was unintentionally funding and which he now believed to be in the local area? Possible, he thought, but unlikely. Scott didn't have the brains to be a con man. No, he had most likely been a minion linked to the brothel Pete Gilmore had heard about. It still came under the banner of organised crime though, and he wasn't ready to rule a link out completely.

"Luke."

He turned to see Maj hovering behind him.

"What is it?" he said.

"Can I ask your advice about something?" Maj asked.

"Sure."

Maj told him what had happened when he'd been shopping with his wife and daughter. "Both women were really scared," he concluded. "Tania, the older one, told me they could be in danger if I said anything to the police."

"She didn't say who from?"

Maj considered this for a second. "The odd thing," he said, "was that she gave me two names but I'm pretty sure they weren't the people she was frightened of."

"Who were they, if they weren't the people she's afraid of?"

"She didn't say, other than asking if I could trace them. To be honest, she was in such a mess I don't know what to make of anything she said. Her accent was pretty strong and I think she may have been Russian. It sounded like the two men are called Laurie and Danny and are in Wales. She gave me the name of the place in Wales too." He paused, trying to remember. "Something like Cheppo or Cheppy."

"Not the Isle of Sheppey then. That's in Essex. Could it have been Chepstow? That's in South Wales."

"Yes, it could have been."

"Do you think these men are friends of hers?"

"Perhaps. I didn't have the chance to ask before she ran off. What do you suggest I do, Luke?"

"I'm not sure there's anything you can do, Maj. No point in telling the police since there's nothing for them to go on. Ask your daughter to keep an eye open for the younger one. Perhaps she can get her to open up if she turns up at the school again."

"Thanks. I'll do that."

Chapter 28

Sam was pleased to have full mobility, but it was weird being able to walk normally without putting half her weight on crutches. There was no longer any pain and she felt lucky to have suffered a clean break rather than a displaced fracture which might have needed plates and screws and taken many months to heal.

It was past lunchtime by the time she got to the office and she decided to start by diving into the mismatch in staff numbers. Perhaps she could find something that would indicate where the mysterious four staff were based, or else lead her to the person who had tried to hide the discrepancy.

She was stopped before she got to her desk by a voice from the kitchenette. It was Chris Nevin.

"Can I get you a cup of tea?" he asked.

She decided this was too good an opportunity to miss given what Maj had seen on CCTV.

"Sure Chris," she said. "I'll be with you in a minute. I'll just pop my stuff down."

Chris was ready with her tea when she returned and she took it from him. "White with no sugar," he said. "Is that right?"

"Perfect. Well remembered."

He gestured to her leg. "It must be great having the plaster off."

"Yes, it feels really good."

"How was your weekend?"

He was smiling, and she was struck again by how pleasant and easy-going he was. Then she remembered Luke's words of warning. *You can't trust anyone*, he had said.

She smiled back at him. "Quiet," she said. "The plaster

only came off this morning so it was a case of being a couch potato for most of Saturday and Sunday. What about you?"

"I was a touch more active. I took up karate last year and now I've really got the bug."

"Really? It's a hobby of mine too. Not that I've been for nearly two months because of my leg, but I love it. I find it oddly relaxing."

"Yes, me too." He hesitated. "Do you mind if I show off a little?"

"Of course not." He was so different from Tony who wouldn't have dreamed of asking permission to boast about himself.

"I was awarded my blue belt at the weekend."

"That's mighty impressive after only a year."

"Thanks. What about you?"

It was her turn to be embarrassed now. "I've been doing it a lot longer than you."

"Don't worry. I won't feel inferior if you're a notch above me."

"I'm a third Dan."

"Wow!" He bent his head down. "I bow to your excellence, madam."

"Thanks, Chris." She raised her cup. "Thanks for the tea too. I need to be getting on now."

"Uh, before you go…" She turned back to face him and he was still smiling but it was a nervous smile now. "I wondered if I could take you out for dinner sometime. I mean," he added hastily, "if you don't want to then just say so, but…"

She replied without thinking. "That would be lovely, Chris."

"You're sure?"

"I'm sure."

She turned and walked back to her desk. She was attracted to Chris, there was no question of that, but should she have said yes after what Maj had seen and Luke had said? Well it was too late now. She made a mental note to ring Maj to see if he had come up with anything else on Chris.

He seemed so nice. Surely he couldn't be working for an international terrorist organisation. No, the idea was laughable.

She had only been back at her desk for a few minutes when Chris leaned over the partition.

"How are you fixed for dinner tonight?" he asked.

"I can do that."

"Great. Where are you staying?"

"The Leonardo."

"Shall I meet you in the lobby? Say at eight?"

"Lovely. I'll see you then."

He gave a little wave as he walked away and her thoughts immediately went to clothes. She hadn't brought anything suitable and could hardly wear what she had on now. There was nightwear in her suitcase as well as more outfits for the office but nothing suitable for a first date.

A first date. Wow! She hadn't had one of those for nearly six months.

She smiled as she thought how nice it would be to go out with someone who didn't talk about themselves endlessly. But then again, perhaps he did. She'd only had a few conversations with Chris so who knows what he'd be like over a full evening.

Better than Tony, she was confident of that.

Sam looked at her watch. Nearly three. She needed to knuckle down if she was going to get anything done.

Starting with October, she began with invoices, doing a search for any documents that contained 'staff' and 'HR'. When this didn't reveal anything of interest she tried 'staff' combined with 'call centre', then 'HR' with 'call centre'. Still nothing. She tried November, then December. Still no joy.

She sat back in her chair. This wasn't working. She

needed to take a different tack. If nothing was coming up for staff, HR and call centre permutations, then…

"That's it!" she exclaimed.

Kevin's head appeared above the partition. "Another breakthrough?"

"I think so, Kevin," she said without looking up. "I think so."

He disappeared again and she made a few notes and then reread what she had written. Yes, that was it, she was sure it was.

She typed in 'staff' and 'contact centre' and hit search.

Nothing.

She tried combining 'HR' and 'contact centre'.

Bingo! Four documents were highlighted.

Sam clicked on them and found that they were almost identical, each itemising the costs for computers, phones and office equipment for one person. Someone had done a superficial check and scrawled 'OK' on each of them and the only element of difference was the name of the recipient. The names were J Duggan, L Peterson, D Spencer and L Boniface. No Christian names, but better than nothing.

Sam switched to the HR system and searched for the surnames. She found a Spencer, but it was a Nancy Spencer. There were no Duggans, Petersons or Bonifaces. As suspected, these four people were not Supracomm employees.

It was six before Sam got away, and she rang Maj as soon as she had checked in and gone to her room.

"Maj," she said when he answered, "did you find anything else on CCTV?"

"A couple of things," he said, "but nothing conclusive. Audrey Manners went to that storeroom again. Do you think you could have a look in there tomorrow?"

"Will do." She paused. "What about Chris Nevin? Has he done anything else to make him look suspicious?"

"Why? Have you noticed something?"

"No, I..." She knew she ought to tell him about their dinner date but it didn't feel right somehow. "It's nothing. I was wondering that's all. He seems such a nice guy."

"It wasn't very nice him leafing through your notebook."

"No, I suppose not."

"Let me know about the storeroom."

"Will do Maj. Have a good evening."

"And you, Sam."

It felt wrong not telling him, but she had a right to her privacy and the more she saw of Chris the more she thought he was a genuinely good person. She decided she would ask him about the notebook. He'd have a simple answer and that would be the end of it.

Chapter 29

The door opened and Greg walked into their bedroom.

"Time to get ready," he said. "You've got two customers tonight. Be in the salon in twenty minutes." He repeated this in German, then turned and left.

This was it then. Tania shivered as she thought of what was about to happen. She'd read on the news about women being trafficked from poorer countries to wealthier ones, then used as slaves or their bodies sold. It had been tragic of course but also distant, something that happened to others.

And now it was happening to her. She looked across at the Germans who were whispering intently to each other. After a few seconds, they got up and left the room.

Izabella hadn't moved since Greg had come in. She was seated on her bed, knees drawn up, her head bent forward over them.

"We have to go," Tania said.

Izabella looked up, tears in her eyes, and started shaking her head.

"There is no choice," Tania went on, and then walked over and held her hand out. Reluctantly, Izabella took it and stood up.

Together they walked out of the room and downstairs. Tania gave Izabella's hand a squeeze as they reached their 'working rooms' and gestured for her to go inside room one.

There were several dresses in the wardrobe in Tania's room. Greg had warned them to make sure they looked attractive and had also made it clear that they would have Anderson to answer to if they didn't do what they were told. She shivered and decided to get on with it, shedding her clothes then grabbing the first dress she saw. It was a black mini-dress, low cut but not indecent. It was something she might have worn herself at home, but when she put it on and looked at herself in the mirror she felt dirty and ashamed.

Sighing, she left the room and knocked on room one. After a few seconds Izabella opened the door. She wearing a pale blue dress which went to below the knees. It was tight-fitting and showed off her curves, but somehow it made her look even younger than her sixteen years.

It was Izabella who grabbed Tania's hand this time and together they made their way to the salon. The German women were already there, eyes wide and wearing expressions that Tania was sure mirrored her own.

Greg followed them in and shut the door.

"They'll be here soon," he said. "You're to smile all the time they're with you. Understood?"

Tania and Izabella nodded, then sat on the sofa opposite the other two women.

Greg left the room and the four of them sat in silence awaiting their fate. Five minutes passed, then ten, and Tania was beginning to hope the so-called customers had decided not to come. Then the door opened and she drew in a deep breath.

Greg was first in, followed by two men each clutching a glass of wine. One was of Asian extraction in his late forties, the other white and about ten years younger. They looked like businessmen and it was clear that they knew each other.

"Here you are, gentlemen," Greg said, and he was smiling now, the perfect host. Tania felt like throwing up. He gestured to each of the four women in turn, telling the two men their names.

"Very nice," the white man said. He turned to his companion. "I told you this would be good."

"Yes, very nice," the other man said, and Tania decided

from his accent that he was probably Indian.

The men turned from one woman to the next, inspecting them as if they were cows in a pen. They exchanged thoughts in low whispers, pointing occasionally. *Not Izabella,* Tania thought. *Please not Izabella.*

After a few minutes, they walked over to the two German women.

"And did you say these two don't speak English?" the white man said.

"That's right," Greg said. "Is that a problem?"

"No. It's ideal. We'll take them."

Greg spoke to the two girls in German and Tania saw their expressions change from fear to horror, though they tried to mask it with smiles, fearful of what might happen if they didn't. Meekly they stood up and followed Greg out of the room, the two businessmen following behind.

Tania stood up and closed the door. She turned to see Izabella looking up at her wide-eyed and went over, sat next to her and grabbed both her hands in her own. Izabella broke down then, sobbing her heart out.

Only a few minutes had passed when Greg came back in and ordered them to return to the top floor. Wearily, Tania led Izabella back upstairs, walking quickly past the German girls' bedrooms, not wanting to hear any noises from within.

Chapter 30

It was gone eight by the time Sam left her room. She'd hummed and hawed about what to wear, eventually deciding on the outfit she had earmarked for the office on Thursday, a navy silk blouse and cream skirt, more business casual than date night but it would have to do.

Chris was waiting in the lobby when she got there and she could immediately see that he'd made an effort. He looked good too in a white linen shirt over black denims.

"You look great," he said as he bent to peck her on the cheek.

"Thanks."

"Are you okay with steak?"

"I love steak."

"Great. I've booked us a table at Gourdans. It's only a ten-minute walk."

They set off for the restaurant and he asked her about her family. From there the conversation flowed easily and they found they had a lot in common, not just karate but also their taste in books and films.

Once they had ordered their mains, a sirloin for her and a t-bone for him, Sam decided to ask about the notebook.

"Do you know Kevin?" she asked.

"Short guy, sits in the cubicle next to yours?"

"That's the one." She hesitated. "Sorry to ask you this Chris, but he told me you were at my desk last week looking through my notebook. Is that true?"

"Sorry, Sam."

"You were?"

"I… Well, the truth is…" He looked her in the eyes and gave a half-smile. "I was looking to see if there was anything in it to indicate you had a boyfriend."

"Really?" She didn't know whether to be relieved or more suspicious.

"Stupid, I know," he said, looking thoroughly embarrassed now. "Rude too. I'm really sorry Sam, I was bang out of order."

It was an excuse, albeit a lame one. Sam decided to forget about it for the time being and come back to it if necessary. For now, she was going to concentrate on enjoying the evening.

"Don't worry," she said and smiled. "So, is Eddie Murphy genuinely your favourite actor?"

"Has been ever since I was eight and my Dad took me to the cinema to see a film he was in. I laughed so much I nearly wet myself."

"Dr Dolittle?"

"No. I'll give you a clue." He coughed then said, adopting his best Eddie Murphy accent, "You might have seen a housefly, maybe even a superfly, but I bet you ain't never seen a donkey fly."

Sam laughed. "Shrek!"

"Exactly. Wasn't it marvellous?"

"Fantastic. My Mum and Dad took me to see it when it came out as well."

"Hey," he said. "They're doing a one-night-only screening of 'The Nutty Professor' on Wednesday night at the Curzon. I was thinking of going on my own but we could make it a second date if you're up for it. Perhaps go to a bar first?"

Sam was a little taken aback. This was moving very quickly. "Well, I don't know if…"

Chris held his hand up. "Sorry, I'm being too forward. Forget I asked."

She smiled. "No, let's do it, although I have an admission to make."

"And what's that?"

"I've never seen it."

Chris smacked his palm on the table. "In that case," he said, "it's compulsory. I'll book our tickets in the morning."

The waiter appeared at the table carrying two plates. "Sirloin?" he asked.

"That's mine," Sam said.

The waiter placed her meal in front of her and then set Chris's t-bone down before moving away.

He smiled at her and said "Bon appetit." She smiled back and they looked into each other's eyes for a second or two before she pulled herself away and looked down at her steak.

"It looks lovely," she said as she started cutting into her meat.

As she ate, she reflected on the evening so far. She was enjoying herself, and Chris came across as very genuine. He'd given a reason for looking at her notebook and that was the only reason for suspecting he might be working for Al Ummah. However, there was still the faint possibility that he was putting on a performance and faking an attraction to her so that he could find out what she had discovered.

She needed to be sure, for her own sake as much as anything else, and decided to move their conversation onto more personal matters and see if he let his guard slip.

They finished eating at almost exactly the same time.

"That was delicious," Sam said. "This was a good find. Have you been here before?"

"Once."

"With a girlfriend?"

Chris hesitated. "Kind of," he said.

Sam was confused. "She was a 'kind of' girlfriend?"

He wiped his mouth with his napkin then folded it and placed it down on his plate. "I, ah…" He swallowed, his eyes still focused on his plate. "I came here with my wife."

Sam drew in her breath. "With your wife?"

He lifted his head, looked into her eyes and put his

hand on hers. "I've been meaning to tell you, Sam. But we were having such a good time."

Sam wrenched her hand away and stood up. "I think I'd better go."

"No, Sam, you don't understand."

"Oh, I think I do. And to think I…"

"She's dead."

"What?"

"My wife died in childbirth three years ago."

"Oh." Sam sat down again. "God, I'm so sorry, Chris." This time she put her hand on his and then gripped it tightly. "That must have been awful."

"This is the first time I've been out with anyone since she died," he said, and attempted a laugh. "Which explains why I've been so useless."

"Nonsense. You've treated me like a lady and I'm having a brilliant time. Don't put yourself down. Now, what about a dessert?"

Chapter 31

Luke reversed up the drive, driving carefully in case his takeaway toppled onto the passenger seat. He had been slightly peckish when he left work, but the twenty-minute drive from the Happy Garden to Norton St Philip accompanied by the aroma of sweet and sour pork balls, peking spare ribs and egg fried rice, had changed that into a desperate yearning for food.

He put the car into park, undid the seat belt and grabbed the carrier bag handles, half his mind on whether he should pour himself a mug of cider before tucking in, the other half on whether he should start slowly with the prawn crackers or dive straight into his pork. He backed out of the car carefully, turned around and…

"Hi, Dad."

Luke jumped and the lusted-after Chinese meal tried its hardest to escape his hold. He wasn't having it though and grasped the handles firmly. No way was this meal getting away from him.

He heard laughter and turned to see his daughter beaming at him from the front porch. "Chloe!" he said. "You scared the bloody daylights out of me."

"Are you having people over?" she said, gesturing to the bag.

"I was hungry."

"Any chance…"

"I'm sure it'll stretch to two."

"Great." She turned to go inside. "I'll get some plates and cutlery."

"How come you're here?" he asked as he followed behind.

"I haven't got any lectures for the next 2 days and

thought I'd surprise you."

"You certainly did that." He put the carrier bag down onto the kitchen table and lifted the foil containers out. "So how's the course?"

"Going well."

"And Tristram?"

"We've finished."

"Sorry to hear that."

"It's not a problem. I dumped him." She took the cardboard lids off the food and started doling it out.

"Why?"

"He's too up himself. More egg-fried rice?" He nodded and she gave him a couple more spoonfuls. "His father's a hedge fund manager and his mother's a QC and all he seems to talk about is how well connected he is and how much money he's going to earn."

"It sounds like you're well rid of him. Do you want any ribs?"

"No, you have them all. I'll stick to the sweet and sour. Yes, he's not my type. Ironic really given our family."

"Yes, but at least Ben won't tease you about shandy now Tristram's out of the picture."

She smiled, remembering her brother's endlessly repetitive non-jokes a couple of months earlier.

"Just make sure you're next boyfriend's not called Irn-Bru," he went on.

"After the river?"

"No, after the Scottish drink." He looked over at her. "You are joking, aren't you?"

She bent her head to one side and smiled at him. "Dad! I'm not stupid. Of course, I'm joking."

"That's a relief. One Josh is enough for anyone." He looked down at his food. "Do you mind?"

"Go for it."

They sat in companionable silence for a while, Luke continually topping up his plate until the foil containers were empty.

"I'll clear away," Chloe said as her father took the last spoonful from his plate.

"Nonsense. Come on, it won't take a second."

They cleared away and then went to the lounge, where Luke took his usual place in the grey armchair and Chloe stretched out on the sofa.

"Talking of snobs," Luke said. "I went to see your grandparents. Mark was there too."

"And Erica?" Her nose wrinkled and it reminded Luke of Jess, who would wrinkle her nose in exactly the same way when she found something distasteful.

"Yes, Erica was there. And she's going to be one awfully happy Erica soon."

"Why?"

"Mark's going to take Borrowham Hall on."

He told her about her grandmother's Alzheimers, and how Mark had become fed up with Canada and was ready to return.

"It sounds like you and Uncle Mark got on well," Chloe said when he'd finished.

"Yes, we did. It'll be nice to see him regularly once he's over here."

"What's going to happen to Grandma?"

"At the moment she's fine at home, but I guess time will tell as to how long that'll last."

"I'd like to see her. I'm sure Ben would too."

"Okay. Maybe we can sort something out when you both finish for the summer."

"Yes, that would be good."

She paused for a moment. "Anyway, Dad, how's work?"

Luke wanted to tell her about money laundering at Supracomm, Evan Underwood and MI6, their belief that it was all for the benefit of an international terrorist organisation. He knew she would be an excellent sounding board, just like her mother had been, but he'd signed the

Official Secrets Act, which meant he couldn't tell her anything.

Sod that for a game of soldiers.

Chloe was his daughter. If he couldn't trust her he couldn't trust anyone.

He made her promise not to tell anyone anything, which she happily did, then told her what he and his team had been doing, how Sam had discovered Supracomm was involuntarily funding four people, and how Josh had uncovered a romance scam operation that they now believed might be using them.

"It sounds like Sam and Josh are doing a great job," Chloe said.

"Yes, they are."

"What about Helen and Maj?"

"Helen's been doing a lot of background work, helping Sam mainly. Maj is a technical whizz which has been really useful." He told her what Maj had found out through studying CCTV footage.

"He sounds like a real find."

Luke nodded. "He is. Something odd happened to him at the weekend though."

"Really? What was that?"

He told her about the two Eastern European girls Maj had encountered while shopping with his wife and daughter. "Maj said they seemed scared," he concluded. "The older one was called Tania and mentioned two men she said were in Cheppy or Sheppy in Wales. We think she meant Chepstow."

"How weird. What's the link to Chepstow?"

Luke didn't answer. Something he or his daughter had said had been relevant somehow. But what was it? They'd talked about Tristram, events at Borrowham Hall and the Supracomm investigation.

"Are you okay, Dad?"

"It's something you said." He put his hand to his

mouth, wracking his brains to try to remember. "Earlier on."

"About Tristram? How much of a snob he is?"

"No, it wasn't that." He thought for a second. "Hang on, it wasn't something you said. It was me. I said you shouldn't have a boyfriend called Irn-Bru."

Chloe's eyebrows went up. "What's that got to do with anything?"

"And then I said it was a Scottish drink not a river."

"I'm not following."

He explained and suddenly it all made sense.

Chapter 32

Laurie was annoyed. It should have been possible to open an account online but no, the bank had insisted he go into a branch to show his id. And now he was stuck behind a big fat woman with a carrier bag full of cash.

She turned around. "Sorry," she said. "I won't be long."

He looked pointedly at his watch. "Good," he said. "I'm in a hurry."

She turned back and passed a dozen or more coin bags over the counter. The woman behind the till was painfully slow as she weighed them individually, making a note after each one. When she had finished she tapped on her keyboard, printed something off and handed it over.

"Thanks, Mrs Overton," she said. "How's your husband?"

Laurie had had enough. "I'm waiting," he said.

The customer turned back to him. "There's no need for that attitude." She said goodbye to the teller and walked away.

"At last," Laurie said. He removed his driving license from his wallet. "I was told to bring ID in."

"Are you opening an account?" the teller asked, her tone cold.

"Trying to." He handed a piece of paper to her. "That's the sort code and account number, but it won't let me use the account until you've seen id."

"Yes, that's normal."

"Will a driving license do?"

"Yes, that'll be fine."

He handed his license over.

"Thank you…" she looked down at his license, "…Mr Peterson."

Shit.

She started tapping on the keyboard. He had to think quickly.

"Sorry," he said. He smiled but it wasn't returned. "Did I set it up correctly? It should be a joint account."

She hit a few more keys. "No, it's a single account."

"My fault, I put Seb's name in and must have chosen the wrong option. He's my partner."

"That's not a problem. I can change it for you now. So to be clear, you want a joint account in the names of Sebastian Crown and Laurie Peterson?"

"Yes please." He paused. "Will Seb need to bring his ID in?"

"He will before he can use the account himself, but I'll set it up so that it doesn't need permission from both of you to initiate transactions. Is that okay?"

"Yes, that's fine."

"Great."

It was just as well he was smart enough to think on his feet.

*

Alex was sitting in Laurie's chair when he returned, idly flicking through one of his notebooks.

Laurie licked his lips. "Is everything okay, Alex?"

Alex put the notebook down and looked up, not much more than his eyes and nose visible through the mass of red hair covering his head and face. His beard hung below his chin in six untidy dreadlocks and beneath it he wore a dark green t-shirt that had seen much better days.

"No, everything's not okay," he said. "Where have you been?"

He didn't want to tell him about the bank account, not after he'd had to use his real name to open it. "I had to post a card to one of my clients," he said. "It's her birthday next week." He hoped Alex wouldn't ask which one and check.

"Yeah, well you kept me waiting." He stood up and Laurie involuntarily took a step back. Alex wasn't just big, he was a man mountain, his biceps the size of most men's thighs. "Mr Anderson's not happy."

"Why? Weren't our numbers up last month?"

Alex looked at each of the four of them in turn. "Has one of you been talking?"

"Of course not," Danny said.

The others nodded their agreement.

"Mr Anderson says there's been a leak. I need to do a full audit."

Laurie swallowed. He hadn't said anything to anyone and his notebooks were good, all up to date. There shouldn't be any problem, but the thought that Anderson was unhappy scared the willies out of him. "How's it going to work?" he said.

Alex looked directly at Laurie. "Prepare me a report." He shifted his attention to each of the others in turn. "I want the up-to-date status of all your clients, what phase they're at and your next steps."

"When do you want it?" Laurie said.

"Tonight."

"But that's…"

Alex bent his face down so that it was inches away and Laurie almost gagged as he breathed in the rancid smell of the other man's breath. "Are you fucking arguing?"

"Not at all."

"Then do it." He stood up and addressed his next comments to all of them. "I'll be back at eight. Have your reports ready." He pushed between Danny and Laurie and left.

Laurie looked at the others and saw his concern reflected in their faces.

"Anyone been talking?" Danny asked. The others shook

their heads. "What about you, Laurie?"

"No, of course I haven't."

He recalled their trip back from filming. He and Danny had been careful to whisper, and even if Greg had overheard it wouldn't matter. And those girls, well they were all Bulgarian or some such, they wouldn't have understood anything. No, he was okay. If there was a leak it must have come from one of the others.

Chapter 33

Luke drummed his fingers on the desk and looked at his watch. 8:20. Soon, she would be in soon.

"Good morning Luke, good morning Josh."

He turned to see Helen walking into the room, a pile of folders under her arm. "A wee bit of homework," she said as she put them down on her desk.

"Helen," Luke said. "Did you finish that list of business parks and industrial estates?"

"Aye, I did. There's a fair few of them mind."

"Could I have a look?"

"Sure. I'll email it over."

A few minutes later Luke's laptop pinged and he opened the file she had sent. Helen was right, there were a lot. She had found eighteen business parks and forty-six industrial estates within a ten-mile radius of Wells.

"Is this all of them?" he asked without looking up.

Helen got up and walked up to stand behind him. "I think so," she said. "Are you looking for something in particular?"

"It's a hunch, that's all."

"What is it, guv?" Josh was looking over his shoulder as well now.

"It's a feeling based on intuition," Helen said.

Josh looked over at her. "Uh?" He paused and then smiled. "Oh, I see. I know what a hunch is. I meant…"

"Got it!" Luke exclaimed. "There, look." He pointed at the screen.

"Rathbone Business Park?" Helen asked.

"No, the one below it. Sheppey Industrial Estate."

"What about it?" Josh asked.

"It's a river."

"Isn't it an industrial estate?"

"Josh, shut up for a minute."

"Right, guv. Gotcha."

"Helen," Luke went on, "I think the romance scamming call centre is on the Sheppey Industrial Estate. Did Maj tell you what happened at the weekend with those two women?"

"He did, aye."

"What the older woman told him was pretty garbled. She said there were two men, Laurie and Danny, in a place called Sheppy or Cheppy in a state in Wales. I assumed they meant Chepstow." He pointed to the screen. "But now I reckon it's highly likely they're in the Sheppey estate near Wells. It'll be named after the River Sheppey." He clicked on the screen. "You've written here that there are 16 units."

"That's right. Do you want me to do a wee bit more digging?"

"Yes, please. See if you can find when each organisation first leased their unit. A rental that started in August, September or October would fit what Sam found."

"Aye, will do." She went back to her desk.

"Josh."

"Yes, guv."

"Give Helen a hand. Dig up what you can on each company and see if anything stands out as odd."

"On it."

"I'll send the list to you now, Josh," Helen said over her shoulder.

Luke sat back in his chair. It was just a hunch, as he'd said, but it fitted and that was enough. He didn't believe in coincidences. But what did these women have to do with a romance scamming operation? Were they being used to blackmail male targets? No, that didn't match the way that Eleanor and Pam had been conned. What had been done to them had been clever but straightforward. It felt like an approach that had been honed to perfection but kept as simple as possible.

He had names for two of the possible con men now though. Only Christian names, but it was a start. He picked up his phone and rang Sam.

"Hi Sam," he said when she answered. "Did you get anywhere with those four unaccounted staff?"

"I did actually Luke. I found names for each of them. Give me a sec." He waited while she leafed through her notebook and read the names to him.

Luke hung up and looked down at the names he had written on his pad.

> *J Duggan*
> *L Peterson*
> *D Spencer*
> *L Boniface*

Laurie had to be the Peterson or Boniface while Danny was the Spencer. He needed to tell Evan and was about to call him when the phone rang and Pete Gilmore's name came up on the screen.

"Pete, Hi. What's up?"

"Sally Croft has just emailed me the report from Jeremy Scott's post-mortem. I thought you'd be interested to know."

"I'm guessing it wasn't accidental."

"A long way from accidental. He was garroted with wire."

"Nasty."

"It gets nastier. He had burn marks down his arm, which Sally thinks were most likely inflicted with a cigarette, and three of his fingernails had been pulled out. All the wounds were inflicted shortly before he was killed."

"So you have a murder case on your hands. Any leads?"

"You know as much as I do, Luke, which is to say, bugger all."

Luke ended the call and remembered back to the interview. Scott had been frightened of someone, for good reason it turned out. Whoever it was, he was operating in Bath or nearby. Was that another coincidence or were there two highly organised criminal outfits operating in an area of the country that was a long way from typical gangster territory?

He needed to talk to Evan, and the phone wasn't going to cut it. He rang and told him they needed to meet urgently

An hour later Luke found himself drumming his fingers again, this time on a table at the Salamander in the centre of Bath. He'd chosen it because it was usually quiet during the day and, true to form, there was only one other customer who was busy doing a newspaper crossword near the front. Luke had taken a seat at a table at the very back of the pub.

He only had to wait a few minutes before Evan walked in, ordered a cappuccino and then brought it over to Luke's table. "You said this had to be face-to-face," he said. "What's happened?"

"This is much, much more than money laundering, Evan," Luke said. "This is heavy-duty organised crime."

"Hang on," Evan said. "We suspect they're using Supracomm to fund a romance scamming operation and I know that's serious stuff, but it's hardly…"

Luke held his hand up. "It's not just romance scamming and money laundering, Evan. I'm convinced the same gang is involved in trafficking women, probably for sex or slavery, and have murdered one of their own people."

"Okay," Evan said. "Tell me everything."

When Luke had finished Evan picked his mug up and sat back. "I agree with you," he said, as he sipped his drink. "Those are not going to be coincidences." He paused. "What were the names of the men the woman told Maj to look for?"

"Laurie and Danny."

Evan smiled and reached into his pocket. "Take a look at this." He unfolded a single sheet of paper, laid it on the table in front of Luke and tapped the name at the top. "This man opened an account at the NatWest in Wells yesterday."

Luke looked down at the name and smiled. "Laurie Peterson, well that certainly joins the dots. It confirms the link between Supracomm, the romance scamming and the two women who spoke to Maj in Bath.

"There's more," Evan said. He clicked on his phone and handed it to Luke. "Camera footage from the branch. No sound, unfortunately."

Luke watched as a man in his early forties remonstrated with a middle-aged woman as he stood in the queue behind her. He wore jeans and a polo neck and was slightly balding but otherwise unremarkable.

"Is that him?" Luke said.

Evan nodded. "Yes, that's Laurie Peterson."

Luke smiled. "It's also Seb, the man who conned Pam Greening out of £8,000."

Evan sat forward again. "This is good work." He gave a bitter smile. "Your team have got further in a week than the United Nations has in two months. The question now is what we do next."

"There are 16 units in the Sheppey Industrial Estate," Luke said, "and right now Helen and Josh are trying to identify which of them is being used by our scammers." He paused. "Is it time to involve the police? Especially given they're already involved in finding Jeremy Scott's murderer."

Evan thought for a moment before replying. "I think we need to do the opposite, Luke," he said. "I'm going to call the Chief Constable and ask that they downplay the murder investigation. The last thing we need is to catch the minnows and miss the big fish."

Luke nodded. "I hate to say this given I'm ex-police,

but I agree with you. It's not just the fact that we might not catch the leaders either. Those two Eastern European women, and almost certainly others, are being held somewhere against their will and if we storm into the Sheppey Industrial Estate they'll be moved and we'll never find them." He paused. "Can you arrange covert surveillance on their unit once we identify it?"

"Definitely." Evan sighed and sat back again. "We're close now, Luke, and I suggest we stay in very close contact from here on."

"Agreed." Luke looked at his watch and stood up. "I'd best get back to the office now and see how my team are getting on."

Luke walked into the Ethics Room to find Helen, Josh and Maj at the whiteboard talking excitedly. "I take it you've made progress," he said.

"We certainly have," Helen said. "Do you want to tell him, Josh? It was you who found it after all."

Helen and Maj stepped back and Josh pointed up at a new post-it with 'Unit 7' written on it. Underneath Helen had written the four names Sam had found, and beneath them 'Laurie and Danny'.

"Unfortunately," Josh said, "Helen wasn't able to find out when leases were taken out."

"I can see why," Luke said. "We'd need police powers for that."

"However," Josh went on, "the Estate is owned by a conglomerate called Marston Platt. They own several similar business parks in the South West and their website has a couple of testimonials on it, including one from a printing company which says they're in unit 3 of the Sheppey Industrial Estate. And I thought, perhaps if I looked at some of their other locations…"

He was going slightly pink in the cheeks and Luke could see he was proud of himself.

"I saw that Marston Platt has just started advertising for

their new Kennford Estate near Exeter," Josh went on. "They're targeting call centres hard and referenced several existing call centres across their parks including one at Unit 7 at Sheppey. They even had a photo of it."

"That's excellent work, Josh."

"Thanks, guv." The pale pink had turned almost beetroot now.

"Laurie's surname is Peterson," Luke said, and told them about the NatWest account he had opened.

Helen updated the board, and Luke told them what he and Evan had agreed about treading gently and keeping the police out of it.

"What should we do now then, Luke?" Maj asked.

Luke thought for a minute. "There are three areas we need to focus on. First, we need to give Sam as much support as possible. Supracomm's systems may well be holding more information that will help us identify who's behind these operations. Helen, I think we ought to place you in Supracomm as well."

"They have a contracts team," Helen said. "Perhaps I could go in there."

"Good idea. I'll have a word with the Client Director and arrange it." He pointed at two names on the board under a post-it with 'Supracomm Plant' written on it. "So far we've identified three possibles for the Supracomm insider, Chris Nevin, Audrey Manners and Mike Swithin. Maj, keep looking will you?"

"Will do, Luke."

"Third, and this is where you come in, Josh, we need to try and use Eleanor and Pam to drive more out of the romance scammers. Let's you and I have a chat and work out the best approach."

"Gotcha, guv."

Chapter 34

Luke felt guilty for not having updated Filchers' Client Director sooner on Sam's progress. Having instigated her placement in Supracomm, Oliver Knight had been keen to find out how she was getting on. The problem was that MI6's involvement made it impossible for Luke to tell the other man what she had discovered.

He sighed and picked up his phone. He wanted Helen placed in the account, so he couldn't put it off any longer.

It was answered immediately. "Oliver Knight."

"Hi Oliver, it's Luke Sackville. How's it going in Oxford?"

"Good thanks. It's timely you should ring because I'm in Bath today. Could you give me an update face-to-face?"

"Sure. I'll come up to your office."

Five minutes later Luke walked into Oliver's office to find him looking more dishevelled than he had on their previous meeting. His hair needed a comb and the top button of his shirt was undone and his tie pulled down.

Oliver gestured for Luke to sit down. "Excuse my appearance," he said with a grimace. "Our Comms Sector Head gave me a rough time on profit margins this morning." He gave a low chuckle, but there was no humour in it. "I'm still recovering."

"Sorry I haven't been in touch sooner," Luke said. "The thing is, there's not much to report."

"No worries. I assumed that was why you hadn't been in touch. There's probably nothing in it anyway."

If only you knew, Luke thought. "You could be right," he said, "but Sam did find something odd with one of the contracts."

"Really?" Oliver sat forward in his chair. "One of the

contracts between Supracomm and a supplier?"

"No, it was the main contract between Filchers and Supracomm."

"What did she spot?"

"Someone seems to have altered the standard clauses around non-performance. It's probably nothing but we need to get to the bottom of it in case it benefits one or other party. Would it be okay if one of Filchers' legal experts joins your contracts team for a few weeks to get to the bottom of it?"

"Yes, that should be fine."

"Thanks, Oliver. Her name's Helen Hogg."

"No problem. I'll sort it straight away."

Josh was tapping away at his keyboard when Luke returned to the Ethics Room.

"So, Josh," he said. "Have you had any thoughts on what we do next?"

"I have actually, guv." Josh paused to collect his thoughts. "On my detecting course last week there was a whole afternoon on surveillance. Arthur White was the lecturer and he was superbo. He used to be in the Met and talked about electronic surveillance, team surveillance, de-bugging, the works. Electronic surveillance was particularly interesting. Mr White told us a story about…"

"Get on with it, Josh."

"Oh, yes, uh, sorry, guv." He went quiet.

"There was a point to this, wasn't there?" Josh remained silent. "Josh?"

"Sorry, guv. Yes, the thing is we know they're there, in Unit 7, and we know that Laurie Peterson is the one who called himself Seb but…" He tapped his index finger on the side of his nose.

Luke's eyebrows went up and Josh got the hint and sheepishly lowered his hand. "Well, what I thought was that if we can get camera footage of Peterson's colleagues when they leave the building and show it to Eleanor she'll be able to tell us which of them conned her by pretending to be John."

"That's good thinking." Josh's trademark smile appeared and Luke struggled to conceal his own pride in the way the lad was continually developing. He was becoming a very valuable member of the team. "I'll contact Evan," he went on, "and see if he can arrange it. I'll ask him to send any footage straight to you."

"To me?"

"Yes, straight to you."

"Gucci."

Luke reflected for a moment. "Actually," he said, "you can ring Evan. There's no reason for me to get involved if I'm just the middleman. Tell him what we've agreed and I'm sure he'll be okay with it. I'll leave you to deal with Eleanor as well. Is all that okay?"

Josh nodded eagerly and Luke could see it was more than okay. He smiled to himself. Despite his irritating moments, well to be fair they could sometimes be irritating half-hours, Josh had a lot of get-up-and-go and he was smart too. He was a real asset.

His phone pinged and he looked down to see a text from Oliver Knight. He called over to Helen.

"Helen," he said, "it's all set up for you to go to Oxford. You're to ask for Tommy Ashcroft, he's the Contracts Manager."

"Great. I'll travel down this evening." She turned to Josh. "Are you okay to keep the whiteboard updated while I'm out of the office, Josh?"

"Definito," he said. "I love doing the crazy wall."

"Luke, come over here." It was Maj, and he sounded excited.

Luke walked over and stood behind him. On his screen was a still image of a man in his late thirties, smartly if casually dressed and with a thick but short beard. He was seated behind a desk in a cubicle, but it was a larger area than was common and had enough room for a small table and three chairs.

The man had his phone to his ear and looked annoyed.

"That's Mike Swithin," Maj said.

"One of the people who refused to help the business process consultant?"

"That's the one." Maj gestured to the screen. "This was a few hours ago. The phone call lasted a few minutes and seemed to get more and more heated. However, it's what happened next that intrigues me."

Maj clicked on play and Luke watched as Swithin shook his head in what looked like disbelief before saying something that looked for all the world like 'Fuck off'. He didn't appear to wait for an answer, pressing the key to end the call and almost throwing his phone onto the desk.

"Not a happy bunny," Luke said.

"He gets even less happy. Watch."

Swithin sat back on his chair, still looking annoyed, and another man came into view. Luke could only see his back as he turned one of the chairs and sat across the desk from Swithin who looked across at him and said something.

Maj hit pause. "I think he said 'What do you want? I'm busy'."

"Could be," Luke said.

Maj pressed play. The visitor was clearly saying something, and it was taking a while. Swithin's expression changed from one of annoyance to one that almost looked like fear. He responded briefly then took a deep breath.

"Can you pause it again," Luke said and Maj clicked on the button. "What do you think he said? It looked like 'You can't *something* me', but I couldn't tell what the missing word was. Can you play that bit again?"

Maj rewound a few seconds, played the clip again and then a third time. "It's 'threaten' I think," he said.

"Could be. One more time." Maj played it again. "Yes, definitely. He's saying 'You can't threaten me'." Luke paused. "Shame we can only see his back."

Maj smiled as he pressed play again. Swithin still looked scared and it was apparent his visitor was still talking. After a couple of minutes, the man stood and turned to leave, revealing his face to the camera as he did so.

"Do you know who he is?" Luke said, pointing to the screen.

"That's Chris Nevin," Maj said. "The man who leafed through Sam's notebook."

Chapter 35

Helen got off the bus at Devonshire Buildings and crossed the road to Tesco Express, humming and hawing for a while before deciding on a box of truffles. The flavour was supposed to be champagne but she doubted the bubbly stuff had ever seen the inside of a Lindt factory.

Chocolates ensconced in her handbag, she made her way to her friend's house. As she pressed the bell of Park Villa she heard laughter and when Joanne opened the door she had a big smile on her face.

"He offered to make the meal tonight and he's only gone and dropped half a dozen eggs on the floor," she said, gesturing down the hall to the kitchen.

There was a male voice from the kitchen. "The dog's clearing it up, shells and all."

"Has he planned something nice?" Helen asked.

"Well, kind of." Joanne lowered her voice to a whisper. "But you know how bloody useless he is at cooking. The eggs were for a creme brulee, so I think that's out of the window now. As for the lamb hot-pot, well that's looking like it's going to be more of a lamb burnt-pot." She paused. "Anyhows, this is rude. Come inside, have a drink."

"I can't, Joanne. I have to race off to Oxford tonight and it looks like I'll be staying there for a few nights. Would you mind looking after wee Popsy for me?"

"Of course not, Helen."

"Thanks." She reached into her bag and pulled the chocolates out. "This is for you."

Joanne took the truffles. "That's very kind of you, but you really shouldn't have bothered. I'm always happy to help, you know that."

"It's the least I can do."

"Mind you," Joanne went on. "These will come in handy later when I need something sweet to disguise the flavour of my dinner."

"I heard that!"

Joanne chuckled. "You were meant to, darling," she called back.

"Thanks again," Helen said.

The door closed and she heard Joanne say something else to her husband followed by more laughter.

She sighed as she turned to walk down the drive. What she wouldn't give to have the kind of relationship Joanne and Dave had. She walked a few yards along the road and then into the short lane that led to her own house and was halfway up when Popsy appeared from the bushes and started rubbing herself against her leg. She absent-mindedly stroked her cat and looked up at the house.

It was big, too big for one person, but she couldn't bear to sell it and move somewhere more sensible. Even after all this time she still felt Archie's absence. They had bought it together, agreeing that it was perfect for bringing up a family and would be their forever home.

Cameron had been born less than eighteen months after their wedding and he was a beautiful baby, bonny and sweet with Napoleon curls and a little button nose. The first of four they decided.

But it wasn't to be. Their son had been six months old when the accident happened, destined never to know his father, play with him and listen to his army stories.

Enough of this, she thought. He's gone and that's it. She unlocked the front door and walked up the stairs to her bedroom. Halfway up she passed the photo of Cameron at his graduation and paused to look at it. She was standing beside him and she remembered how proud she had been that day. It was only nine years ago but it seemed like a lifetime. He had been so excited to be joining a law firm, talked endlessly about becoming a barrister, and then, less than a year later…

She shook her head and rushed up the last few steps, pulling her case down from the top of her wardrobe and almost throwing clothes into it. After a while she stopped and grabbed a tissue from the dressing table to wipe her eyes. This was stupid. They were gone and she had to accept it and move on. But it was hard. First Archie and then Cameron. It was all too much.

Helen took a deep intake of breath, grabbed her phone and rang for a taxi. The sooner she was on her way the better.

The driver dropped her off at Bath Spa just in time to catch the 5:45 train which would get her into Oxford at just after seven. Once on board she slid in behind a table, pleased that she could get one to herself, and rang Sam to arrange to meet for dinner at eight. Then she signed on to the train's wifi, opened Spotify and selected some chilled jazz to listen to on the journey.

She tried her hardest to relax but her thoughts kept returning to Cameron. Had she been a bad mother? Was that why it happened? Perhaps she had spoilt him, trying to make up for the lack of a father or siblings?

Helen, stop it. With new-found determination, she turned the music off and pulled a folder out of the suitcase on the seat beside her. She opened it, extracted some papers and her notepad, and continued working her way through the contracts she had printed off earlier in the day.

Chapter 36

Sam was pleased that Helen was joining her in Oxford. It would be nice to meet up and talk about their investigation, even if they did have to keep their friendship a secret when at work.

It was more than that though. Helen was a genuinely nice person and funny with it.

She was a good fifteen minutes ahead of time when she got to The Plough, but Helen was already there, seated at a table set for two next to a small bow window and staring out, deep in thought.

"Penny for them," Sam said as she slid in opposite.

Helen turned around. "Oh hi, Sam. Sorry, I was miles away." She called over to the bar. "George, can I have the same for my friend please?"

"Be right up, Helen," he said.

"Do you know him?" Sam asked, slightly taken aback.

"We go way back," Helen said and smiled. "Five maybe ten minutes." Sam shook her head. "I know," Helen went on. "What am I like?"

The barman brought Sam's Prosecco over and gave them each a menu.

"Before we order," Sam said, "I'm itching to know what's happened. You said on the phone there have been a few developments."

"Aye, there have." She lowered her voice. "It's way beyond simple money laundering. Luke's now convinced the same gang is involved in romance scamming and trafficking women. They've murdered someone too."

"Murdered someone!"

Helen told her about Jeremy Scott and then about Sheppey Industrial Estate near Wells. "Josh used his initiative, bless him, and found out that the romance scamming team are renting Unit 7."

"Wow, good on him."

"One other thing. It seems pretty certain that Chris Nevin is their man on the inside."

"What?"

Helen leaned forward over the table and grasped Sam's hand. "Are you all right? You've gone pale."

Sam swallowed. "It can't be him. It just can't."

"Why do you say that?"

"I…" Sam hesitated. "I'm kind of dating him."

"Holy shite! Please tell me you're joking."

Sam shook her head. "I'm serious. He invited me out to dinner and I'm seeing him again tomorrow evening. We're going to a bar and then onto the cinema afterwards."

"Not The Godfather I hope."

Sam half-smiled. "No, Helen, not The Godfather." She paused before continuing. "How can you be so sure it's him?"

Helen told her about the video of Chris Nevin threatening Mike Swithin.

"And he was definitely threatening him?" Sam asked.

"Definitely, or in the words of our youngest team member, definito."

"Do you think he's asked me out because he knows what I'm up to?"

"Probably."

"I've been an idiot, haven't I?"

"You need to tell Luke."

"No!" She wasn't sure why, but Sam didn't want Luke to know she was dating Chris.

"These people are evil," Helen said. "Look what happened to Jeremy Scott. If he knows you're investigating them you could be in real danger."

"He wouldn't…" Sam stopped as she remembered Luke's advice about not trusting people. She sighed. "What should I do, Helen? We got on really well and it'll look suspicious if I cancel our date."

"As I said, you need to tell Luke. He'll know what to do for the best."

Chapter 37

Sam woke up at five, went to the toilet and then tried her hardest to drop off again but it was impossible. Her mind was churning, her head full of thoughts of Chris, then of Tony. Luke's face kept appearing too and she dreaded having to tell him what she had done.

It was no good, there was no way she was getting back to sleep. She leaned over to the bedside lamp and turned it on, then rolled onto her back, stared up at the ceiling and wondered why she was so rubbish at relationships. Was there something about her that pulled in the wrong sort of man?

She thought she had been careful with Tony and that she had let things develop slowly. But when she thought back to their first few weeks together she realised she had let her physical attraction to him overrule her brain. In truth, she had known from the start that they had little in common. And now he was back in touch, talking nonsense about wanting her to meet his new girlfriend of all things.

As for Chris, she found him attractive but unlike Tony they also shared many of the same interests. He liked karate, they shared a love of the same kind of films and he loved long walks in the countryside. Conversation had been easy too, and he had seemed genuinely interested in her rather than forever wanting to talk about himself.

The bastard.

It was obvious now why he asked about her so much. As for sharing the same interests, well that was easy to fake. He must have found out somehow that she loved karate and then used google to beef up his background story. She shook her head and half-laughed but there wasn't any humour in it. His favourite films were probably gore-filled slasher movies.

This last thought made goosebumps appear on her arms. This wasn't just a relationship problem, a case of connecting with someone unsuitable. From what Helen had said, it was almost certainly Chris who was Al Ummah's man inside Supracomm. And that meant he had courted Sam deliberately, which in turn meant he knew what she was up to.

She was in danger and Helen was right. She had to swallow her pride and tell Luke. He would know what to do.

The hotel had a small gym and the dining room opened at six. She cleaned her teeth and had a quick wash before pulling on a pair of leggings and her sports bra and top. A workout would do her good and use up her pent-up energy. Better that than letting it fester inside her. Then she'd have a shower and an early breakfast. There was loads to do once she was in the office and she needed to keep her mind active.

By the time Sam got back to her room after breakfast it was nearly seven. Was it too early to ring him? No, he was bound to be up. She had to get it over with. Sighing, she sat on the end of her bed and pulled his number up on her mobile. She held her finger over the green button for a few seconds then pressed it and put the phone to her ear.

It rang a few times and she was beginning to think he might be showering or not yet up when his voice came on the line.

"Not another bloody pigeon!" There was a pause then, "Put it down!"

"Luke," Sam said.

"Oh, for fuck's sake!"

"Luke," she said again, louder this time.

After a few seconds, there was a rustling sound and then his voice came on the phone again. "Sam?"

"Hi Luke. Is everything okay?"

"Sorry, it's… No, Wilkins!"

"What's he doing?"

"He's trying to bury a pigeon and the poor bugger isn't even dead. I'll ring you back." He hung up.

Several minutes passed before her phone rang. "Is everything okay?" she said.

"Yes, it's fine. I managed to rescue the bird and amazingly it seems to be okay. Gave me a nip for my troubles then flew away. Wilkins has run off looking for another one." He paused. "It's only just gone seven. Is everything okay?"

"I need some advice?"

"Sure. What's up?"

"Helen told me you believe Chris Nevin is working for Al Ummah."

"It looks like it, yes."

This was it. She swallowed. "I, ah, I'm kind of seeing him."

"Seeing him." There were both silent for a few seconds and then the penny dropped. "You mean as in…"

"We're dating."

"Bloody hell."

Her next words came out in a rush. "We've only been out once but it went well and he's asked me out again."

"Mmm."

"Sorry, Luke, I didn't think. What should I do?"

"Do you think he's onto you?"

"He must be. Why else would he ask me out?"

"You're not exactly…" Luke stopped, then started again. "You may be right."

"Any thoughts?"

"Let me think about it. I'll give you a ring in half an hour."

"Thanks, Luke."

Sam ended the call and looked at her watch. Thirty minutes seemed like a long time. She decided to get some fresh air and put on a light jacket before heading downstairs, spotting Helen walking towards the dining room as she stepped out of the lift. She almost called to her until she remembered they weren't supposed to know each other.

She sighed. This secret squirrel stuff was hard and it didn't seem like she was cut out for it. The business with Chris proved it. She should go back to number-crunching for a living, perhaps leave Filchers altogether and join an accountancy firm.

She hadn't long left the building when her phone rang.

"That was quick," she said.

"Is anyone in earshot?" Luke asked.

"No. Why?"

"We need to be careful, that's all."

Was he having a go at her, subtly telling her she hadn't been careful enough? She hated to have let him down.

"What should I do?" she asked.

"Can I ask you a couple of questions? They're kind of personal."

"Of course." She wondered what was coming.

"Am I correct in assuming he asked you out, rather than the other way around?"

"Yes."

"And how did it get to that stage? Did he appear to go out of his way to be with you?"

She thought back to their meeting at the water dispenser, then his suggestion of lunch. "It didn't seem that way."

"And was your date for dinner?"

"Yes."

"And afterwards did he ask to come back to your hotel?"

She felt her face flush. "I'm not that kind…"

He interrupted her before she could finish. "Sam, what I want to establish is whether he tried to get close to your notes or your computer."

"I see." She hesitated. "He asked if he could come back and I said no, but that I'd love to see him again."

"Right. Well, I think you should go ahead with seeing him. Saying no would seem odd since you got on so well."

Sam felt her cheeks reddening again and was thankful they were talking on the phone and not face-to-face. "Okay," she said.

"Are you sure you're up to this?"

She gulped. "Sure."

"Is it another dinner?"

"No, we're going to a bar and then on to see a film."

"Good. But you need to be incredibly careful. If he's what we think he is you're putting yourself in grave danger."

Chapter 38

Luke was worried about the risks Sam was taking. She had to tread so bloody carefully. If Chris Nevin was indeed Al Ummah's inside man then every contact she had with him put her at risk. The trouble was that short of pulling her out of Supracomm completely there was little option.

But dating him! He shook his head. Sam was a strong individual, and smart too, but she was really going to have to be on her mettle. He made a mental note to keep in more regular contact with her.

Luke sat on the hall settle, tied his shoelaces and then called Wilkins over. "Come on boy," he said. "In your bed."

Wilkins obediently walked into the dog crate and looked up at him eagerly anticipating what he knew would happen next.

"Here you go," Luke said as he shut the gate and passed the cocker a bone-shaped biscuit through the bars. It was down the dog's throat before he was out of the door.

Luke sat in the company BMW and looked up at the house, remembering Jess leaning out of the upstairs window, her hair tousled and her eyes full of sleep. She had blown him a kiss and then gone back to bed.

It was the last time he had ever seen her.

He sighed and reversed the car back before turning around and heading for the office. It was a twenty-minute drive but he enjoyed the scenery. It was mostly rural and took him through Hinton Charterhouse and Midford, both lovely villages, before turning towards Bath at The Globe roundabout near Corston.

After a few minutes, he felt more relaxed and flicked the audiobook on. Bob Hoon's never-dulcet tones immediately came through the speaker, the latest invented expletive from the pen of JD Kirk making him laugh out loud.

He was approaching Midford when his phone rang. It was Mark.

"Good morning, Mark," he said. "How's everything?"

"Not so good."

"Oh dear. Is it Mother?"

"No, it's Erica."

Somehow, Luke wasn't surprised. "What's happened?" he asked.

"I found out she…" Mark paused for a moment.

"Are you okay?

"We had a massive argument last night, and, well, she kind of kicked me out."

"Of Borrowham Hall?" Luke marvelled at the cheek of the woman, kicking her husband out of his own family home.

"You wouldn't believe what she can be like when she's upset." Luke decided it was best not to comment. "Anyway," Mark went on, "I drove and drove and decided I needed someone to talk to so made my way north. It was about three in the morning by the time I reached Norton St Philip and I didn't want to wake you so I crashed out at The George."

"I'm surprised they found you a room at that time."

"They didn't. I slept in the Range Rover in their car park."

"Christ, Mark. You should have come around."

"Yes, well I thought I'd catch you early before you went to work. The trouble is I've only just come to. I take it you've left for the office?"

"Yes, I'm about halfway to Bath. Tell you what, there's a cafe called Three Ways opposite St Martin's Hospital that's open for breakfast. Let's meet there." He gave Mark the postcode.

Twenty minutes later Luke was ordering his second

double espresso when Mark walked in. He was immediately struck by how awful he looked, his eyes bloodshot, his clothes a mess and his curly brown hair all over the place.

"You look like you slept in your car," Luke said.

Mark gave a sardonic grin. "Very funny." He looked around. "You didn't tell me the cafe was part of a school."

"This place is great. I tend to stop here once or twice a week during term time. What will you have?"

Behind the counter, a middle-aged lady and a lad of sixteen or so were looking expectantly at Mark. The boy was sporting a badge saying 'Neville', and underneath in smaller letters 'I'm in Training - Please be patient.'.

"The English Breakfast is excellent," Neville said and smiled.

"That sounds good, Neville," Mark said. "I'll take one. An extra sausage too please, and a black coffee."

Neville turned to the woman beside him and smiled at her. She showed him how to enter the order into the system and Mark paid.

"So what happened?" Luke asked once they were both seated in the corner of the cafe. "You said you'd found something out. Has she been with someone else?"

"Gosh no!" Mark said, then looked over at his brother. "Well, kind of."

"What do you mean kind of? How can you 'kind of' be with someone?"

"It was before I met her."

"Then, why…"

"And she had a child, a girl."

"What!" Luke found this hard to take in. "How long have you been together?"

"Nearly eight years."

"And her daughter is…"

"Eight."

This left Luke with so many questions he didn't know where to start. "Why didn't she tell you? And where's her daughter now?"

Mark let out a long sigh and pushed his hand through his hair. "Erica was raped, Luke."

"My God!"

"A man grabbed her in St James Park when she was walking home after work and pulled her into the bushes."

"In Toronto?"

"No, in San Jose. She didn't go to the police, couldn't face it, and then a few months later found out she was pregnant."

"Did she consider abortion?"

"No. She decided to have the baby but have it adopted as soon as possible after birth."

"That must have been incredibly traumatic."

Mark nodded. "The only people she told were her parents and she stayed at home for the entire pregnancy. If anyone asked after her they were told she had had a breakdown. Then after the birth she moved to Toronto and it was six months after that that we met."

"How did you find out?"

"We were talking about having children and she suddenly went quiet and then it all came out. I was sympathetic of course, but after we'd been talking for a good half an hour I asked if that was why she was always so nasty to Jess and she completely lost it."

Luke didn't need to think. "You have to go straight back and talk to her," he said.

"Don't you think I should give her space? Time to calm down?"

"No." He paused. "I know she can be difficult."

Mark raised his eyebrows. "You don't know the half of it."

"But," Luke went on, "she needs you now more than ever. She's been bottling this up for eight years, Mark, and she's probably desperate to tell you everything."

"You're right I guess. I'll go back now."

There was a noise behind them and Mark turned around to see Neville smiling down at him. "I've given you two extra sausages instead of one," he said.

"Thank you," Mark said as he took the offered plate.

"You're very tall," Neville said, "and you look a mess. I figured you needed a big breakfast."

"That's lovely of you, Neville. I really appreciate it."

Neville's smile widened and he nodded to Luke before returning behind the counter.

"Right," Luke said. "Get that down you and then head back to Dorset. And be sure to ring me as soon as you can and let me know how it's going."

Chapter 39

"Why are you wearing that suit?" Noah asked. "Are you going to a wedding?"

Josh looked disparagingly at his younger brother then back to his reflection in the glass, intent on moussing his hair to exactly the shape he wanted, and irritated that their only full-length mirror was in the hall rather than the privacy of his bedroom.

"That's a pen-stripe suit, isn't it?" Noah went on

"It's 'pin-stripe', you moron." Sometimes he could be a lot stupider than his thirteen years.

"Have you got an important meeting?"

"Yes." He knew what Noah was like and if he didn't give him an answer the little half-pint would go on and on and on. He tilted his head to the right. His hair wasn't correct over his left ear. "Can you pass me my styling brush? It's on my chest of drawers."

Noah retrieved the brush and passed it over. "Is this your first ever important meeting?' he asked.

"Of course not."

"Why the posy suit then?"

The little sod could be so irritating at times. "None of your business."

"Are you trying to impress a girl?"

Josh squirted a little mousse into his palm, rubbed it on the disobedient curl and used the brush to curve it into shape. He stood back and smiled to himself. Yes, that was a lot better.

"Won't Leanne be upset?"

"What?" He turned to his brother as what he had just said sunk in. "Why would Leanne be upset?"

"Because you're trying to impress a girl."

"I'm not trying to impress anyone, okay? It's an important meeting, that's all." He sighed, grabbed his jacket and headed downstairs.

Noah called down after him. "She'll stop letting you put your tongue down her throat."

Josh ignored him and went into the kitchen. His Mum was seated at the breakfast bar, a bowl of cereal in front of her.

"You look smart," she said as she looked up. "Who are you trying to impress?"

"I'm not, Mum. I've…"

She laughed. "It's all right, I'm only joking. I heard what Noah was saying. What's the meeting about?"

He wanted to tell her, he really did, but he thought back to his course and what they had said then about confidentiality. There was the Official Secrets Act to think about too.

"I can't tell you Mum. I've signed the Official Secrets Act."

"Liar, liar, pants on fire."

Josh closed his eyes and let out a long breath before turning around and glaring at his brother. "Why would I lie, idiot?"

"Because it's a girl and you don't want us to know."

"Noah," his mum said. "Stop winding your brother up. Now, what do the two of you want for breakfast?

"I've got to go, Mum," Josh said and leaned forward to give her a peck on the cheek. "I've got lots of prep to do."

"Bye, darling."

"Have a good meeting," Noah said, holding his fingers up as air quotes as he said the last word.

Josh felt like thumping the little twerp but instead said, "Bye little brother. Have a good day at nursery," before walking quickly to the front door and out before he had a chance to reply.

Once outside, Josh decided he would walk to work and

use the time to plan his approach. He turned off Cedric Road and headed off down the hill towards the Lower Bristol Road.

He had been nervous ringing Evan but the MI6 man had talked to him as an equal which was awesome. Evan had said that he would get straight onto it, and to ring him in the morning for an update.

He was working alongside MI6! How cool was that? Josh Ogden OO7, now that had a certain ring to it.

"A good agent doesn't need gadgets," he said out loud, affecting a Sean Connery accent and causing an elderly woman to stare at him before veering off the pavement and onto the road to walk quickly past. "The only gadgets I've ever needed," he continued, "are a sharp eye, sensitive hearing and a whole bunch of bigger brains."

He smiled, then remembered it had been Johnny English who had said those words and not James Bond. Ah well, it didn't make it any less relevant.

By the time he got to the office, he had more or less worked out how he was going to approach his meeting with Eleanor. But first, he needed to ring Evan.

Maj was already there when he got to the Ethics Room, standing at the whiteboard and looking pensive.

"Spotted something?" Josh asked

"Maybe." He turned and looked Josh up and down. "That's a posh suit. Have you got an important meeting?"

Josh sighed and decided he'd go back to his normal light grey suit from here on in. "I'm seeing Eleanor Jones this afternoon," he said.

"I see." Maj pointed to her name on the whiteboard. "We could certainly do with finding out more." There was an arrow linking it to Unit 7 at Sheppey Industrial Estate but unlike Pam Greening's, which was connected to Laurie Peterson, there were no other connections. "Are you hopeful of finding out who her mysterious John really is?"

"That's the aim, yes."

Josh put his jacket over the back of his chair, sat down and rang Evan. It was answered immediately

"Good morning, Josh."

He's got my number on his phone, Josh thought but said, "Good morning, Evan. Any news?"

"It's all sorted. They fitted a couple of cameras two hours ago."

"Gucci."

"What?"

"Sorry." Josh gave a little cough. "Thanks, Evan. That's excellent."

Josh took note of the access codes as Evan read them out.

"You know how to use the codes?" Evan asked.

"Yes, Luke gave me the URLs."

"Great."

Josh ended the call and turned his laptop on, tapping his fingers on the desk as he waited for Windows to fire up. As soon as he'd entered his password he went to the secure website and entered the first of the two access codes.

"Superbo," he said, as a crystal clear image of the front of a set of warehouse units came up. He opened a second browser window beside it and keyed in the other code. It also worked, bringing up an image that he assumed was of the rear entrance. "Superbo duo!" he exclaimed, earning a stare and a shake of the head from Maj.

He watched the live feeds for a few minutes but the only action was a cat idly walking past the rear entrance. No surprise there. The men would be inside Unit 7 conning some other poor innocents out of their life savings. He thought for a moment then keyed in 07:00 on the front feed and fast-forwarded from there.

He smiled to himself as he saw four men enter the building at 8:31, 8:38, 8:50 and 8:59. The camera only caught their rear but he was pretty sure the third of them was Laurie Peterson. The view of the others was poor though, certainly not enough to show Eleanor. He needed to see faces. Did that mean he'd have to wait until they came out to go home, or would they keep their heads down, ever wary?

Bollocksy, bollocksy, he thought. Eleanor Jones was coming in at 2 pm and he wasn't going to have anything to show her.

Chapter 40

Sam had barely sat down at her desk when Chris Nevin made an appearance. He put his hand on her shoulder.

"Good morning, Sam," he said.

She turned, hoping the smile on her face didn't look as artificial as it felt. "Morning, Chris."

He was beaming down at her. "I've booked our tickets. It's at 8:45. Is that okay with you?"

"Sure, it's fine." Her smile was still plastered across her face, but she was finding it hard to keep it there.

"I thought we could go to Angels Cocktail Bar first. It's a terrific place with a great atmosphere."

"That's great." She paused. "I really need to get on though." She gestured to her desk. "I've got a mountain of work to get through."

He looked past her at the papers on her desk. "What have you got on?"

"Oh, ah, bits and bobs. It mounts up though."

"Sure." He was still looking at the papers on her desk. "Catch you at lunchtime?"

"Fine."

He raised his eyes to hers and smiled. "I'll come past at one."

"Great. See you then."

He left and she stared after him. Gosh, this was hard.

With a sigh, she turned back to her desk. She had been telling the truth when she said she had loads to do, but it was focused work and not the bits and bobs she had claimed.

She had the names of the four people Supracomm was unknowingly funding, and someone had put their kit through the accounts. But who? She now knew Chris was involved, but he wasn't in a position to have that kind of access which meant there had to be someone else working alongside him.

Mike Swithin was the obvious suspect. As Lead Accountant, he could access any system and Helen had told her about the CCTV footage showing Chris threatening him. Yes, it had to be Mike.

She had found account entries for each of J Duggan, L Peterson, D Spencer and L Boniface and Supracomm's Audit Log, or 'Saul' for short, would have logged who made them. The problem was that Saul wasn't a system she had access to, and asking for access would look suspicious.

After a few minutes thought she made a decision and picked up the phone.

"Audrey Manners."

"Hi Audrey, it's Sam. I wondered if you could do me a favour. Can I pop up and have a word?"

"Of course. I'm between meetings so now would be good."

"Great. I'll be there in a sec."

When she got to Audrey's office she was cradling a coffee in both hands and looking a lot happier than she had the previous week.

"Thanks for taking all that work on for me, Sam," Audrey said.

"No problem." She hesitated. "If you don't mind me saying so, you look a lot happier than you did last week."

"Yes. Things are looking up. I..." She stopped when her phone rang and looked down at the screen. "Sam, I have to take this. Would you mind stepping outside for a moment?"

"Not at all."

Sam closed the door behind her and looked back through the glass. Seeing her do this, Audrey swivelled her chair around. After no more than a minute, she turned back and gestured for Sam to return. As she approached she saw that the other woman looked drained and close to tears.

"Are you okay?" she asked.

"I put my trust in him and now he does this," Audrey said, almost under her breath.

"Is it your boyfriend?"

"No, of course not," she snapped. "As I told you, we're finished."

"Perhaps I should come back later."

"No, I'll be fine." She hesitated. "Sorry if I was a bit abrupt. I was told something rather shocking, that's all." She paused and tried to smile, but it was a ghost of a thing. "How can I help, Sam?"

"I'm trying to tie together some entries for March for the annual accounts and I found a duplicate invoice. One copy needs to be deleted but I don't know who made the entry."

"Do you need access to Saul?"

"Yes, I think that's the only way."

"Sure, no problem." Audrey grabbed a pen and post-it from her desk. "Here's my Saul user id and password," she said as she scribbled them down. "Make sure you destroy it when you've used it, won't you?"

"Yes of course," Sam said as she took the note. She gestured to Audrey's phone. "I hope everything sorts itself out."

"I'm sure it will," she sighed. "One way or another."

Sam headed upstairs and back towards her cubicle. After twenty yards or so she reached a gap in the wall on the left. She checked no one was looking then turned into the corridor, hoping it was the right one. It was a dead-end, with a fire exit at the end, but halfway along she found what she was looking for, the word 'Storeroom' large and visible on the door.

She looked back down the corridor then pressed the handle, pushed the door open and turned the light on.

When she closed the door behind her she took in the

myriad of items on the floor and on shelves at the sides and back of the room. They ranged from boxes of pens and pencils to printer cartridges and paper. Everything you would expect in a storeroom in fact. It could be that Audrey had been there for a valid reason, but she had been seen entering holding several sheets of paper and leaving with nothing. It was suspicious, to say the least, and suggested she had an ulterior motive for going there, possibly to use a hidden phone.

There was a waste bin on the floor and she started there. It was full to the brim with cardboard cartons, plastic wrappers and paper, possibly the sheets of paper Audrey had brought in, but no phone. She looked at a few of the documents. They were call centre documents, but nothing confidential and this was the call centre storeroom so no surprise there.

Next, she investigated the shelves. They were crammed and it was going to take ages to search through the mass of various-sized packets and boxes. She had to look, that was all, and she also had to be as quick as she could.

Sam started with what was on the ground, then moved to the lowest shelf, working her way from left to right. She glanced at the door, hoping that no one would need supplies. If someone stumbled in looking for a box of envelopes she was going to struggle to give a good reason for being there.

She was about to start on the second shelf up when something clicked in her brain. She had seen something out of place, but what was it? There had been paper clips, erasers, staplers, in-trays and out-trays, but there had also been something unusual. But where?

She looked back along the shelves, then down to the items on the floor. When she reached the end opposite the door her eyes fell on the bin and she remembered. Bending down, she moved some of the rubbish aside and there it was. She picked it out, held it up and smiled. *Audrey*

Manners, she thought, *I know exactly what you've been up to.*

Chapter 41

"Are you Helen Hogg?"

Helen looked up from her newspaper. "Aye, that's me." She held out her hand. "You must be Tommy."

He shook her hand and laughed. "Sorry, no. Tommy wouldn't thank you for thinking that. He's much younger and fitter than me." He tapped his belly as he said this but it looked perfectly flat to her. "My name's Oliver Knight. I'm the Client Director for my sins. Tommy's in a meeting so I thought I'd welcome you rather than keep you hanging about in reception."

"Thanks, Oliver."

"No problem. I always like to greet new team members personally anyway. Come up to my office and I'll tell you what's what while we're waiting."

As she followed him up he pointed out some of the teams they passed, introducing her to a couple of people as 'our new legal whizz'. Once there he asked his secretary to fetch coffee and tea and asked Helen to sit down.

"Thanks for coming in," he said. "First your colleague Sam and now you." He chuckled. "I'm beginning to think there's something amiss in this account."

"I suspect what I'm looking at is purely a case of poor drafting," Helen said. "Part of the Ethics Team's job is to ensure Filchers takes corporate social responsibility seriously and it looks like one of the clauses inserted in the main contract downplays Supracomm's compliance with the energy mandates that the government imposed in their 2019 bill on industrial and commercial climate levelling."

"I see."

She tried not to smile when she realised she had successfully lost him.

"It leaves us open to legal challenge," she went on, "and we wouldn't want that would we?."

"No, of course not." He paused before continuing. "So there's no link with what your colleague is looking at?"

"To be honest, Oliver," she said, despite having no intention whatsoever of telling the truth, "I haven't the faintest what she's looking at. It's a completely separate investigation, to the extent that we don't even acknowledge we know each other when we're here."

"That makes sense. And will you tell Tommy what you're investigating?"

"Oh aye, no need to keep it a secret. As I said, I'm pretty sure it's a simple error."

There was a knock at the door and his secretary walked in, followed by a slim man in his early thirties. He wore Harry Potter glasses and was dressed in a dark grey suit, his navy blue tie tight to the collar of his white shirt

"Ah, Tommy," Oliver said looking up. "That was quick."

"Aye, my meeting ran short," Tommy said, then looked at Helen. "You must be Helen."

"I am," she said as she shook his hand. "And you're a fellow Scot I see."

"I am that. Edinburgh born and bred."

"As am I. We've got a wee bit more than deep-fried Mars bars in common then." Her eyes twinkled as she added, "We're about the same age too."

"I, ah…"

She laughed. "I'm teasing you, Tommy."

"Aye, right." He heaved a sigh of relief and turned to Oliver. "I'll take it from here."

"Great," Oliver said. "Nice to meet you, Helen."

"And you, Oliver."

Tommy led Helen to the area where the contracts team sat and introduced her to the others in the team, two men of about her own age and a woman in her early to mid-forties. It was clear that they were busy, their in-trays bulging with folders.

"We're up to our eyes in sub-contract reviews," Tommy said once he'd shown Helen her cubicle. "Oliver kicked this off eighteen months ago and it generates a lot of work as we approach year-end. Your arrival is a godsend."

"You know I have an anomaly to look into in the main contract?" Helen asked.

"Oh aye, but from what Oliver told me it shouldn't take long. Are you okay if I pass you a few subs to look at once you've resolved it?"

She felt she had little choice. "Sure," she said.

"Won't be a sec." He disappeared and returned a few seconds later holding a document wallet. He handed it to her. "You'll find access instructions and so forth in here."

"Thanks." She put it down and he smiled and vanished again, this time coming back with a pile of eight or nine paper-clipped documents. "These are the sub-contracts I'd like you to review," he said with a sheepish smile as he put them onto her in-tray.

"Thanks again."

"No problem. I'll leave it to you, then."

"Great."

Helen sighed as she looked at the small mountain of paper in her in-tray.

She and the three permanent team members were in a pod of 4 cubicles while Tommy sat in his own, slightly larger, area off to the left against a wall. The partitions were low, meaning she could see each of the others. Not ideal for her non-contract-related investigative work but she would have to make do.

She sent a WhatsApp message to Sam to say she was settled and had all her access rights. The response came back immediately. 'I found out what Audrey Manners is up to. Tell you this evening.' She was about to reply when she saw Sam was typing again. A few seconds later her message appeared. 'Please can you do more digging on Chris

Nevin?'

She confirmed that she would and retrieved a lever arch file from her bag, opening it and leafing through the hefty document inside to the section on corporate social responsibility. She needed to look like she was investigating an anomaly in the master contract between Filchers and Supracomm.

Next, she opened her notepad and jotted down what she knew about Chris Nevin:

- high-flyer

She smiled to herself, put her pencil to her lips and thought for a moment. There were a number of avenues she could pursue. Social media was a great source of information, but there was no point in doing that from the office. Likely as not access to sites such as Instagram, Facebook and LinkedIn wouldn't be possible from the office computer anyway. She sent a WhatsApp to Maj with Chris Nevin's personal details and he agreed to look at his profiles and activity and get back to her.

Helen keyed 'Chris Nevin' into the search bar on the Supracomm intranet and hit enter. It returned five results. The first entry was his staff profile. Underneath his photo it had his age, his job title and his interests. She added to her list:

- aged 31
- Senior procurement specialist
- Likes karate, films, reading, travel

The next entry was six months old and promoted the new staff karate club with Chris named as one of the instructors.

The third entry was a duplicate of the article in the staff magazine naming Chris as one of Supracomm's high-flyers., while the fourth was headed 'Promotions in May' and listed him as one of the people moving up to Grade 5. The fifth and final result was only eight months before the fourth and was another promotions article.

She updated her list and read through what she now knew:

- high-flyer
- aged 31
- senior procurement specialist
- Likes karate (instructor), films, reading, travel
- Joined Supracomm three years ago
- Promoted to grade 4 in June last year then to grade 5 this February

It was this last bullet point that intrigued her. His second promotion had come incredibly quickly. Her phone pinged and she looked down to see a WhatsApp from Maj. *You bonny wee superstar*, she thought as she read his message. She added more entries to her list:

- has a daughter (aged 2 or 3?)
- ex-Army

Chapter 42

By 12:30 Josh was beginning to despair and wondered if he should ring Eleanor and cancel. There had been nothing to see on either feed, not even one person stepping out of the rear exit for a cigarette.

He was watching live, hoping and praying something would happen. They should be thinking of lunch about now, and surely they wouldn't all have brought sandwiches in.

What he didn't expect was for someone else to arrive. Again it was only a rear view but the man would be hard to miss if he saw him again. He was a giant, almost as tall as Luke but a good thirty kilograms heavier. His hair was long and he had a shaggy beard which even from the side Josh could see had been plaited.

Like the others, the man had a key and used it to enter Unit 7.

Another twenty minutes passed and Josh was on the verge of phoning when the door opened and the giant walked out. He didn't lock the door behind him which gave Josh hope, and sure enough a few minutes later two men followed, neither of whom was Laurie Peterson. He waited, his eyes glued to the monitor, but no one else appeared and fifteen minutes later the two men returned carrying a carrier bag and four coffees in styrofoam cups. The giant didn't return.

Josh looked at his watch. It was 1:30. He worked his way back through the recorded feed making notes, and had just finished when his phone rang.

"Hi, Josh Ogden here," he said.

"It's Leanne."

"Oh, uh, hi." He paused. "I'm kind of busy. Can I ring

you in a couple of hours?"

"I'm working on reception today." Her voice was cold.

"Yes I know, but can we talk later? I've got an important meeting. "

"Really?"

"Yes, I'm…" He hesitated as he remembered the last time Leanne had said 'really' in that tone of voice. *Buggery, buggery, shittedy-shit.* What had he done wrong now? He swallowed. "Has my visitor arrived?"

"Yes."

"Great. I'll come down and welcome her."

"I'm sure you will." She said the words so quietly he almost didn't catch them.

"What?"

"She's not on her own."

"She's not?"

"No. She's brought her mother."

She ended the call and Josh looked at the phone for a minute, stood up, sat down again, then shrugged his shoulders and stood up again. He looked at his jacket on the back of the chair and decided against wearing it.

Normally Josh didn't so much walk somewhere as bounce there. Today, however, his journey to reception was at a snail's pace. In his head were images of Mandy and Leanne rolling around the reception area floor, hands pulling at each other's hair, burly security men trying but failing to separate them, and all the while Mandy's Mum screaming for an ambulance.

When he walked out of the lift he was delighted to see a complete absence of blood or carnage. Leanne was at the reception desk signing a visitor in while Mandy and her Mum were seated on the large gold sofa opposite talking in a low voice.

Leanne turned when she heard the lift and gestured to the sofa with her pencil. Josh tried to smile at her but she avoided his glance and turned back to the visitor without acknowledging him further.

He walked over to Mandy who to his horror stood up as soon as she saw him, gave him a massive beaming smile and leaned forward to peck him on the cheek. He swallowed, looked back over his shoulder and then back at Mandy.

"Hello," he said, his voice almost falsetto. He turned to her mother and attempted to lower his voice to its normal pitch. "Hello again, Mrs Jones."

"Eleanor, please."

"Please can you both follow me."

"You're very serious today," Mandy said.

Josh didn't reply and walked quickly to the lift, looking sideways at Leanne like a frightened turtle as he did so. He heaved a sigh of relief when they emerged from the lift on the first floor.

"This way," he said and led them along the corridor.

"Is that a Norton?" Mandy asked when they reached the Ethics Room. She bent down to look at the fingerprint scanner. "It is," she went on. "It's a Norton FS-433." She looked up at Josh. "I'm surprised you've got that. We had one at work but it was swapped out for the FS-444 when it was recalled."

"It's only just been fitted," Josh said. "Why was it recalled?"

"Problems with recognition." She put her finger against the sensor, pressed the handle down and pushed the door open. "See what I mean?"

Josh made a mental note to tell Luke about the sensor and showed them in. "I've ordered coffee and tea," he said. "It should be here any minute."

"Well, at least we won't need to let them in when they bring it," Mandy said with a smile.

Josh pulled up two chairs behind his and invited the women to sit down. "I managed to find some clips of the scammers when they went out to fetch lunch today," he said. "I'd like you to watch them, Eleanor, and see if the man claiming to be John is one of them."

"Will do."

Josh played the first clip and they watched as the front door opened and two middle-aged men came out talking animatedly, one appearing to be laughing at something the other man had said. Neither was Laurie Peterson so there was a decent chance one of them was John. He kept his fingers crossed as he watched Eleanor for any sign of recognition.

She moved closer to the screen. "Can you pause it?" She hesitated. "Rewind a little."

This was it. They had their man.

"No," she said. "It's neither of them."

Shitstick, Josh thought. "Would you mind looking at them when they return?" he asked.

"Might as well," Eleanor said.

He moved the recording forward to the point where the two men returned and pressed play. Eleanor was sitting back now, resigned to the fact that she wasn't going to see John, when she suddenly leaned forward and pointed.

"Pause it," she said. Josh pressed pause. "Are you able to zoom in?"

"Sure," Josh said. "Which part?"

"His head." Josh zoomed in and Eleanor moved even closer to the screen. "That's him!" she said.

"Wowza," Josh said and punched his hand in the air.

Both Mandy and Eleanor turned to look at him.

"Sorry," he said. "Uh, how can you be sure?"

"It's John's ear. He lost the bottom of it in an accident when he was young."

Josh looked at the screen and sure enough there was a small part of the man's ear missing. He rewound to the earlier footage. "Have a more careful look at them when they came out," he said.

Eleanor watched, and after a few seconds gave out a

gasp. "It is John," she said. "He's the one laughing. I didn't recognise him before because he hasn't got a beard and he's not wearing glasses." Her voice started to break. "He's not as pale either. He looks the picture of health."

Mandy put her hand on her Mum's arm.

"I'm sorry," Josh said.

"It's definitely him," Eleanor said, and he could see that she was struggling to hold it together, "but it's still hard to believe he's not my John." She swallowed and looked at Josh. "I know that sounds stupid."

"Not at all, Eleanor," he said. "Not at all."

Chapter 43

Greg was frightening, but Tania's biggest worry was that Anderson would return. The way he had killed the girl on the lorry had been truly horrific. He had done it with no more thought than if he was swatting a fly. The man was evil, pure evil.

She was concerned for herself, naturally, but it was Izabella who was putting herself in more and more danger all the time. She was becoming increasingly withdrawn and hadn't eaten for twenty-four hours, saying that the food made her feel sick. Now, as had been the case for an hour or more, she was sitting on her bed, legs pulled up, staring blankly at the wall opposite.

"You must be strong," Tania said. "You saw what happened on the lorry. If they see you are weak, they will think you are no use to them."

Izabella lifted her head and looked at her, her eyes bloodshot and rimmed with tears. "It would be better if they kill me," she said, her voice flat and lifeless. These were the most words she had spoken for some time.

"Why don't you go for a walk? It's your free time in a few minutes and the fresh air will be good for you."

Izabella ignored the question. "How can they be like that?" she said, gesturing to the two German girls who were on one of the top bunks talking and occasionally laughing.

"It's their way of coping." Tania hesitated for a second before continuing. "You also have to find a way. It won't be for long. I will get us out of here."

Izabella shook her head and half-laughed. "How? We are slaves, Tania. They allow us out one at a time and if one of us says anything we know the others or our family will suffer. They have made that very clear. I don't see how there can be a way to escape. And soon they will make you and me go with men like they had to.' She gestured to the Germans again. "I don't think I can face that."

The girl was right. These men viewed them as no more than possessions, held against their will so that they could be sold on to other men who would abuse their bodies. It was only a matter of time before they started giving them drugs to ensure their full compliance and cooperation.

But she would not let it get to that stage. Somehow, she would find a way to escape.

There had to be a way of exploiting their daily free time when they were allowed out for ninety minutes. But how? What she had said to the man in the city centre had been impulsive and stupid and had achieved nothing. She had left him confused, that was all. She dreaded to think what might have happened if he had followed her back and Greg had seen him.

"I miss my Mother and Father," Izabella said. "Will I ever see them again?"

In that moment she looked ten rather than sixteen, and it broke Tania's heart. "Of course you will," she said. "You have my word."

Izabella swung her legs off the bed. "I will go for a walk as you suggest," she said.

"It'll do you good." She pulled Izabella's shoes out from under the bed and passed them to her. "Where will you go?"

"I am not sure, but I'll make sure I'm back on time." She put her shoes on, stood up and walked to the door.

Tania smiled, but it wasn't returned. "I will think of something," she said. "I promise."

Izabella opened the door and left, walking down the stairs to the front where one of the men who guarded them was sitting by the door bashing away on his phone.

He looked up when he heard her footsteps. "Where are you going?" he snarled.

"For walk. My ninety minutes."

He pulled a handwritten note from his pocket, studied it for a second and then looked at his watch. "Name?"

"Izabella."

He looked at the piece of paper again. "Be back at three."

She nodded and left the building, his attention back on the phone before she closed the door. Once out on the street she turned left and walked quickly, keen to make the most of her time. She was sorry to have lied, but it had been necessary. If she had told Tania where she was going she would have tried to stop her and what she planned would do no harm. It would help her in fact, make her stronger in the face of everything that was happening, and wasn't that what Tania wanted?

A man walked past her talking earnestly on his mobile phone and she thought about asking if she could use it to call her mother. But no, Greg had told them all that they knew where their families lived. She had seen how ruthless Anderson was and knew he wouldn't hesitate to send men to hurt or possibly kill her parents if she stepped out of line.

She had to put her faith in Tania and hope that she came up with some kind of plan. And she did have to be strong, but it was so hard. What would happen when more men came and one of them decided to choose her? She felt tears coming and wiped her eyes with her sleeve.

She was nearly there now. It was around the next bend and she could already hear the sound of laughter. This time she would stay slightly further away, so that she could watch them but didn't attract the attention she had last time. That girl had been so nasty, seeming to dislike her just for being there.

Sitting on the wall opposite the school she saw four girls of her own age in a huddle next to an outbuilding. After a few seconds three of them went around to the back. She almost smiled as she realised the remaining girl was keeping a lookout while her friends sneaked a cigarette. They were worried they would be caught, but what would happen if they were? A telling off probably, a warning not to do it again. How she wished she was in their world where the worst that could happen to you was a few harsh words.

With a start, Izabella realised there was someone crossing the road and walking towards her. She stood up quickly and turned to go, but before she could leave her arm was grabbed.

"Must go," she said, trying to wriggle away.

"Please, wait."

Izabella turned back and looked at the other girl. She was about her height but no more than 13 or 14. She realised it was the girl who had helped her the last time she came to the school, the one she had also seen in the centre of Bath.

"I leave now," she said.

"At least tell me your name. I'm Sabrina."

"I cannot. Is danger."

"Please sit down for a second. You look frightened. What has happened?"

Izabella looked at her blankly. The body language was clear. This girl meant well and wanted to help her. But she was struggling to understand more than the odd word. She tried to hold her emotions in check but it was hard, so hard. She shook her head. "I no understand," she said.

Sabrina gestured for Izabella to sit down, then sat on the wall beside her. "Just a moment," she said and reached into her pocket for her phone.

"No! No!"

"It's all right," Sabrina said, putting her hand on Izabella's arm. "I'm not going to phone anyone." She clicked on the screen a couple of times and then showed it to the other girl. "This is an app called SayHi," she said. "I put it on my phone for our last holiday to France but it translates lots of languages."

Izabella looked blankly at her and Sabrina clicked once more then spoke into the phone. "My name is Sabrina and I want to help you." After a few seconds a female voice issued from the phone. "Menya zovut Sabrina, i ya khochu vam pomoch."

"Ah!" Izabella said. "Nie jestem Rosjaninem. Jestem Polakiem." It was Sabrina's turn to look blank. "Nie rosyjski." Izabella went on, pointing to her chest. "Krakova. Polski."

Realisation dawned. "You're not Russian? You're from Poland?"

Izabella nodded. "Yes. Polski."

Sabrina tapped on her phone a couple more times and said into the microphone "You look frightened. What has happened to you?" After a few seconds, the female voice translated it into Polish.

Sabrina clicked again and held the phone to Izabella's mouth indicating that she should speak. She did so and a few seconds later the voice said, "I cannot say. It would be dangerous for me and for you too. My friend is finding a way to escape."

Sabrina took a deep breath. "Why can't you tell me? Is someone doing bad things to you?"

Izabella listened to the translation and then said, "You cannot possibly understand. There are bad people but there is nothing you can do."

"Why can't you come with me? I'll take you to the police where you will be safe."

Izabella shook her head in horror. Sabrina was about to reply when they heard a bell and she looked across the road to see everyone filing back into school.

"You must go. I will be fine." Izabella said through the app.

Sabrina didn't believe this for an instant, but it was clear she wasn't going to get much more out of the girl. "At least tell me your name."

"Izabella." She paused then clicked on the app and spoke. "Thank you for saying you will help," the voice said after a few seconds, "but there is nothing you can do. I am sorry to have worried you. I will go now and I will not return."

She stood up, gave a weak smile and turned away. Sabrina watched her go, looked across at the school and made a decision. Izabella needed her help and needed it badly. She would follow her so that at least she knew where she lived.

Chapter 44

Anderson was incandescent with rage.

They were in a garage, the door pulled down and a single bare bulb casting shadows onto the hard concrete floor. He was pacing back and forth, the three men sitting in a line in front of him on plastic chairs.

"You lot had better pull your fucking fingers out of your arses!" he said. They exuded self-confidence, arrogance even, and he needed to wipe those smug expressions off their faces.

"I've had to take serious measures twice in the last few weeks," he went on, and they all knew what 'serious measures' was a euphemism for. "I need to be sure you're all up to this." He stared at each of them in turn. "I need an update. Greg, you first."

"We had our first customers for the new girls," Greg said. "It went smoothly."

"How many?"

"Two of them. The Germans."

"When are you breaking the other girls in?"

"Some time in the next few days. We're getting the word out, but as you know it's always slow at the start."

"Well get a fucking move on. It costs money to get 'em here and they need to start earning their keep."

"Yes, sure."

Anderson caught the expression on Alex's face and walked over to him. "Don't think I can't see you smirking inside those stupid fucking dreadlocks. What's so funny?"

"Nothing, Mr Anderson."

"And what the fuck were you thinking when you let your guys share the lorry with those girls?"

"I did it to save money. I know how important it is to

increase the bottom line."

"It was stupid, a risk not worth taking. Haven't I said we keep your three operations separate at all times? Or is the brain under that stupid fucking hairstyle too small to take that in? Increase the bottom line, my arse." He jabbed Alex in the chest with his finger. "Are you up to this, Alex?"

"Of course I am."

"What's turnover looking like?"

"Good. We've made a few new acquisitions in the last few weeks. A couple have ended because they ran out of money but overall we're going to be up on last month. My guys are doing pretty well."

Anderson sniffed. "Did you find out where the leak came from?"

"I don't think there was a leak."

"That's not what I heard. Keep looking." He moved to the end of the line and addressed his next words to the oldest of his three reports, a skinny man in his early fifties with ragged greying hair that fell to his shoulders. "What about you, Stefan?"

"Going well," Stefan said, his voice as rough as his pock-marked face. "Got three cabbage farms up and active and the pigs ain't got the foggiest."

"Yeah, that's all very well but what about the big stuff?"

"Doin' okay. Steady income from dingers. The girls love 'em at the clubs."

"Steady isn't fucking good enough. You need to get more MDMA out there. There's loads in stock. What about crack?"

"Yeah the candy's doin' good."

Anderson grunted. "You recruiting?"

"Sure. Not easy though, is it?"

"I don't care how fucking hard it is. We've got imports to sell and can't afford to back the stuff up. Get more guys on board."

"Will do, Mr Anderson."

Anderson took a step back and addressed his next words to all of them. "I'm keeping an eye on all of you so don't fucking let me down. I have a boss as well and I'm not prepared to disappoint him. Do you understand?"

They all nodded.

"I'm holding you three responsible and you'd better improve your game." He waved his arm. "Now get the fuck out of here."

Greg was the first up, opening the door and marching out. Alex followed but Stefan remained seated.

"What do you want?" Anderson said when it was apparent Stefan wasn't leaving with the others.

Stefan sniffed. "Greg's not up to it," he said.

"Did I ask for your fucking opinion?"

"I could do a better job. I used to run girls."

"Yeah, a few street girls.'

"Same thing."

"You want to move sideways then?"

"Nah, I could manage both."

Anderson laughed. "The fuck you could. You need to concentrate on getting your own house in order and not worry about trying to spread your wings. All you gotta do is organise distribution and yet your numbers are piss poor. Hell, Alex is making more money than you and all he's got is a few scammers." He paused. "Perhaps Alex could take your side of the business under his wing."

"No, Mr Anderson, I'm on it. Numbers'll be up soon."

"They'd better be. Now get out."

After Stefan left, Anderson closed the garage door and reached for his phone. It was answered after only one ring.

"Hello, Mr Anderson." The voice was deep, each word carefully enunciated with just the slightest of Arabic accents.

"I've seen the guys," Anderson said, "There have been a couple of problems but I've dealt with 'em."

"Is there anything I should be concerned with?"

"No, Mr Rasul. They were minor."

"Good. How are the numbers?"

"Improving."

"They need to improve significantly. At the moment you are well below what you promised. Do you have a plan in place to improve your results?"

"Oh yes, we're recruiting and some new girls were brought over…"

"I do not need to know the details. Update me this time next week."

"Very well, Mr Rasul."

He had to ensure his people improved their performance. To be fair Stefan was doing okay, and Alex was bringing in decent money even if he had been careless letting two of his men travel with those girls. Greg was the major concern.

Greg's man Jed had told Anderson he'd been pulled in by the police after a random stop and search and hadn't said anything. His methods of persuasion were normally good enough to extract information from anyone, but there had to have been a reason for the police wanting to speak to the little shit. If Greg was running a loose operation he needed to know about it, and if necessary replace him. This business of giving the girls so-called free time was ridiculous too. He'd tell Greg to stop it.

He decided to go to Number 42 and check things out for himself. But first he had another call to make.

This time it took a little longer before the call was answered. No surprise though given his plant was in the Supracomm team and had to find somewhere quiet to talk.

"What about that Sam woman you told me about?" he asked. "Is she getting anywhere?" He was reassured by the answer, but couldn't afford to take any risks. "I want you closer to her," he went on. "Get her confidence and make absolutely sure she's as thick as you think she is. You got me?"

He waited for confirmation and then ended the call. He would call again tomorrow to make sure everything was in hand. If not he would have to take serious measures.

Anderson closed and locked the garage door and was at the house within fifteen minutes. He was pleased to see it looking smart, the small front garden tidy and the windows recently cleaned. For the prices customers were paying they expected something upmarket and the house presented well.

He opened the front door to find a man in his early twenties slouching in a chair just inside the entrance. The youngster looked up from his phone and did a double-take when he realised who the visitor was. He stood up quickly, his back straight, and seemed to be fighting the urge to salute.

"Hello, Mr Anderson," he said. "Do you want me to find Greg for you?"

"Who are you?"

The man gulped. "I, ah, I'm Sean."

"What are you doing?"

"I'm monitoring the door."

There was a sound behind him and Anderson turned to see Izabella walk through the front door. She drew back when she saw him, her mouth open in shock, and raced past to the stairs.

"Where's she been?" Anderson asked.

"For her daily free time," Sean said. "That's okay isn't it?"

"Well shut the fucking door after her then." Sean stood up but he put his hand on his chest to stop him. "Hang on. Who's that?" He gestured to the front gate where a young black girl was standing clasping the railings and looking up at the top-floor windows of the house. She dropped her eyes, saw him and her eyes widened. She turned to walk away.

Anderson grabbed Sean by the shoulder and pushed

him out. "Fetch her inside," he said. "I wanna have a word."

Chapter 45

Luke's phone rang and he answered immediately when he saw the name on the screen.

"How's it going?" he asked.

His brother hesitated for a second. "So-so," he said. "She's still furious with me, but she hasn't kicked me out again, and she's beginning to settle down now she's got something to occupy her mind."

"I can't believe she's still annoyed about what you said about Jess."

Mark grunted. "She's moved on from that, Luke," he said. "She's angry with me for all manner of other things now, everything from the fact I wake up earlier than her to my taste in ties."

"It sounds like she's back to normal."

Mark laughed. "I suppose so." He hesitated. "I know she can be a little difficult and the two of you don't always see eye to eye."

That's the understatement of the century, Luke thought but said. "We've had our differences."

"But now we're settling down here in the UK, and what with Mother ill, and me taking on the reins of Borrowham Hall…"

"I see where you're going with this, Mark."

"We ought to try and mend things and what Erica has come up with, and I'm up for it as well, is the idea that we have a little welcome-back-to-the-UK do. Just for the family."

"Yeah, I guess we could do that. I'd have to check when the twins are free."

"Oh, don't worry. Erica's excited about the idea and she's already spoken to Ben and Chloe."

"She has?"

"Yes, she loves organising a party. It's her thing."

"Party? I thought you said it was just family."

"Oh, it is." Mark hesitated. "And a few close friends. Anyway," he added quickly, "Ben and Chloe are both free so as long as you are as well…"

"You haven't said when, Mark?"

"Oh sorry, what a berk. It's two weeks on Saturday."

"What if I'm busy?"

"Chloe told Erica you're free."

Luke decided he would be having a few words with his daughter when he got home. "Fine," he said. "What time?"

"Cocktails at six. Erica's organising a chef."

This sounds ghastly, he thought but said, "Wonderful. I'll see you then."

"Good stuff. Tally-ho."

Luke smiled at this last expression as he ended the call. *Jeeves and Wooster look out,* he thought. *Mark Sackville is returning to the aristocracy.*

He was still smiling when Josh called over.

"Guv," he said, "I rang Security about the fingerprint sensor and they said they'd send someone over around lunchtime. It's nearly three now. Shall I chase them?"

"Yes, give them a ring."

A few minutes later he heard Josh's voice raised. "What do you mean?" There was a pause then he said, "Of course it's urgent."

Luke got up and walked over, gesturing to Josh to hand the phone over. He took it from him and said, "This is Luke Sackville, Head of Ethics. Is there a problem?"

"No problem." The voice was male and his tone dismissive. "You're on our list."

"I thought you were fixing our sensor this lunchtime."

"As I said, it's on our list." Luke could almost sense him yawning as he said it. "We should get to it this week, although it might be next week."

Luke hesitated. "What priority is it?"

"Glen said it wasn't urgent."

Luke had heard enough. He hung up without another word. "Leave it with me, Josh," he said.

"Right, guv."

Luke smiled and rubbed his hands together. "I'm looking forward to this."

He made his way to the Executive Floor and walked into Glen Baxter's office without knocking. It was empty. He stepped outside again and along the corridor to where Edward Filcher's secretary was sitting. She looked up as she saw him and smiled.

"Hi, Luke."

"Gloria," he said. "Have you seen Glen?"

"He's in with Mr Filcher," she said.

"Just the two of them?"

"No, there's a woman from 'Solid Doors' with them." She winked at him as she added, "And of course, you're not to interrupt them."

"I'll tell him you said that," Luke said as he gave a peremptory knock on the door and walked into Filchers' office.

Filcher was in his usual specially-elevated chair with Glen and the external visitor sitting facing him across the desk. She was an attractive brunette, no more than thirty-five with blue eyes and halo-white teeth, and was holding a brochure open on the desk, clearly in the middle of explaining something. Neither of the men was looking at the pamphlet, however, their eyes fixed on the woman's face.

Filcher forced his gaze away and looked up at Luke as he approached. "I'm in a meeting," he said.

"Yes, I know and I hate to have to interrupt," Luke lied. "Gloria warned me not to, but it's urgent." He nodded to the saleswoman and smiled. "My apologies."

She smiled back and stood up. "It's not a problem." She

turned to Filcher. "I'll wait outside."

As soon as the door closed behind her, Filcher stood up. "I will not have this," he bellowed, and Luke sensed Glen smirking beside him. "That girlie was…"

"Mr Filcher!" Luke said, stopping him in his tracks. "That young woman is a professional and deserves your respect. You cannot refer to her as a 'girlie'." He turned to Glen. "And you can wipe that stupid expression off your face. I need a word with you."

"I don't think…" Filcher started but Luke interrupted him again.

"I need an urgent word with you as well, Mr Filcher," he said. "It's about Cheltenham." He nodded his head towards Glen, giving a clear indication that he couldn't say more in his presence.

"Cheltenham?" Filcher said. "What do you mean…" The penny dropped. "Oh, you mean, uh…" He tapped the side of his nose, then dropped his voice to a whisper. "Bond stuff. Shaken not stirred. That kind of thing."

Glen looked at Filcher then at Luke then back to Filcher. "What's going on?"

"Step outside, Glen," Filcher said. "Vital things to discuss with Luke. Jolly secret and hush-hush. Intelligence information."

"Yes," Luke said. "We need to talk about intelligence so it's well outside your remit."

"Eh?" Glen said.

"Out," Filcher said, gesturing to the door. He waited until the door had closed then asked, whispering again, "Did you go to GCHQ?"

"Oh yes, Mr Filcher," Luke said. "I saw Evan and I met his superior too."

"Really? His superior? Should I meet him?"

"I'm sure that can be arranged when the time is right."

Filcher nodded. "Time is right. Indeed. Yes." He paused. "Have you got further with the, you know," he tapped his nose again, "people concerns?"

"Almost."

"Excellent. Bravo."

"Also, the Deputy Chief Constable has asked me to help with a case."

"Has she?" Filcher nodded his head a few times. "Perhaps I should phone her. Demonstrate that Executive Management at Filchers are totally behind you."

"Later, perhaps. However, she told me how much she values your support."

"Did she? My support? Did she indeed?" A smug look came over his face.

Luke stood up. "Thank you, Mr Filcher. Your backing means the world."

"It must do, yes. Uh, can you tell Glen and the girl... uh, the Solid Doors, uh, professional woman, to come back in."

"Of course. I need to have a brief word with Glen first though, if that's okay?"

Filcher nodded and waved him out, smiling as he left. "Values my support," he said under his breath.

"You can go back in now," Luke said when he got outside. The saleswoman nodded and went back into Filcher's office. Glen made to follow but Luke put his hand on his chest to stop him. "I need a word with you first, Glen," he said.

"We're buying fire doors. I need to be in the meeting."

"I told Filcher you'd be a few minutes. I'm sure one pair of eyes that can't tear itself away will be fine for a few minutes."

Glen looked back at him blankly. "Uh?"

"Let's talk in your office." Luke turned and walked back down the corridor and after a few seconds Glen followed. Once they were both inside he closed the door, stood in front of the other man and glared down at him.

Glen started fidgeting, and in that moment he looked

like a naughty schoolboy brought before the Headmaster to be reprimanded. A naughty boy who was 6 foot 2 and boosted with steroids.

"What's so important?" Glen asked.

"The sensor on the Ethics Room door is still broken."

"Is that all. Can't this wait?" He gestured to the door. "I've got…"

"…young women to stare at?"

"Eh?"

Luke poked him in the chest. "You fitted a device that had been recalled." he said.

"Nonsense. I tested it. It recognised my finger and the door opened."

"It recognises a carrot."

"What?"

Luke sighed. "If you hold anything up to the fingerprint sensor it opens. It is completely ineffective and that's why it was recalled by the manufacturer."

"Okay. I'll tell someone to replace it. Now let me past."

"No."

"What do you mean 'no'?"

"Who normally fits these sensors?"

"Craig, but he's…"

"Call him and tell him to bring the new model to the Ethics Room now. Say we'll meet him there."

"I can't just pull him off what he's doing."

"Do it!"

Glen grunted, pulled his phone out of his pocket and passed the instruction on. "Craig's fully capable of doing it without me there," he said when the call had ended.

"I'm sure he is," Luke said. "To be honest he'd probably be quicker without you. However, I don't trust you not to pull him away as soon as you leave here."

He turned and Glen followed meekly behind him. His man was already there when they got to the Ethics Room, kneeling on the floor and looking intently at the fingerprint sensor.

He looked around when he saw Luke and Glen approaching. "I don't know which moron fitted this," he said. "Not only is it the recalled model but it's been wired all wrong."

"Must have been a complete numpty," Luke said and then turned to Glen. "Who was it, Glen?"

"I, ah…" Glen swallowed and then looked down at the man on the floor. "This is urgent, Craig," he said, his tone aggressive. "Stop complaining and get a move on."

Craig shrugged. "Will do. Shouldn't take more than five minutes."

"How are you going to discipline the member of your team who cocked this up, Glen?" Luke asked. "Are you going to make him watch one of your, ah, acting performances."

This elicited a chortle from the man on the floor. "Oh no," Craig said. "That would be a fate worse than death."

Glen opened his mouth but before he could say anything Maj called from inside the Ethics Room.

"Sorry to interrupt, Luke," he said. "Have you got a minute?"

"Sure." He turned to Glen. "Stay here."

"Do you mind if I leave now?" Maj said when he got back inside. "I've just had a call from my daughter's school to say she went home at lunchtime feeling poorly but she's not answering her phone. She's probably gone to bed if she's ill but I'd like to make sure she's okay."

"Of course. I'll see you in the morning."

"Thanks."

Chapter 46

As Maj walked to his car he wondered what was wrong with Sabrina. She had seemed fine when he dropped her off in the morning, so whatever it was it had certainly come on quickly. A virus perhaps, or it could be something she ate that had disagreed with her.

Once he was in the car and on his way he rang Asha. "Sabrina's poorly," he said when she answered.

"Oh no," his wife said. "Any idea what's wrong?"

"Not yet, but she's gone home. It was one of the deputy heads who rang. He said she left after lunch."

"Okay, let me know how she is, won't you?"

"I will."

It was only a ten-minute journey from Filchers to Oldfield Park, and as he drove Maj reflected on how different his life was from that of his parents when they were his age. They had been farmers in Somalia, but not in the British sense of the word. They had a few goats and a field of maize but it was subsistence living. When his mother was shot dead by rebels, his father had taken the courageous decision to take his two children and leave. Three months later, after a hazardous trip by sea and land, they arrived in England and were granted asylum.

He was so grateful for his father's bravery. Somalia was even more dangerous now than it had been when they had left nearly thirty years ago. If they had stayed he and his sister would probably be in poverty, whereas she earned a reasonable living as a nurse and he had been equally successful. Neither of them would ever be rich, but they had enough money to pay the bills and put food on their family's plates and that was what mattered.

England was safe, and that counted for a lot. He still

had relatives in and around Mogadishu and the stories he heard, none of which ever seemed to reach the British news channels, were chilling. He pulled up outside the modest terraced house on Third Avenue that was his home and smiled to himself. He was lucky, so very very lucky.

Maj unlocked the front door, walked into the small hall and called up the stairs. "Sabrina. Are you in bed?" There was no answer which meant she was most likely asleep. He walked slowly and quietly upstairs, not wanting to wake her, and gently opened her bedroom door. To his surprise, there was no sign of his daughter.

He called again. "Sabrina?"

Nothing.

He opened the doors of the other two bedrooms and the bathroom before going back downstairs and checking the lounge and the kitchen-diner. No sign of her so she definitely wasn't in the house. Perhaps the deputy head had been wrong and she had gone to a friend's house. Idil or Susan was the most likely.

He pulled his phone out, navigated to his contacts and found Idil's mother's number. He was about to call when the phone rang and he looked down to see 'caller number withheld' on the screen. He clicked the green button.

"Hi, Mr Dawson," he said. "Sabrina's not at home. Could she have gone to a friend's house?"

"My name's not Dawson."

Maj was confused. He could swear it was the same man who had called him earlier. The London accent memorable. "I don't understand," he said.

"Shut your fucking mouth and listen."

Maj felt his heart start pounding in his chest. "Who are you?"

"I said shut it." There was a pause. "Your daughter's a fucking pain, did you know that?"

"What are you talking about?"

"If you ever wanna see her again, you gotta do exactly

what I tell you. Do you understand?"

Maj didn't know what to say.

"I'm taking your silence as acceptance. So listen to every fucking word."

"How do I know she's safe?"

The man at the other end laughed, but it was cold and completely lacked humour. "She ain't fucking safe," he said. "That's why you gotta do what I say." He paused again, then said, "Bring 'er over here." There was the sound of scuffling. "Tell him you're okay."

Sabrina's voice came on the phone. "I'm okay, Dad," she said between sobs. "I followed that girl. I'm at number…"

Maj heard her scream, then there were two thumping sounds. "Leave her!" he shouted.

There was silence for a few seconds.

"What have you done?" Maj said.

He heard the man say, "Shut her the fuck up," then a muttered reply and then, "I don't care how. Use a fucking tea towel or something."

He addressed his next comment to Maj. "She's got a pretty face, your daughter. Be a shame if it was scarred." He paused to let his words sink in. "First thing is you don't tell no-one nothing, 'cos if you do I'm gonna have to take serious measures." Another pause. "I need you to confirm you understand."

"I understand."

"Good. Second thing is she told me you been talking to one of my girls when you was out shopping. I need to know what she told you."

"She didn't tell me anything."

There was that bitter laugh again. "Well, see, I don't fucking believe you, do I? I need you to tell me face to face."

"What about Sabrina?"

"She's staying here. Call it security, in case you don't

turn up or you tell someone else."

"Okay." Maj realised he was shaking. "Where do we meet?"

"I'll text you an address. You go there and I'm gonna check there's no one watching and text you a second address. We'll meet there. Understand?"

"I understand."

The ring tone sounded and Maj stared at his phone, unable to believe what he had just heard.

Chapter 47

Anderson pulled his gun from his pocket and pointed it at Sabrina. She was sitting on the floor against the wall, a tea towel stretched between her teeth and tied at the back. Her wrists were tied together with rope.

She saw the pistol and shook her head from side to side, her eyes wide and staring, tears running down her cheeks.

"I'm tempted," he said, "but I reckon you're a keeper." He looked her up and down. "Young body like you've got has to be worth a bit. Get the word around and there's rich men who'll pay a fair whack. Thousands possibly. Ain't that right, Greg?"

"There's a couple of men come across special from Saudi for young girls," Greg said. "They'd pay a lot."

"Not here, though," Anderson said. "Too many people she knows in Bath. We'll need to move her to London. Can you contact Cloughy in Tottenham, see if you can cut a deal?"

"Will do, Mr Anderson."

"The tea towel can come off now. It looks tight and we can't afford any damage to her face."

Greg untied the tea towel and pulled it away.

"What are you going to do to my father?" Sabrina gasped.

"You heard me," Anderson said. "I'm going to find out what he knows." He smiled. "He'll tell me everything. I can be very persuasive."

"And then what?"

He bent down and clasped her chin in his right hand. "Unfortunately, he may have an accident and die. But by that time he'll be wanting it to happen."

Chapter 48

Maj's phone beeped and he clicked on the text message. 'Society Cafe, Kingsmead Square,' it read. 'Be outside in 30 minutes.'

Thirty minutes was ample time. Ten minutes to drive into Bath and a few minutes to park. He could leave straight away and be there with fifteen minutes to spare.

It was important to use the time carefully. Tell no one, the man had said, and he certainly wouldn't tell Asha. There was no sense in scaring her when there was nothing she could do to help. The police were a no-no too. They would doubtless fly into action but there was no way he would trust them to be low-key.

Sabrina's life depended on the decisions he made and he couldn't afford to delay any further. There was only one person he could trust to help.

The phone was answered straight away.

"Hi Maj," Luke said. "Is everything okay?"

"Not at all," Maj said, and he told Luke everything that had happened.

As soon as he'd finished Luke said, "I need a few minutes to think. Get in the car and drive to Bath, I'll ring you while you're on your way."

Maj hung up and raced out to his car. He started the engine and did a three-point turn, cutting up a Subaru and earning the middle finger from the driver as a consequence. He ignored him and headed towards the centre of Bath, trying his hardest to keep his speed down while his heart was telling him to rush, rush, rush.

He hadn't travelled more than a mile when his phone rang and it was with relief that he saw Luke's name come up on the screen.

"Go ahead as planned," Luke said when he answered. "He'll likely keep you waiting for a while to check you're alone but as soon as he sends you the second address I want you to forward it to me."

"What then?"

"Do as instructed, but if you see anyone you know, and I mean anyone, you have to pretend you don't know them." He paused. "We'll get Sabrina back safely, Maj. I promise you."

Maj wished he could believe him, he really did. But the man had been so cold and for all he knew Sabrina might already be dead.

He drove into Kingsmead Square car park and was relieved to find someone leaving. He nabbed their space and walked out to the square where he soon spotted the Society Cafe on the corner opposite Tesco Express. It was a pleasant afternoon and there were a few groups of people sitting outside. He decided to take a seat and didn't know whether to look around or fix his eyes down. He settled for taking his phone out of his pocket and staring at it.

A few minutes passed then there was a voice at his shoulder and he almost jumped out of his skin.

"What can I get you?"

Maj looked up at the smiling waiter, his mind suddenly a complete blank. "Oh, I, ah…" He tried to compose himself. "I'll have a cappuccino, please."

"Can I tempt you with anything else? We have an excellent coffee and walnut cake today."

Christ all-bloody-mighty. "No thanks. Just the cappuccino."

"Be with you in a minute."

Maj looked down at his phone then up then back at his phone again. After two or three minutes the waiter returned and placed his drink in front of him.

"Thanks," Maj said absent-mindedly and gave him a ten-pound note. "Keep the change."

"That's very generous. Thank you. You're sure I can't tempt you with…"

Maj gave him a look that would have melted graphite then returned his gaze to his phone.

A few seconds later it beeped and he gasped as he read the message. Of all the locations in the world, this was the last one he expected to be sent to. He forwarded the message to Luke as surreptitiously as possible then stood up.

"You haven't drunk any of your cappuccino," the waiter said

"No," Maj said over his shoulder as he marched to his car. "Help yourself, and have some cake too."

Chapter 49

Luke read the message in disbelief.

"Where am I going, guv?" Josh said.

Luke read the message out. "17 Third Avenue, Oldfield Park."

"Isn't that Maj's address?"

Luke nodded and it suddenly hit him what they'd done. He thumped his palm against his temple. "I've been bloody stupid."

"Do I need to go to his home then?"

Luke ignored him and rang Maj, hoping and praying he got hold of him in time. After about ten rings it went to voicemail. He thought for a second and looked at his watch. It was 4:30.

"Do you know when Maj's wife gets home from work?"

"I'm not sure but she's usually at home before Maj leaves here so it can't be late."

"Okay. I want you to go to his house and tell her some but not all of what's happened. There's no point in frightening her before we know exactly what's what. You'll have to be as tactful as you can."

"Do you trust me to do that, guv?"

Luke put his hand on Josh's shoulder. "Yes, I trust you. Don't let me down."

"I won't, guv. What are you going to do?"

"Me? I'm going to Kingsmead Square."

They headed out together, Josh to his battered old Renault Clio, and Luke to his company Beemer.

Chapter 50

Each of the two burly men sitting on either side of Maj held one of his arms down. He tried to squirm free but their grip was too firm.

"Where's my daughter?' he asked.

Anderson turned around in the front passenger seat. "I wouldn't worry about her," he sneered. "It's too late for that."

Maj wanted to ask what he meant but knew there was no point. "Where are you taking me?"

"For a little ride." Anderson looked across at the driver. "Greg, take us to that place where I had a chat with your guy, uh, what was his name?"

"Jed, Mr Anderson."

"That's him. Take us there." He turned around to look at Maj and smiled coldly. "It's a quiet spot. We can talk there and no one will hear anything."

"There's nothing I can tell you."

Anderson was still smiling. "When it comes to it I think you'll find you talk plenty." He turned back to face the front. "You was talking to one of my girls and I want to know what she told you and who you've passed the information on to. It's as simple as that. And when you've told me everything I'll reunite you with your daughter and the two of you can go home and play happy families."

Maj didn't believe him for a moment and dreaded to think what Anderson would do once he'd forced the information out of him. Sabrina was his biggest concern. If, and it was a big if, she was still alive then he had to find a way of escaping and getting to her.

He looked at the two men on either side of him. They were looking forward, their expressions blank, identikit thugs with short brown hair and five-o'clock shadows. He suspected they weren't the smartest tools in the box but they had muscle and that was all they needed to keep him in check.

The driver, the man Anderson had called Greg, was something different. He was as well-built as the two thugs but taller, perhaps 6ft 2 or 6ft 3, and despite his ragged black hair, and a face that told tales of acne when he was younger, had an aura of intelligence about him.

As for Anderson himself, his coarse accent didn't deceive Maj for a moment. He was undoubtedly smart and despite being the shortest person in the car and verging on the obese had to be the scariest person he had ever encountered.

He had to think and think quickly. If he let them get to their destination he was done for.

"What the fuck is this?" Anderson exclaimed as they came to a halt behind a line of cars.

"Roadworks I think," Greg said.

"Is there another way?"

"Only the toll bridge. Probably quicker to wait though."

Chapter 51

Luke had a hunch and he hoped and prayed he was right. He was forced to wait at the Filchers car park exit for a gap in the traffic and drummed his fingers on the steering wheel, impatience getting the better of him. How he wished he could blue light it all the way.

A lady in a silver Volvo let him out and he raised his hand to thank her before turning right onto the Lower Bristol Road towards Bath. He pressed a button and told the car to phone Evan, then drummed his fingers again as he waited for it to connect and ring.

"Hi Luke," Evan said when he answered.

"Evan, I need your help urgently. Maj and his daughter have been taken. She was abducted first and I don't know where they're keeping her, but I'm pretty sure they've got Maj now as well."

"What happened?"

"They told him to go to Kingsmead Square where he would receive a text with a second address, but I believe that was a ruse to put us off the scent. My suspicion is that they picked him up there and are taking him to Bathampton. I'm heading there now."

"To the place where Jeremy Scott was found?"

"Yes. I'm only about ten or fifteen minutes away but they picked him up in the centre of Bath so they're going to arrive first."

"I can get my guys there but it's going to take time, probably half an hour minimum."

"That's going to be too late."

"I'll do my best." Evan paused. "You realise this is going to blow the whole thing open? If the men who have Maj get away they're going to close down operations and vanish."

"I know, Evan, but right now our priority has to be rescuing Maj and his daughter."

"Agreed. I'll get on it now. Good luck, Luke."

The call ended as Luke joined the London Road at the bottom of Guinea Lane. He hoped Cleveland Bridge wasn't a bottleneck. It could be busy early in the evening as people started to leave work.

With a start, he remembered a conversation he'd overheard in the canteen. Someone had been complaining about the snarl-up at the top of Bathwick Street, massive hold-ups caused by a badly programmed three-way set of traffic lights.

With luck, they had taken Maj that way, which meant he might beat them to Bathampton if he took the toll bridge across the river.

He drove through the traffic lights and looked to his right across Cleveland Place to the bridge. Sure enough, there was a queue of traffic. *Please be stuck in the queue,* he thought as he gunned it towards Batheaston.

Luke thought about what Evan had said. He was right, the whole thing was going to blow open. He needed to make another phone call.

Chapter 52

Josh was relieved when his Clio started first time and equally pleased when each gear engaged without too much grinding and screeching. "Good work Horatio," he said, patting the top of the dashboard.

He was struggling to get his mind around what had happened and even more about what he was going to say to Maj's wife. With shock he realised he couldn't remember her name. Maj had said it often enough but it hadn't stuck, probably because it was uncommon. Was it Masha? Or could it be Sacha?

His phone rang and he glanced down to see it was Luke calling. He fumbled around the centre console trying to accept the call and put it on speaker while keeping his eyes on the windscreen, nervous in case a policeman saw him using his mobile while he was driving.

"Hi, guv," he said when he finally managed it.

"Change of plan, Josh," Luke said. "I still want you to go to Maj's house and speak to Asha though."

"That's it," Josh said. "Asha."

"What?"

"Sorry, uh, carry on, guv."

"Make sure you get her somewhere safe then head to the Sheppey Industrial Estate. I think it's all going to kick off there this evening. Wait at the Estate where you're out of view of Unit 7 until Evan or I contact you. Understand?"

"Gotcha, guv. What about you?"

"I'm going to the canal where they found Jeremy Scott's body. My gut tells me that's where they're taking Maj."

Josh hung up. This was quite a development, and he wondered why Luke thought it was going to all kick off. It had to be linked to what had happened to Maj and his daughter, but why would that impact the scamming operation? He guessed all would become clear later.

He pulled up outside Maj's house, climbed out of the car and rang the doorbell. As suspected, Asha wasn't back yet, so he got back in the Clio and looked the Industrial Estate up on his maps app. It told him the journey would take about 45 minutes, which probably meant 50 to 55 if there were any hills.

It was possible the scammers would have finished for the evening by the time he got there, but then again they might have Zoom or FaceTime calls with their victims during the evening which meant they stayed later.

His thoughts were interrupted by a knock on the glass by his side. He gave a yelp and turned to see a woman in a headscarf bending down and smiling at him through the glass. He lowered the window.

"Josh?" she said.

"Yes, but how…"

"Maj pointed you out in the car park when I picked him up last week. Are you looking for him?"

"No, I, ah, I wanted a word with you actually."

"Is everything okay?

He ignored her question. "Can we talk inside?"

"Sure."

She led the way to the house, unlocked the door and gestured for him to follow her into the lounge and sit down. He sat on the front edge of a blue armchair and she sat opposite him on the matching sofa.

"Nice furniture," he said. "Lovely shade of, uh…"

"Blue."

"Exactly."

"Would you like a cup of tea?"

"I won't thanks." He sighed as he tried to decide how to play things. He needed to persuade her to leave the house, but do so in a way that didn't terrify the poor woman.

"Are you okay?" she asked.

"Sorry, I was miles away." He swallowed. "The thing is, Asha, Maj asked me to come here and speak to you because he's had to go somewhere. It's all a bit hush-hush." He tapped the side of his nose, though he didn't quite know why.

"He mentioned he's working on a top secret project."

Josh leapt at this. "Yes, that's the one." He tapped his nose again, unable to stop himself. "He said could I ask you to put some, uh, clothes together for him, just a small bag. And toothpaste. Overnight things. You know. For overnighting."

"Sure, I can do that. Are you going to take it to him then?"

"No!" He swallowed again. "Sorry, I didn't mean to snap. Uh, Maj said you've got a friend who lives near here. I can't remember her name…" He stared at Asha, then at the ceiling, then back at her again, eyes wide, willing her to suggest someone.

After a few seconds, she said. "Could it have been Sahra?"

"Does she live near here?"

"Sahra's a man."

"Right, yes, of course he is. I remember now. Sahra, a man friend. That's exactly what Maj said."

Asha's eyebrows furrowed and she gave him a quizzical look. "He described Sahra as a man friend?"

Josh laughed. "Well, not in so many words. He actually… Anyway, it doesn't matter. Sahra lives nearby does she, uh, he?"

"Yes, not much more than half a mile away, on Shakespeare Avenue off Bear Flat."

"That was him. Definitely. Maj said to take his, uh, overnighty things to Sahra and for you to wait for him there."

"Okay, I'll take them later."

"Now!"

"What?"

"Sorry, I think Maj wanted you to take them soon, in case, uh…"

"In case he arrives at Sahra's soon?'

"Gotcha." Josh flicked his fingers together. "In case he arrives at hers, uh his, soon. Exactimo."

"Right, I'll pack a bag now." She stood up and walked to the door.

"Great." He sat back in the chair.

She looked back at him. "There's no need for you to stay though, Josh. I'm sure you need to be getting on."

"No, I don't."

"Why do you…" she started to say, then stopped when she saw the rabbit-in-headlights look on his face. "Okay, you stay there and I'll get Maj's stuff together."

He smiled and gave her a double thumbs up. Asha shook her head and went upstairs.

Chapter 53

Luke was pleased to find there was no hold-up at the toll bridge. He paid and drove over the river then past The George, keeping a careful eye open for any unusually parked cars or suspicious activity. He slowed as he approached the bridge over the canal and looked carefully as he passed a lane to the left. He saw nothing and carried on over the bridge then used the next turning to the left to turn around and retrace his steps.

He parked in the car park of The George and walked past the pub to the bridge where he followed the track down to the towpath. A few yards beyond the bridge there were three narrowboats moored up and it was here that Jeremy Scott's body had been spotted in the water. Other than a few ducks there wasn't a living soul in sight.

Luke desperately wanted his hunch to be proven correct. If it was, then clearly the roadworks had held them up as he had hoped, but they could be there at any moment. He looked around for a place to hide, then on impulse walked to the bow of the nearest narrowboat and knocked hard on the door. There was no answer.

It was then that he heard the sound of voices. He hunched down so that he was hidden and listened carefully.

"Have you got proper hold of 'im, Greg?"

"Yes, Mr Anderson."

"You two, back to the car."

Luke crept to the side of the narrowboat and peered back towards the bridge. Two men were walking away from him up the bank to the road. The man who had spoken first was under the bridge and facing away. He was middle-aged, bald and overweight and blocked the view of the others who he assumed were Maj and the man he had called Greg.

Luke stepped back out of view, worried that Greg might see him. The bald man spoke again.

"Hold 'im tight."

He heard a soft thump followed by an exhalation of breath and realised he had punched Maj, presumably in the stomach.

"That's just a taster. Tell me what she said to you."

"Not a chance." It was definitely Maj.

Luke heard the thumping sound again, and again Maj gasped.

"Pass me my cigarettes," the bald man said, then gave a bitter laugh. "They're bad for me I know, but they're gonna be even worse for you."

Luke knew what he was going to do next. Sally Croft had found burn marks down Jeremy Scott's arm. He shivered as he remembered that three of Scott's fingernails had also been pulled out.

He didn't have the time to wait for Evan's men to arrive. He had to act, and he had to act quickly.

Chapter 54

Luke stepped lightly from the narrowboat onto the towpath, took a deep breath and charged. It was ten years since he had last played rugby but the muscle memory and the ability to accelerate rapidly from zero to plenty were still there. He covered the twenty yards from the narrowboat to the bald man in less than three seconds.

Anderson heard the steps and turned, his hand reaching into his pocket for his gun, but Luke was on him before he could pull it out. He was knocked sideways as over 16 stone of muscle and determination barged headlong into his shoulder. As intended, Luke's momentum carried him on and into Greg who was flung against the bridge. There was a loud crack as his head connected with stone.

Maj had also been thrown to one side by the impact, and had one knee on the ground and his hand to his stomach.

"Are you okay?" Luke asked.

"Watch out!" Maj screamed.

Luke turned to see Anderson had staggered to his feet, breathing heavily but with a defiant look on his face and his gun in his hand. He sneered and raised his arm so that the pistol was pointing at Luke's forehead.

"Who the fuck are you?" he said

"I'm his boss," Luke said, gesturing to Maj.

Anderson gave a derisory laugh and, without looking away from Luke, "Greg, come over here."

Luke looked down at Greg who was lying on the floor and immobile. "He's unconscious or worse," he said. "He's not going to be of any use to you."

Anderson shrugged. "I don't need his help." He waved the gun up and down. "I've got this."

"Yes, but I've got a team."

"You call that a team," Anderson said, pointing at Maj. "He's nothing but a lanky black streak of piss."

"There's more than just Maj in my team," Luke said, then added with a smile, "Not forty others like one of my colleagues, but any one of my team is worth a dozen of his."

"What the fuck are you talking about?"

"Glen. He's Head of Security."

"I've heard enough." Anderson turned his gun so that it pointed at Maj. "He's getting it first." He put his finger on the trigger, then hesitated and put his head to one side as he heard something behind him. "What the…"

He started to turn around but was too late. He was hit for a second time, the body that hit him considerably smaller than Luke's but big enough to cause him to fly backwards. The gun flew out of his hand, hit the towpath then fell into the murky water of the canal. Luke fell on Anderson.

"If I was still a policeman," he said as he twisted the other man's arm behind his back, "I'd arrest you and read you your rights."

"Madonna rights is that, guv?" Josh said with a smile.

"If you like, Josh. If you like."

Chapter 55

"I need you to tell me where Sabrina is," Luke said. He jerked Anderson's arm up behind his back and forced him to his feet.

"Not a fucking chance," Anderson said.

Luke spun him around and backed him to the underside of the bridge, his hand against his chest. He was disconcerted to see the other man smiling.

"What's so amusing?" he asked.

"I ain't stupid and it's all set up."

"What's set up?"

Anderson gestured at Maj with his head. "If I don't return then his daughter gets it."

Maj leapt at him and grabbed him by the shoulder. "Where is she?"

"Let him go, Maj." Luke said. "I'll get it out of him. Don't worry."

Maj stepped away from Anderson. "If she gets hurt…"

Anderson was still smiling and looked Maj in the eyes. "She'll get more than hurt," he said and smirked. "Pretty young thing, isn't she?"

Maj lunged again but Luke pushed him back with his free hand. "Stay over there with Josh," he said, his eyes firmly on Anderson, "while I decide what to do with this low-life." He kept his hand firmly against the bald man's chest so that he was pinned to the wall.

"Guv!"

Luke turned around to see two men on either side of Josh. He recognised them as the thugs who had run up the bank before he charged at Anderson. The one on the left was pointing his gun directly at him but keeping an eye on Maj as well. The other had his pistol pressed hard against

Josh's neck.

It was the one threatening Josh who spoke. "Let Mr Anderson go," he said.

"Don't!" Josh said and then flinched as the muzzle of the gun was pushed even harder against the side of his throat.

Luke was left with no option. He pulled his hand away and Anderson ducked to one side then walked quickly over to his men. He gestured to the gun that was pointed at Luke. "Give me that."

The thug obliged and Anderson raised it and pointed it at Luke's forehead. "We've been here before, ain't we?" he said.

"Do you want me to shoot this one?" the thug holding Josh said.

"Nah. Gotta cut our losses and get out of here before others in his fucking brilliant team arrive."

"What about Greg?"

Anderson looked over at the man still and unmoving on the floor. "Oh yeah, Greg," he said. "I almost forgot about poor Greg." He waved his gun at Maj and Luke and gestured towards the narrowboat. "Step back over there."

"We'd better do as he says," Luke said, and he and Maj walked slowly backwards to the stern of the boat.

Anderson kept his eyes on them as he stepped over to Greg and bent to put his fingers against his neck. Still pressing his finger down he looked across at Luke and said, "He's still got a pulse so you didn't kill him you lanky piece of shit."

"He needs to go to a hospital," Luke said.

"No, he don't."

Anderson pressed the gun to Greg's forehead and fired. The sound was deafening and a mass of blood and bone fragments exploded out of the back of his skull. Luke instinctively started forwards but Anderson pointed the gun back at him.

"Stay right there," he said. "As you can fucking see, I ain't afraid to use this." He paused for a second, enjoying the power the gun gave him. "We're going to leave you now. Madame de Pompadour there," he gestured to Josh, "is coming with us. Call it security."

Luke was powerless to do anything. He watched as the four men stepped from under the bridge to the towpath, the gun still pressed to Josh's neck.

"Take him to the car," Anderson said, his eyes on Luke and Maj, the gun unwavering.

Luke could feel Maj tensing beside him. "Don't, Maj," he said.

"Good advice," Anderson said. He backed up the path until he was at the top, then moved the gun slightly to Luke's left and fired before turning and running away.

Maj screamed and Luke turned to see him falling sideways and to the floor.

Chapter 56

Luke bent over Maj who was lying on his side, his hand pressed to his knee.

"I don't think I'm badly hurt," Maj said.

Luke removed Maj's hand from his trousers and saw that they had been ripped by the blast. There was a small trickle of blood and he grasped the torn edges, ripping through the trouser leg before looking closely at what was revealed.

"I think you're right, Maj," he said. "It doesn't look bad but it might need stitches."

Another pistol shot sounded, followed by the sound of a car accelerating and being put rapidly through the gears.

"God, no!" Luke shouted. He stood and raced up the path in the direction the men had taken Josh, his mind working overtime. If they had killed him he was going to make them pay. He would throttle the cocky bastard with his own bare hands if he had to.

When he got to the top he was vaguely aware of a black SUV accelerating through the corner by the pub as he tried to see where Josh had fallen.

But there was no sign of him anywhere.

Then he heard someone calling, the sound getting nearer all the time.

"Guv! Guv! Guv!"

He raised his eyes to see Josh running towards him from the direction of The George. He reached Luke and bent over, panting, his hands on his thighs.

"Are you okay?" Luke said.

"Yes, I'm fine." Josh looked up, still breathing heavily. "They stopped and bundled me out of the car once we were around the corner. Is Maj…"

"He's okay. The bullet nicked him but it's only a graze." Luke paused. "What was the gunshot?"

"That was Anderson. He said he wanted to frighten you, then shot into the air." Josh swallowed. "He's scary, isn't he? I can't believe what he did to his man Greg."

Maj stepped up beside them. "Thank goodness you're okay, Josh."

"What do we do now, guv?" Josh asked.

Luke was about to answer when a silver Mercedes pulled up and Evan climbed out and walked over to them. "I take it your hunch was wrong and they haven't turned up," he said.

"Oh, they have," Luke said. He told him everything that had happened. When he'd finished he said, "I think we know what we have to do now."

"There's no choice," Evan said.

"Josh, " Luke said. "You go with Evan."

"What about Horatio?" Josh asked.

Evan gave him a bemused look.

"It's what he calls his car," Luke said before turning his attention back to Josh. "I think we'll leave that rust bucket here and give you a chance of getting to the destination. I'm sure you'd rather do that than break down in a country lane and spend the evening waiting for the AA."

"I'm not in the AA."

Luke shook his head in despair "That's hardly... Oh never mind." He turned to Maj. "Maj, you come with me."

"I'll give you a call en route," Evan said, "and we can agree on the best approach to take."

Chapter 57

Sam thought long and hard about how to play the evening. If Chris Nevin was indeed Al Ummah's insider in Supracomm, and it was becoming harder and harder to rule him out as time went on, then he was going to read something into every word she said. He would pry too, try to force her to reveal how much she had discovered. And all the while she had to keep calm and ensure she didn't slip up.

It was going to be a game of cat and mouse.

She took a sip of her tonic water and almost spat it out when there was a tap on her shoulder.

"Sorry, Sam," Helen said. "I didn't mean to frighten you." She slid onto the next stool, called the barman over and ordered a glass of Prosecco. "Same for you?"

"No, I daren't," Sam said. "I'm going to have to stay stone-cold sober tonight."

Helen put her hand on Sam's arm. "You'll do fine," she said. "I have every confidence in you."

"I wish I felt the same."

"I've found more about Nevin," Helen said, "but first, spill the beans. You said you'd found out what Audrey Manners was up to in the Storeroom."

Sam reached into her handbag and pulled out an empty navy blue box. She placed it on the bar, smiled and read what it said on the cover. "Trojan Pleasure Pack - Will stimulate you where it counts." It was only when she finished reading that she realised the barman had returned and was staring at her, his mouth wide open. He tore his eyes away and held out Helen's glass of bubbly.

"Thanks," Helen said as she took it from him. She pointed to the box and then to Sam, her eyes still on the barman. "My girfriend's always preferred older women." She winked.

"It's got to be Mike Swithin," Sam said once the barman had left. "They've got back together and they're meeting in the storeroom for you know what."

"I bet you're right, the randy wee buggers." Helen took a sip of her drink. "Here's what I've got on Nevin so far." She put down her glass and retrieved a piece of paper from her purse, unfolded it and laid it on the bar next to the empty condom packet.

Sam read what it said with interest.

- high-flyer
- aged 31
- senior procurement specialist
- Likes karate (instructor), films, reading, travel
- Joined Supracomm three years ago
- Promoted to grade 4 in June last year then to grade 5 this February
- has a daughter (aged 2 or 3?)
- ex-Army

"I'm shocked to see that he's a karate instructor," Sam said.

"I thought you knew that."

"He told me he's just got his blue belt. That's far from skilled enough to be an instructor."

"Did you know about his daughter?"

"No," Sam said. "He told me his wife died in childbirth, but didn't mention the baby survived. I assumed she'd died as well." She paused. "The fact that he's ex-Army is interesting as well. How did you find those last two things out?"

"I didn't," Helen admitted. "I'm not brilliant at social media and I asked Maj to help." She paused. "Why don't you give Maj a call and ask him?"

"Good idea."

Sam rang Maj and he picked up immediately. "Sorry to bother you in the evening, but…" She stopped when she realised she could hear Luke talking in the background. "What's going on, Maj?"

"Luke's on the phone with Evan," Maj said. "I'll ring you back in a minute." She could hear a tremble in his voice as he added, "They've got Sabrina." He ended the call.

Sam stared down at the screen.

"What's up?" Helen asked.

"I don't know." She looked up at Helen. "He said they've got Sabrina."

"Who are 'they'?"

Sam shrugged. "He didn't say. He's going to ring me back." She looked at her watch. "I'm supposed to be meeting Chris in ten minutes at The Alchemist. I need to leave."

"I'll text Maj and tell him to ring me not you, then I'll WhatsApp you."

Sam stood up. "Thanks, Helen."

"As Josh would say, be careful out there."

Sam half-smiled and then turned and left. By her reckoning, the cocktail bar wasn't much more than a five or ten-minute walk which gave her enough time to get her head into gear.

It sounded like Maj's daughter had been abducted, and if that was the case Chris was bound to know about it. Her so-called date was even more important than ever now and she couldn't afford to waste time sitting next to him at The Curzon. No, she had to pretend to be enjoying the bar and their conversation so much that she wanted to skip the film.

Chapter 58

Chris was waiting outside when Sam got to The Alchemist. He bent forward to kiss her on the cheek and then grasped her hand in his. It was all she could do not to pull away.

"Come on," he said and led her into the bar and to a table by the window.

"This is a nice place," Sam said once they were seated.

He looked her in the eyes. "While I was waiting for you I was thinking about what I need to do to get you to tell me everything." He was smiling but this evening she found it sinister rather than attractive.

"You were?"

He laughed. "Let's start with a cocktail. I can recommend their mojito. It's excellent."

"What do you mean tell you everything?"

"I want to know more about you." He grasped her hand tightly and squeezed. "Everything about you." He paused. "So, shall I order two mojitos?"

She swallowed and decided she needed Dutch courage. "Sure," she said and put on her best attempt at a smile. "Why not?"

Chris let go of her hand and walked to the bar to order their drinks. When he returned he reached for her hand again. "Tell me what you've been up to today," he said. "Did you find out everything you needed to find out?"

Sam's phone pinged and she flinched. She should have put it on silent.

"Who's that?" Chris asked. "Not Supracomm-related I hope."

"It'll be my mother."

"Problems at home?"

"No. She's probably asking for advice again." Chris

raised a questioning eyebrow. "Uh, it'll probably be about her investments."

"Investments?"

"Yes, she's trying to decide whether to invest in stocks and shares or not."

"Tell her to be careful. There are a lot of con men out there." He smiled and gestured to her bag. "Don't mind me if you want to see what she's asking."

"No, it's fine, Chris. I'll get back to her later." She was itching to read Helen's message, but it would look too obvious if she went to the toilet straight away.

The barmen brought their mojitos over and put them on the table in front of them. They picked up their cocktails and Chris leaned forward and clinked his glass against hers. "Here's to finding out more about you," he said.

"Right," she said and took a small sip of her drink then put it to her lips and drained about half of it.

"Thirsty?"

"Dry throat." She put her glass down.

"This is nice," he said. "I've been really looking forward to getting to know you better. Tell me, where does your family live?"

No way was she giving him that information. "The other side of the country," she said, and decided to turn the conversation around. "What about yours? You told me your wife died in childbirth. Did the baby…"

"She survived," he said and a wide smile creased his lips. At that moment she found it impossible to believe he could be working for terrorists. "My daughter will be three in a couple of months. Her name's Clarissa."

"What a pretty name. Does she live with you?"

"No. I went to pieces afterwards and I was in no fit state to look after a baby. My sister took her in. I see her regularly of course." He looked Sam in the eyes again. "It's awful when your daughter is taken from you."

Sam shivered. Was he alluding to what had happened to Maj?

"I need to visit the ladies' room," she said, deciding she couldn't bear to wait any longer. "I think it's the mojito." She tried to laugh but it was brittle and weak.

"Sure," he said and stood up, ever the gentleman. "Don't worry. I'll still be here when you get back."

She walked to the toilets, relief pouring over her when she found a vacant cubicle. She locked the door, pulled her iPhone out of her bag and clicked on Helen's WhatsApp message.

'Sabrina's been abducted,' it read, 'but we don't know where she's being kept. Luke, Evan, Maj and Josh are heading for Unit 7. It will take them thirty minutes to get there. Luke wants you to see if Nevin knows anything about it.'

Sam typed a response. "I will do what I can. Keep me updated." She sent the message, put her phone on silent and then flushed the toilet. Another woman was at one of the sinks when she came out so she gave her hands a quick wash before returning to their table.

"I've ordered you another mojito," Chris said when she sat back down. "Is that okay?" He was smiling again.

This time she looked him in the eyes but didn't smile back. The message from Helen had convinced her that there wasn't time to pussyfoot around. There was no doubt he was dangerous but she was in a bar and it felt safe. Okay, there weren't a lot of customers but there were a few and a couple of bar staff too.

"What's wrong?" he asked. "Is it your mother?" He tried reaching for her hand again but this time she pulled it away.

"I know what you're up to," she said, her voice cold.

"You do?" He paused. "How?"

"You threatened Mike Swithin."

"You saw that!" He looked genuinely shocked.

"It was caught on CCTV."

Chris hesitated before replying. "I had to. He let me down. He was letting us all down."

"Did he refuse to cook the books for you? Was that what it was, Chris?"

He raised an eyebrow. "You genuinely don't know what he was doing, do you?"

"Please tell me."

"I'll do better than that," he said, and he was smiling again.

He reached into his pocket.

Chapter 59

"It's just going to be the four of us then," Maj said.

"Looks like it," Luke said. "We'll plan the details at the petrol station." He looked at the clock next to the speedometer. "It's eight now so they could well have finished for the evening. Even if they have, there's still the chance Chris Nevin let's something useful slip while he's with Sam."

"Maybe. It seems like a long shot though."

Luke thought the same but he didn't want to say it. The truth was that Sabrina was in immense danger and they needed to get to her quickly. Anderson was one of the scariest men he had ever come across, and in his police days he'd encountered a fair few.

"It's along here on the left," Maj said.

Luke pulled into the forecourt of the Esso filling station to find Evan already there, leaning against the side of his Mercedes, his phone to his ear.

"Where's Josh?" Luke asked.

Evan pointed his finger to the building next to the kiosk and mouthed 'Toilet'. A few seconds later he ended his call. "I've had my guys check the video feeds," he said, "and it looks like there are three men still inside Unit 7." He turned as he heard Josh approaching. "Five went in around 2 pm and two of them left at around 6:30 and haven't returned."

"Did they say if a large man with a dreadlocked beard was one of the ones who left?" Josh asked.

"He's still in there."

Josh turned his attention to Luke. "I wonder if he's the boss, guv," he said. "He's not got the looks to be charming women out of their savings."

"Good thinking, Josh," Luke said. "Any of your guys going to be here in time to help, Evan?"

Evan shook his head. "Unfortunately not."

"And I don't suppose you have a gun?"

He shrugged his shoulders, "Sorry. They're not standard issue."

"We've got one more man than them and we've got the element of surprise," Luke said. "We're going to have to make our advantage count. And if all three come out at once, and I suspect that's highly likely, we can't afford for any one of them to get away." He hesitated. "I don't need to tell you that Maj's daughter's life may depend on it. Here's what I suggest we do."

He explained his proposal and gained their agreement then said, "I need to make one phone call then I suggest we make our move."

Chapter 60

Anderson paced up and down the hall of Number 42 muttering expletives and giving vicious looks to the thugs who had driven him back from Bathampton. Both men stood against the wall trying to avoid eye contact.

"This is a clusterfuck!" he screamed and slapped his palm against the wall before turning to the two men. "Did one of you idiots lock the bitches in?"

The slightly older of the two nodded. "I did it, Mr Anderson," he said. "They're upstairs in their room."

Anderson grunted. "We've got to get 'em out of here." He was talking more to himself than to them. "Take 'em to London or Birmingham or up North. Too many prying eyes around here now." He raised his voice. "Where the fuck is Stefan? You!" He pointed to the younger man. "Ring him. Make sure he's on his way."

"He said he was leaving straight away," the man said.

Anderson marched over, poked him in the chest and put his face up to his. "Did I ask for a fucking debate?"

"No, Mr Anderson."

"Then do it. Christ all-fucking-mighty!"

The man retrieved his phone from his pocket but before he could call up the number the front door opened and Stefan Kaplinski walked in.

"Everything okay?" he asked.

"No, it ain't. Where's the girl?"

"I locked her in my boot."

"Good. Now listen. I'm gonna give you a chance to prove yourself, Stefan. This operation needs moving out of Bath but I want you to take it on."

Stefan could barely hide his delight. "You won't regret it," he said. "What about Greg?"

"Don't you worry about him. He's decided not to come back." He hesitated. "You gotta prove yourself though."

"Not a problem, Mr Anderson. Anything."

Anderson turned to the thugs. "You two, upstairs. This is confidential." He waited until they were out of earshot then turned back to Stefan. "You gotta finish the girl."

"What, the one…" Stefan pointed back to the door.

"Yeah, her. Who else would I be talking about, dumbfuck?"

"You want it to look like an accident?"

"No. I wanna send a message. Make sure those fuckers know not to mess with me." He glared at the other man. "You up to this?"

"No problem," Stefan said and Anderson could swear he almost smiled. "What do you want me to do?"

"Up to you. Send a photo to me and to this number." He passed the other man a piece of paper. "And make sure the photo shows the story. Got it?"

"Sure. Whose number is this?"

"That's my business. Do it soon."

"This evening?"

"Yes, this fucking evening." He poked Stefan in the chest. "And don't let me down. Is that clear?"

"Yeah."

"Go on then." Anderson gestured to the door. "And don't take too long. I want this done."

Chapter 61

Helen was still in the bar where she'd met Sam, cradling a glass of orange juice and trying to work out what she should do. Luke, Maj and Josh were a hundred miles away but Sam was around the corner. There had to be a way of helping her.

She shivered as she thought of the danger her friend was in. Sam was meeting a terrorist who more than likely knew what she was up to. What if Nevin had already confronted her, taken her somewhere or even hurt her?

She made a decision and called the barman over.

"My friend went to a cocktail bar called The Alchemist," she said. "Do you know where it is?"

He looked at her sympathetically. "You might be best cutting your losses if she's dumped you," he said.

"Aye, right." She repeated her question. "Do you know where The Alchemist is?"

He smiled. "You turn right out of here, left onto Speedwell Street and take the second or third turn on the right. I think it's Greyfriars Street."

"Thanks." She passed him a twenty-pound note as she climbed off her stool. "Is that enough?"

"Ample. I'll get your change"

"It's okay. Keep it."

"Thank you. And good luck with your girlfriend."

"Aye, I think I'll need it."

She left the bar and followed his directions. Five minutes later she turned onto Old Greyfriars Street and saw the sign for The Alchemist ahead on the left. She hesitated but only for a second. Nevin had never met her and Sam was shrewd enough not to flinch when she saw her. She would go in, find a table with a view of them and watch carefully.

If they were still there and he hadn't already taken Sam somewhere else that was.

Helen opened the door, walked in and immediately felt out of place. The clientele were without exception twenty or more years younger than her. Ah well, what the hell.

She looked around and spotted Sam sitting alone at a table by the window, her back to her, and sighed with relief. She was in time. But where was Nevin? She ordered a virgin bloody mary at the bar and then found a table where she had a good view of her friend's table. As she sipped her drink she realised that Sam looked incredibly tense. She was sitting bolt upright and kept pulling her hand through her hair

She thought of going over, but if he returned…

A man passed her table and walked over to Sam. He stopped, put a firm hand on her shoulder, bent down and whispered into her ear. He had to be Nevin.

Sam looked up at him, her eyes wide and staring, and shook her head. It looked like he was telling her to do something and she was resisting. Was he threatening her or one of her family? Helen wanted to intervene but knew that could make the situation worse.

Nevin walked to the other side of the table and sat down, enabling Helen to see his face for the first time. His eyebrows were furrowed and he was leaning forward as he talked. He was speaking too quietly for her to make out what he was saying but it was clear that he was angry. At one point Sam tried to say something but he held his hand up to stop her and Helen heard him this time as he almost shouted, "No! You listen to me."

The situation was heating up and Helen was pleased she was there. If he tried to do anything to Sam she would wade in and show him she meant business, all eight stone of her.

Chapter 62

Luke's biggest concern was that one or more of the men was armed. The biggest of them, the one Josh thought might be the boss, was the main worry. It was unlikely the scammers would have guns but if the giant was indeed the main man they had to be extremely careful. He had agreed with Evan that he would tackle him while Evan took the other two with Josh and Maj's help.

Unit 7 was the left-hand unit in a block of four. Luke looked over at Josh and Maj who had positioned themselves around the corner so that they were out of view of anyone leaving. He had confidence in both of them, but Maj's frame of mind could cause problems. He was upset and would do anything to secure his daughter's freedom. As a result, he might take unnecessary risks.

He and Evan were crouched behind a skip outside the unit opposite. It meant they were thirty or more yards from where the men would emerge which diluted the element of surprise. They would have to move quickly.

The big question was whether all three men would leave the building at the same time. It would be much more straightforward if they came out one at a time.

"When's your guy due?" Evan said in a hushed tone.

Luke looked at his watch. "He should be here," he whispered. "I've told him to park at the Estate entrance."

A light came on behind the glass door to Unit 7.

"Let's go," Luke hissed.

Both men stood up and Luke put his arm around Evan's shoulders and slumped forwards. They stepped past the skip and along the road until they were directly in front of Unit 7. The door clicked open and a man in his late forties emerged. As he did so Luke stumbled and fell to the ground.

"Bugger!" Evan exclaimed. He called over. "Excuse me, would you mind giving me a hand? My colleague's banged his head and I'm trying to get him to my car so that I can take him to the hospital."

The man looked up. "What happened?"

"We've been working late and he tripped and fell. I think he'll need stitches."

The man grunted, suspicion etched on his face. "Where do you work?"

Evan pointed to his Mercedes which was parked at the end of the opposite block about a hundred yards away. "At Marshall's printers in Unit 4. I'm Robin Marshall and that's my car parked outside."

"Right." The man grudgingly accepted what he was saying and walked over to Evan's side.

"If you get his right arm, I'll get his left," Evan said.

As the man bent down Luke swivelled onto his back and swung his arm at his legs, knocking them from under him. As the man fell Evan grasped him from behind by the hair and put his hand over his mouth. He leaned forward to his ear and hissed, "Don't say a word."

Luke stood up, took his phone out of his pocket and clicked on the top number in his list of recent calls. It was answered straight away. "Bring them to Unit 4," he said, then gestured for Josh and Maj to come over. "This is the guy who called himself John and conned Eleanor out of her savings.," he hissed, trying to keep his voice low. "Grab his arms. I want to ask him some questions."

Their prisoner put up no resistance and looked defeated and more than a little scared as they led him away from the building. "Who are you?" he said. "Are you with the Delaneys?"

Luke knew the Delaneys. They were a father and son who ran drug operations in Bristol and were known for their violent tempers. "To make things simple I'm going to call you John," he said, "and I need you to answer a few questions. For starters, when are the other two coming out?" he asked.

"What other two?"

"Don't mess with me, John," Luke said. He towered over the smaller man and there was real menace in his voice. He bent down and grabbed the man's shirt beneath the lapels with both hands. "When are they coming out?"

"I, uh, I don't know. They were finishing up with a few emails. Twenty minutes perhaps."

There was a noise from behind and Luke turned to see Detective Inspector Pete Gilmore walking towards him, his eyes fixed on their captive. "I don't want to know what's going on, Luke," Pete said, "but this had better be good. My career's on the line here." He handed over three sets of handcuffs.

"And the van?" Luke asked.

"On its way."

"Thanks. I owe you."

"Too bloody right you owe me. Ring me later." He shook his head and then turned and walked back the way he had come.

Luke jerked their prisoner around, fastened the handcuffs to his wrists behind his back then twisted him back to face him again. He bent down and the man tried to back away but Josh and Maj had his arms again. "What do you know about Anderson?" he asked.

"Nothing. I've heard of him but I've never seen him."

"Do you know what other operations he runs?"

"Not really."

Luke clasped his hand around the other man's jaw. "Not really isn't good enough, 'John'. Tell me everything you know."

Luke was towering over him now and even Josh felt intimidated. "I'm pretty sure he runs at least one brothel," John said. "Danny and Laurie travelled back from Poland last week with a bunch of girls and Anderson was there to meet them when they arrived."

"Where's the brothel?"

"I haven't the faintest."

"And what about Greg?"

"Never heard of him."

"Josh, Maj - take him to Evan's car. I want both of you to stay with him and keep him quiet. The others could come out at any time. There'll be time for more questions later."

Josh and Maj led their prisoner to Evan's Mercedes. Maj opened the back door and Josh put his hand over the man's head as he bundled him into the back seat. "There you go," he said, the corners of his mouth turned up in a wide smile. "Just like in the movies." He climbed in beside him and looked up at Maj, "Are you getting in the other side?"

"No, I'm going back to help Luke and Evan."

"Didn't Luke say both of us were to stay with him?"

"Yes, he did,"

Maj turned away and headed back towards Unit 7.

Chapter 63

Stefan couldn't take the little bitch looking at him any more. He had gagged her to stop her moaning and now she was alternately sobbing and staring, tears running down both cheeks

"Fuck, I can't be doing with this!" he shouted.

He grabbed a tea towel and walked over to where she was sitting, her hands tied behind the back of an old wooden chair. Her eyes widened as she realised what he was going to do and she started shaking her head from side to side. He grasped her hair and pulled hard until she stopped and then stretched the blindfold tight around her head. She tried to scream through the gag so he tightened that as well.

He returned to his armchair. Taking her to his house had been a mistake. No one had seen him bring her in, he was sure of that, but it meant he had to get her out again. There was a large rug across the floor of the upstairs bedroom, perhaps he could put her in that.

He should have taken her to a park and done it there. He was stupid, fucking stupid.

She was still shaking her head. Sobbing too, though at least he didn't have to watch her eyes now. Those eyes would haunt him for the rest of his days.

He thought about what Anderson had said. 'Make sure the picture tells the story'. That wouldn't be difficult. She already looked scary enough with most of her face hidden by the blindfold and gag. A bit of blood on her face and she'd look like fucking Carrie.

Stefan smiled, pleased with what he planned to do. The girl wasn't going to like it but it would all be over quickly. She wouldn't have to suffer for long. He was smart and he was cunning and managing drugs and girls was what he was good at. And when he had to be brutal with people he was good at that too.

Anderson had also said not to take long. That wasn't a problem either. With her fucking sobbing and whimpering the sooner he got this over with the better. All he had to do was prove himself and he was in. It was all going to be worth it.

He wondered whose phone number Anderson had given him. It had to be someone he wanted to send a strong message to. It could be someone senior in the police, he supposed. Somebody who was already on his payroll that he wanted to keep in check. Yes, that made sense.

Stefan came to a decision, pushed his hands down on his thighs and stood up. It was time to get to work. Much as he wanted to put it off, there was no point in delaying any further.

The miserable bitch's whining stopped when she heard him move and she turned her head to follow the sound of his footsteps as he made his way to the kitchen.

Once there, Stefan inspected the rack of knives and chose the smallest. He pulled it out and pressed it to the index finger of his left hand. A spot of blood appeared and he smiled. It was plenty sharp enough.

He returned to the lounge and edged towards Sabrina. She pressed herself back against the chair as she heard him approach and he felt her trembling as he bent to kneel next to her. Taking in a deep breath to compose himself for what he was about to do, Stefan lifted the blindfold over her head. She turned to look at him and he raised the knife to her throat, trying to ignore her staring eyes as he pierced the skin with the tip of the blade.

Chapter 64

The conversation had become less heated and Nevin was almost smiling now. He said something and then stood up and walked in the direction of the toilets. As soon as he was out of sight Sam pulled her phone out of her bag, clicked a couple of buttons then put it to her ear.

Helen heard the dulcet tones of Auld Lang Syne and looked down to see Sam's name on her now-vibrating phone. She hesitated for a second and then accepted the call.

"Hi Sam," she said. "I'm actually…"

Before she could finish Sam said, "It's not him."

"What?"

"Chris isn't the plant."

"I'll come over." Helen hung up and walked the few paces to Sam's table. "Hi," she said as she tapped her on the shoulder, earning a surprised look from Sam. "I've been over there for about twenty minutes," she added, indicating the table she had been sitting at. "I wanted to keep an eye on you in case he tried anything."

"Are you her chaperone then?"

Helen turned to see Chris Nevin standing behind her, a perplexed look on his face.

"This is Helen," Sam said. "She's a work colleague of mine."

"And a friend," Helen said.

Sam smiled. "And definitely a friend. Chris, I think you need to sit down."

He sat down and Helen pulled a chair across from a neighbouring table and joined them. "So where have you two got to on the explanation front?" she asked.

"Chris told me why he was threatening Mike Swithin

and it makes sense given what I found in the Storeroom." Sam reached into her bag and pulled out the empty condom packet and placed it on the table.

"I'm close friends with Mike's wife," Chris said. "We went to school together, so when I found out he and Audrey Manners were meeting for sex I confronted him. I told him I'd tell executive management and end his career if he didn't break up from her."

"I see," Helen said. "And how much has Sam told you about what we're investigating?"

"Not very much. I'm at a bit of a loss as to what the hell is going on, to be honest. When Sam confronted me about Mike and told me about studying CCTV footage of me, well, I kind of lost my rag." He half-laughed. "It's almost as if you two are spies."

"We kind of are," Sam said.

Chris opened his mouth in horror. "Tell me you're joking."

"She's not joking," Helen said.

Chris's eyes were on Sam. "So when you agreed to come out with me it was all a ploy? A way of finding out more about me?"

Sam swallowed and reached for his hand but he pulled it away. "I like you, Chris," she said. "I really do."

"Let's go back to the beginning," Helen said. She looked at Chris. "I think we owe it to you to tell you everything." She turned to Sam "Do you agree?" Sam nodded her head.

"Chris," Helen went on, "I can only tell you if you agree to be bound by the Official Secrets Act."

"Bloody hell." He looked at Sam then back at Helen. "Are you serious?"

"Deadly serious."

"Well, okay then. Yes, I agree to be bound by it."

Helen told him everything, from the initial request for someone to look at abnormal accounting practices at

Supracomm to their meetings with Evan and the discovery of romance scammers and what appeared to be sex trafficking. "It's come to a head in the last 12 hours," she concluded. "The daughter of one of our team has been abducted by the man who we believe is behind it all."

"God, that's awful," Chris said. "If there's anything I can do to help…"

"There is actually," Sam said.

Chapter 65

Luke wasn't happy that Maj had returned but understood why. His daughter had been taken and the last thing he wanted was to be sitting in a car twiddling his thumbs.

The trouble was that they had now spent a further fifteen minutes waiting behind the skip and Maj was becoming increasingly restless. "What about the guy who's with Josh?" he said. "Should we see if he knows anything else?"

"He won't," Evan said.

"How can you be sure of that?"

"Evan's right," Luke said. "He's a minion in the operation. The guy with the dreadlocked beard is our best bet."

An engine sounded behind them and Luke turned to see a van driving towards them, the word 'POLICE' emblazoned on the bonnet in large blue letters. "Shit," he said. He stood up and ran to the driver's door.

The window was lowered as he approached and a gruff voice shouted, "Are you DI Gilmore?"

"For heaven's sake be quiet," Luke hissed. "I'm Luke Sackville. You'll have passed DI Gilmore on your way in."

The man lowered his voice. "I was told there were some men to be taken to the custody centre."

"There will be. Can you return to the entrance, find the DI and wait with him? I'll let him know when you need to come back."

The officer shrugged. "I suppose so." He reversed his vehicle.

Luke ran back to the others. "Maj, can you get that guy's keys." He gestured towards the Mercedes. "I'm worried the two inside heard or saw the van."

Maj ran to the car and a few seconds later returned with a small bunch of keys.

"This is a hell of a risky approach to take," Evan said.

"We've got to go in," Luke said. "If they've heard or seen us and they contact Anderson…"

Evan nodded. "I guess you're right."

"Hopefully, we've still got surprise on our hands. Maj, you and I will tackle the big man. Evan, you take the other one."

Luke walked to the entrance, unlocked and opened the door as quietly as he could and stepped through, the others immediately behind him. To either side were two steel doors with the entrance to Unit 7 on the left. He inserted the most likely key into the lock and it gave a satisfying click as it turned.

"Are you ready?" he whispered.

They nodded.

Luke pressed the handle, pushed the door and stormed in, screaming "Lie on the floor or we'll shoot," at the top of his voice.

The men inside looked around in shock. The smaller of the two was sitting in front of a laptop, the other standing behind him. Josh had been right. He was massive.

Their hesitation only lasted for a split second. The larger man reached into his trouser pocket and pulled a pistol out. He raised his arm but Luke charged into him and there was a deafening boom as the gun went off, the bullet slamming harmlessly into the ground.

There was a yelp and Luke was vaguely aware of Evan wrestling the smaller man to the ground, but his focus was on the giant who had rocked backwards but stayed on his feet and was raising his pistol hand again. This time it was Maj who was on him, grabbing him by the wrist and twisting and pushing with all his might. The big man snarled and swung his other arm, his fist targeting Maj's jaw, but Luke smashed into his shoulder before it could connect. This time the impact was too much and the giant fell to the ground, the pistol flying from his hand as his elbow hit the floor.

Luke swung his own fist and there was a satisfying crack as it connected with the man's nose. The giant tried to get up but Luke pinned him by the arms.

"I've got his gun," Maj said from somewhere behind him.

Luke stood and backed up to stand beside Maj. He took the gun from him and pointed it at the big man's face. "Glock 21 so I'm guessing there are twelve rounds left. Adrenaline's got me wired so I wouldn't make any sudden movements if I were you." He turned to Evan, who had the other man in a neck hold. "Everything okay?"

"No problems." He released his grip and shoved his captive in the back. "Lie next to your friend."

The man obliged, looking like a midget when he lay on his back next to the other man.

"I'm going to need some answers," Luke said, "and I'm going to need them quickly."

"Fuck off," the giant said.

Luke pointed the gun at the man's knee. "I'll start with an easy question. What's your name?"

The only response was a vicious stare and a sneer. Luke fired and the bullet caught the edge of the man's grubby denims. "The next one connects," he said. "What's your name?"

"Alex."

"Right, Alex. First off…"

Luke stopped mid-sentence as Maj screamed "No! No!" behind him.

"What is it," Luke said, his eyes still on the men on the ground.

"It's Sabrina." The distress was evident in his voice. "He's killed her."

Chapter 66

Anderson had to admit that even he was a little horrified. He hadn't been sure Stefan would do what he had asked, but the photo was proof that he'd done the deed. It would serve the fuckers right but the girl must have been through hell to end up looking like that.

The imperative now was to get out of Bath pronto. Once they'd got over the shock, that big bastard and the girl's father would redouble their efforts to find him. He couldn't afford to waste any time.

He called upstairs. "Are they away?"

"Yes, Mr Anderson," came a voice from the upstairs landing. "They're locked in their room."

"Good. Come down here." The man trotted downstairs. "Where are the other two?"

"They're fetching the van."

"Why the fuck does it take two of them?"

"I think they wanted to…"

Anderson put his hand up to stop him continuing. "Have you ever heard of a rhetorical question?" he shouted.

"You mean it's old?"

"That's historical," Anderson sighed. "For fuck's sake, have you got peanuts for brains?" The thug opened his mouth, but he held up his hand to stop him. "I don't want an answer, you moron." He looked at his watch. "When did they leave?"

`Anderson waited but the man just stared back at him blankly. After a while, something clicked and he said, "Oh, do you want me to answer that one?"

"Yes, I fucking want you to answer that one."

"They left about fifteen minutes ago."

Anderson grunted. The van wasn't far away so they shouldn't be long. He got his phone out and rang Stefan.

"What's taking so long?" he snapped when the call was answered.

"I've been clearing up," Stefan said. "Making sure nothing can be traced back."

"When will you get here?"

"I've just left. Got half a dozen black bags to dispose of on the way but should be there in fifteen minutes, twenty tops."

Anderson shook his head when he hung up. Stefan was one ruthless bastard, a man after his own heart. He would go far.

Chapter 67

Chris had been working for Supracomm for several years and knew just about everyone. They had discussed Mike Swithin and Audrey Manners in depth but agreed there was no longer any reason to suspect them.

"What about the other senior managers?" Sam asked. "Surely it has to be someone high up to have the access needed."

"I'm not senior and you thought it was me," Chris said.

"True, but you did leaf through my notebook when I was away from my desk."

He blushed at this. "You know my reasons."

"Back to the point," Helen said. "If it's not Mike or Audrey who else could it be?"

"It has to be someone who's been employed for Supracomm for a while," Sam said. "And not necessarily senior but someone with access to key financial systems."

Chris made a list of the senior team. There were eight. "We've said we can rule out Mike and Audrey," he said. "And we can rule Oliver Knight out too. He came across when Supracomm outsourced to Filchers so he hasn't been here long enough." He crossed the three names out. "That leaves the other five. Of course you know Ron Young, Sam."

"I certainly do," Sam said, shivering as she remembered the feel of his hand on her shoulder.

Helen looked at the list. "And I've met Tommy Ashcroft, the Contracts Manager," she said. "What about more junior staff?"

"It can't be anyone reporting to Audrey in the call centre," Chris said, "They don't have access to any of the key financial systems. However, it could be any of Mike's team. He's Lead Accountant and his staff need access to all systems to pull together the annual report."

"How many report to Mike?" Helen asked.

"Five. Sam, you met Anne and Mary when we had lunch with them." He added them to the list, thought for a moment then added three other names.

Sam looked at the list. "We've got ten possibles so far. Anyone else?"

"I don't think so," Chris said. "I'm pretty sure their insider is one of these."

Sam shook her head. "I took an immediate dislike to Ron Young, but other than the fact he's creepy as hell there's no evidence he's our man."

"It's a long list," Helen said. "How are we going to..." She paused mid-sentence as a thought struck her. "Hang on a moment."

"What is it?" Sam said.

Helen looked up at her friend. "I've just remembered something someone said." She smiled. "We were talking about deep-fried Mars bars."

"Eh?" Chris said.

Helen pointed to a name on the page. "That's our man," she said. "I'm sure of it."

Chapter 68

The first thing DI Gilmore noticed when he walked in was the two men with their hands handcuffed behind their backs. Evan had the Glock and was pointing it at them.

"I got your message, Luke," Pete said. "The van's outside." He spotted Maj who was sitting on one of the chairs with his head in his hands. "What happened to him?"

Luke lifted Maj's phone and showed it to him. "He's just been texted this image."

"My god!" Pete said when he saw the screen. "What a mess. Do you know who it is?"

"It's Maj's daughter." He took the phone back and held it up so that the bearded man, Alex, could see the photo.

"That's nothing to do with me," he said, shaking his head.

"This is Anderson's work," Luke said. "She was a schoolgirl, only thirteen years old." He paused. "Where is he?"

"I don't know, do I?"

"Where does he keep the girls?"

"What girls?"

Even though Alex was a giant, as broad as he was tall, Luke still had two or three inches on him and the man flinched when he saw the look on his face.

Luke spoke slowly and deliberately. "I'm not going to take any more shit," he said. "Do you understand?"

There was still no response.

Luke leaned forward and dialled the menace up to eleven. "I'm going to ask you one more time. Where does he keep the girls?"

Alex sighed. "Number 42."

"What's the name of the road?"

"I can't fucking remember. He just calls it Number 42."

"Not good enough."

Alex hesitated but another look from Luke was enough. "It's something like No Mash Terrace."

"That'll be Beau Nash Terrace," Pete said from behind them. "It's one of the roads between The Royal Crescent and The Circus. Do you want me to get some cars up there?"

Luke looked at his watch. It was a fifty-minute drive from the Sheppey Industrial Estate to the centre of Bath and they had no time to waste. "Yes, Pete," he said. "You had better line up the Armed Response Unit to go with them as well. Once you've done that you can charge these two and their friend outside."

His phone rang and he looked down to see 'number withheld' on the screen. He stepped away from the others and accepted the call. "Luke Sackville."

"Evening Luke. How's your face looking these days?" The man's voice was rough and it took a moment for Luke to place it then the memories came flooding back.

"Stefan Kaplinksi?" he said.

Stefan laughed. "You thought you was so fucking clever that day but poor old Vinny taught you a lesson, didn't he?"

"What do you want, Stefan? Much as I would love to have a reunion I'm kind of busy right now."

"I can give you Anderson."

Luke's ears pricked up. "What?"

"There's conditions."

Of course there were conditions. Stefan's sort never did anything for nothing. "What do you want?"

"Immunity from prosecution."

"No deal. We know about number 42 and armed police are heading there now."

Stefan laughed again. "He's long gone. You may be big mate but you're too fucking slow."

"Why do you suddenly want to help?"

"He's murdered Greg, ain't he? I heard all about that and I can't risk him doing the same to me. He's a fucking lunatic and I need out. All you gotta do is get the high-ups to agree and he's yours. You'll find his girls with him too."

Luke hesitated, but only for a second. "I'll see what I can do."

"Good. Once you've had the buy-in we need to meet face to face."

"Why?"

"You'll see. Where are you?"

Luke didn't see any harm in telling him. "Wells."

"The Sheppey Industrial Estate by any chance?" Stefan chuckled and when Luke didn't respond he went on. "Meet me in Radstock, that's about halfway. There's a Co-op Funeral Shop in the centre which is kind of appropriate." Another chortle. "Come alone and park outside where I can see you. And get the Chief Constable, or whoever the fuck it needs, ready to be on the phone. I want his personal guarantee I won't be charged with nothing."

The line went dead.

Luke didn't know if he should trust Kaplinski. It was over twenty years since Luke had been key to his arrest, but was it possible he still held a grudge and this was all a ruse to get his revenge?

Pete walked back into the room. "All sorted," he said. "They're on their way to Number 42 now."

"Good," Luke said. "We need to talk. I've just taken a very interesting call." He looked over at Evan. 'You too, Evan."

Pete turned to his sergeant and told him to charge Alex and the other two men and take them to the custody centre. When he'd finished he followed Luke and Evan outside.

Luke led them across to the block opposite and told them about his conversation with Stefan Kaplinski.

"Do you really think he can deliver Anderson?" Pete asked when he'd finished.

"It's all we've got," Luke said. "It's worth a shot."

"Why face to face though?" Evan asked.

Luke shrugged. "He'll have a reason."

"I'll speak to the DCC," Pete said. "See if I can line up the immunity from prosecution."

"Are you going to meet Kaplinski on your own?" Evan asked.

Luke nodded. "I think it's safest. But can you bring Maj and Josh and stay somewhere out of sight just in case?"

"In case of what?"

"I'm not sure, but I don't trust him one iota."

Chapter 69

Anderson stood watching as the women were hustled into the back of the lorry. All four were quiet, even the mouthy older one. The stupid bitches hadn't understood anything he'd said, and yet he'd cowed them with his words. Fucking hell, he was good at this.

Once they were securely in Birmingham he would find someone to manage that part of the operation. He or she, he wasn't sexist, had to be a whole lot tougher. There wouldn't be any more of this free-time bollocks for a start. Greg had been much too soft. It cost a lot to get the girls over from Eastern Europe and they needed to earn their keep, not wander around enjoying themselves. Over a week they'd been here and there had been a grand total of two punters.

Stefan Kaplinski would have been ideal given his experience of running street girls and his ruthlessness. The edges of Anderson's mouth turned up as he remembered what Kaplinski had done to the black girl.

That idea was shot though. The bastard had done the dirty on him and he would pay, and pay good. Just as well he'd learned never to trust anyone. Fuck, most of the time he didn't even trust himself.

Planting a listening device in Kaplinski's car had been a smart move. Okay, the bug hadn't picked up what the other person was saying but one end of the conversation had been enough. He even knew where they were meeting.

He realised the three men were standing in a line in front of him and staring expectantly.

"What's up?" he snapped.

"Shall we go, Mr Anderson?" It was peanuts-for-brains who spoke. "I thought one of us in the back and the other two in the cab."

"Why not more in the back where the girls are?"

"We can't have all three of us in the back."

"I know that, numbnuts." Anderson paused and spoke his next words slowly. "How many do you need to drive the van?"

"One, Mr Anderson."

"So why not two in the back?"

He could almost see the cogs turning as the idiot worked his way through this. "Yeah," he said eventually. "That would work."

"Are you related to Einstein by any chance?" The man's mouth opened and Anderson held his hand up. "No, don't answer." He sighed before continuing. "I've got something to do. I want you to stop at Michael Wood and wait for me there. And before you ask it's the name of a fucking service station on the M5 not a member of the public.'

He walked to his Audi where he googled Co-op Funeralcare in Radstock and then entered the postcode into his SatNav.

Chapter 70

Luke was halfway to Radstock when his phone rang.

"Luke Sackville."

"Hi Luke, this is Shirley Davenport. DI Gilmore rang me about this guy Kaplinski. He says he's well known to us and did a spell inside a couple of decades ago. Has he stayed on the right side of the law since then?"

"I very much doubt it. I had a couple of run-ins with him and he's a nasty piece of work. He's cunning too, and I suspect he's been breaking the law at every turn but clever at avoiding capture."

"If he's a persistent offender then why should I grant him immunity from prosecution?"

"Believe me, Shirley, the man he says he can lead us to makes Stefan Kaplinski look like Winnie the Pooh. His name's Anderson and I've seen him kill someone in cold blood."

"Yes, I heard from DI Gilmore what he'd done to his man Greg. And you think Kaplinski is being straight with you?"

"To be honest I don't know, but I think it's worth a shot."

"Okay, Luke. I'm going to trust you on this. Ring me when you're with him."

Luke drove through Midsomer Norton and then down the hill towards the Centre of Radstock. He spotted Co-op Funeralcare on the right and used the roundabout to turn around. He parked outside as Kaplinski had requested and almost immediately saw Evan's Mercedes coming toward him. It passed by without slowing and in his rear-view mirror he watched as it turned right at the roundabout, presumably with the intention of parking around the corner.

Luke sat and waited. Five minutes passed, then ten. He was beginning to give up hope when a small Peugeot van pulled up behind his BMW. A thin man in his early to mid-fifties stepped out and darted up to Luke's door.

Luke lowered the window and was struck by how little the years had changed Stefan Kaplinski. His hair was grey now and receding at the temples, but it was just as long and stringy and his face was as cratered as ever.

"Get in the van," Kaplinski said. "And bring your phone." He ran back to the driver's side and clambered in while Luke went to the passenger door.

"What have you got for me?" Luke asked

"A couple of things," Kaplinski said, and there was almost glee on his face. "A way of capturing that fucker Anderson for starters. But first, ring the geezer who's gonna guarantee me immunity."

Luke rang DCC Davenport and Kaplinski snatched the phone from him before it was answered.

"Davenport," she said when she picked up.

"Who are you?" Kaplinski rasped. "What's your job?"

"I'm Deputy Chief Constable Shirley Davenport. I take it you're Stefan Kaplinski?"

"Too fucking right, darling." He laughed but it came out as more of a wheeze than a chortle. "You giving me immunity?"

"I am."

"And I'll have that in writing?"

"Of course." She paused. "It's conditional, of course."

"On what?"

"On us capturing this man Anderson."

It was Kaplinski's turn to hesitate. "Fair enough," he said after a moment's thought. "Nice speaking to you."

The line went dead.

Kaplinski turned and there was a broad and apparently genuine smile on his face as he handed Luke his phone back. "I've got a surprise for you, big man," he said, and then his head exploded.

Chapter 71

Luke was momentarily deafened by the explosion and closed his eyes as blood and pieces of flesh splattered into his face. He blinked them away and became aware of someone speaking but the voice was hollow and almost inaudible, as if it was coming to him through thick pillowcases pressed against his ears.

He forced his eyes open and saw the grinning face of Anderson at the now smashed driver's window. Kaplinski was slumped to the side of his seat, the right side of his face obliterated.

"I might have known it would be you, you fucker," Anderson said. He raised the gun, pointed it at Luke's face and then disappeared down and out of view. There was a clatter as his pistol hit the road and then shuffling and expletives and finally the satisfying sound of a fist connecting with a jaw.

A face appeared at the window again, but this time it was thirty years younger and with considerably more hair and one less gun. "We've got him, guv," Josh said. He was smiling but it disappeared and his complexion turned ashen when he spotted Kaplinski's body. "Shittedy-shit-shit," he said. "Where's his face gone?"

Luke leapt out of the car and around to the other side to see Anderson lying front down on the floor. Maj was standing a couple of paces away rubbing his bruised knuckle while Evan was fastening handcuffs around Anderson's wrists.

"Is he unconscious?" Luke asked.

"No, I fucking ain't," came a voice from the floor.

"You killed my daughter," Maj said.

"She shouldn't have meddled," Anderson said. "Anyway

it wasn't me. It was Kaplinski what done the deed." He let out a snort that was almost laughter. "The man with no face made her the girl with no face."

"You bastard!" Maj started to move towards him but Josh held his hand up to stop him. "What was that?" he said, his hand to his ear.

Luke shook his head, his hearing still at half-cock.

"I didn't hear anything either," Maj said.

"There it is again," Josh said, and there was a tremor in his voice. He raced to the back of the van and threw open the doors. "I knew it!" He reappeared and gestured with his hand. "Maj, come here, quick!"

Maj followed him and peered into the van. It was dark and it took a few seconds before he realised what was in there.

It was Sabrina's eyes he saw first. They were wide and staring and a cloth was stuffed in her mouth.

Maj jumped up and into the van, pulled the gag out and then untied the ropes that bound her wrists and ankles. She leapt into his arms and he hugged her tighter than he had hugged anyone in his life, the tears flowing freely again, but this time tears of happiness.

Sabrina was also sobbing and Josh silently stepped away from them and back to Luke and Evan. "Best leave them to it," he whispered as he rubbed the moistness away from beneath his eyes.

Chapter 72

Tania was on edge, adrenaline firing through her veins. She had heard part of Anderson's conversation with the three men taking them to Birmingham and it was clear that they were not, as they said in Ukraine, the brightest bulbs in the chandelier. This was her best chance, perhaps her only chance. She had to take matters into her own hands and act quickly.

But how? They were big beefy guys so she couldn't achieve anything physically. Would seducing them work? Perhaps she could offer them sex and, while their attention was on her, rely on the other girls to take advantage and attack them.

She felt nauseous at the thought of even flirting with these monsters. Was it really the only way?

She looked around at the others and realised that it wouldn't work anyway. Izabella had withdrawn into herself, something she seemed to be doing more and more, and the two German girls weren't much different. There was no light behind their eyes, and their half-hearted attempt at joviality a few days earlier was long forgotten.

What options did that leave? There had to be a way, had to be. All four of them would be scarred forever by what had happened, but at least they would have a life if they could escape.

And this journey probably presented the best chance she was going to get.

They were all thrown to one side as the lorry stopped suddenly and then started to move backwards and turn. It dawned on Tania that the driver was reversing into a parking space.

After a few seconds, the engine was turned off and the

fluorescent light brightened for an instant before weakening again. In that moment she saw something glint in the corner next to the two thugs. She stared at it for a second. If she could grab hold of it, then perhaps…

It was now or ever. She needed to use their intelligence, or rather their lack of it, to outwit them.

She stood up.

"Sit down," one of the thugs said and glared at her. He was on one of two wooden chairs, the other man seated next to him. The women had been told to stay on the floor opposite, their backs to the side of the vehicle.

She walked over to stand in front of him. "I heard Mr Anderson call you peanuts-for-brains," she said. "Is it a British compliment?"

"I said sit down."

The second man echoed him, his voice slightly deeper and even slower. "Yes. He said sit down."

She edged sideways so that she was in front of him. "What about you?" she asked. "If he's peanuts-for-brains does that make you pretzels-for-brains?"

He looked at her blankly.

"Actually," she went on, "pretzels are more complex. Do they more brain cells than peanuts or less?"

This was too much for either man to cope with.

"Sit down," they said in unison.

"I mislaid my necklace."

"Uh," Peanuts said, struggling to cope with the sudden change of topic.

"Yes, it is solid and thick and I lost it. Have you seen it anywhere?"

The two men looked at each other and then back at her.

"Ah, there it is," she said, and pointed to one corner of the lorry. As if watching a tennis match, both men's heads swung in unison to follow her gaze and she leapt to the opposite corner and reached down for what she had seen lying there.

"Found it," she said, as she turned back to face them. "I'm not sure if it is as solid and thick as you two though."

They looked at what she was holding and started to stand but she was too quick. She swung hard and the solid iron coupling whipped across Peanuts' nose and then into Pretzels' jaw.

They both grunted in pain. Peanuts was bleeding profusely and he fell back into the chair, grabbed his nose with his hand, then yelped as the pain hit him. Pretzels continued rising despite the pain so she swung again, this time catching him across the side of his head. He staggered back, fell over the chair and off the front of his fellow thug onto the floor.

Tania darted to the back of the lorry and reached for the lever, but just as she got there the door swung open to reveal the driver standing outside. He stared at her for half a second before his eyes flitted to the other two men, one lying prone on the floor and holding the side of his head, the other seated but clutching his bleeding nose and trying to stem the flow with his sleeve.

"What the fuck?" he yelled. He jumped onto the lorry in one leap.

Tania swung her arm back but he was too quick and charged into her, his weight sending her barrelling to the front where she crashed into the steel partition that separated the cargo area from the cab. She managed to stay upright but the chain had fallen to the floor and in that split-second she knew all was lost. An image of her mother flashed through her mind.

"I'll fucking kill you, you bitch," he screeched and bounded towards her, fists raised. She raised her hands to fend him off but he was massive, well over six feet tall and almost twice her weight, and she knew she didn't stand a chance.

He sneered, flattened his left hand and pushed her chest so that she was pinned to the wall. Then he drew his right arm back, his hand still in a fist. He towered above her and she drew a deep breath as she tried to prepare herself for the pain when he hit her.

"You deserve this, you mouthy cow," he said, but instead of punching her he smirked and pushed his entire body into hers.

My god, she thought, not this. Was this monster going to force himself on her and rape her? She had to push him away but he was so big, so strong.

He was staring into her eyes, his face a mask of evil. "I'm going to give you...AAHHH!"

He let out an almighty scream before pulling his hand from her chest, putting it to his throat and staggering backwards.

Tania was shocked to see a much smaller hand pressed to his neck. It was covered in blood and was twisting and tearing at his skin. He grabbed the hand and pulled it away before swinging around to look down at his attacker. Tania looked past him to see Izabella, wide-eyed and staring, wiping her bloodied hand across the side of her skirt.

The thug reached for Izabella but before he could take hold his legs gave way and he fell to the ground with a resounding crash, blood pumping from the artery in his neck. Just visible through the spray was the pearled end of Izabella's hairpin sticking out from his skin.

She turned to see Peanuts starting to get up from his chair. He was almost standing when the chain crashed into his nose for a second time causing him to flop back down with a loud whimper. The taller of the German girls almost smiled as she stood over him, holding the chain in both hands as if she was about to throttle him with it.

"Nimm das, du Arschloch," she said, and somehow Tania knew she wasn't calling him darling.

"We have to go," Tania said.

The German girls were quick and immediately leapt off the back of the cargo bay. Izabella hadn't moved and was staring at the prone body of the man on the floor.

"Come, Izabella," Tania said. "Quickly."

She grabbed the girl's hand, pulled her to the rear and then pushed her off the lorry before jumping off herself. She immediately saw that the other two girls had run to one of a number of lorries parked a few yards away. Tania followed and saw first one man, then a second and finally a third, clamber down from their cabs. They were all big men, rough-looking, their arms covered in tattoos.

Let them be nice, she thought. *Please God, give us a break.*

She turned to see one of the two thugs clambering out of the rear of the van. It was Pretzels, the one who now had a broken jaw. She grabbed Izabella and pulled her close.

"What's going on?" the nearest truck driver said. "Has that man hurt you?"

"Will you help us?" she asked, trying to keep her voice from quavering.

"Of course."

"Then please call the police."

Chapter 73

Luke walked into the Ethics Room and was greeted by a standing ovation from his team, Sam and Helen having returned from Oxford the day before.

"We all wanted to say what a fantastic job you did, guv," Josh said. He shook him by the hand.

Helen followed suit, then Sam stood on tip-toes to peck him on the cheek.

She stepped back and Luke put his hands in the air. "I appreciate the thanks," he said, "but this was a team effort all the way."

"Aye, but we wouldn't have got anywhere without your leadership," Helen said.

Maj was last and he went for a full-on man-hug. "I can't thank you enough," he said.

"How's Sabrina?" Luke asked.

"Amazing. She's having counselling but she's a strong girl and she's doing really well."

"And what about where Kaplinski cut her?"

"She'll have a small scar." Maj smiled before continuing. "Nothing to match yours mind."

Luke automatically put his hand to the scar on the left side of his face and grimaced. "Just as well for her."

"What exactly happened?" Sam asked.

"Kaplinski never intended to kill her," Maj said. "He wanted her to be genuinely scared and gave her a real cut for the first photo. Once he'd done that he produced a container of pig's blood and told her his plan. She told me that the rest of the photos were staged."

"He was a nasty piece of work," Luke said, "but cold-blooded murder was a step too far even for him. I believe that when Kaplinski found out Anderson had killed both

Jeremy Scott and Greg he feared for his own life if he didn't agree to kill Sabrina. His intention was to fake it and then shop Anderson to the police in exchange for immunity from prosecution."

"What about the Eastern European women?" Sam asked. "Have you heard how they are?"

"They're physically fine and can't wait to go home," Luke said, "but those women went through hell and it's going to stay with them for the rest of their lives. Tania was incredibly strong and it was only through her bravery that they got away. She was the oldest, but having said that she's only twenty-three. Maj, you spoke to her yesterday didn't you?"

Maj nodded. "Evan gave her my number and she rang me at home," he said. "She was embarrassingly grateful and you're right, Luke, her courage was incredible." He blinked away the tears as he remembered Tania's raw outpouring of emotion. "Sorry," he said with a half-laugh. "It really got to me talking to her."

"It makes what we do worthwhile, though, doesn't it?" Sam said.

"It definitely does," Maj said. "She can't wait to be home with her family and we agreed to stay in touch. Sabrina's going to keep in contact with Izabella too." He swallowed. "Tania told me she's only fifteen."

There was silence while they all reflected on this.

"What about Al Ummah, guv?" Josh asked after a minute or two had passed. "Has Anderson given the police any names?"

"One name," Luke said, "but he knew him only as Mr Rasul and they never met face-to-face. Evan doesn't think they'll be able to track him down."

"And where are we at with Al Ummah's insider?"

"Helen and I have got a meeting to confront him in…" Luke looked at his watch. "Five minutes. It shouldn't take long and then all of us are going home for the day."

"Wicked," Josh said. "The day off."

"On one condition," Luke went on. "You all meet me for a drink in the Saracen's Head this evening at seven."

There were no objections.

Luke and Helen made their way to the Executive Floor where Evan and Pete Gilmore were already waiting outside.

"He's already with Mr Filcher," Gloria said. "You're to go straight in."

Luke led the way, opening the door without knocking. Filcher was seated behind his desk and looked to be in the middle of a long story. The man opposite was trying hard to conceal a yawn.

Filcher stopped when he heard them enter. "Good," he said and looked at his watch. "About time. Need to get on." He looked at the man opposite. "I'll finish telling you later."

"Pleased to meet you," Luke said, holding out his hand. "Tommy Ashcroft, isn't it? I'm Luke Sackville."

Tommy shook his hand. He appeared confused. "What is this?" He spotted Helen. "Oh, hi."

"Hi," Helen said.

"This is Evan Underwood from MI6," Luke said, and Evan leaned forward to shake Tommy's hand. "And this is Detective Inspector Pete Gilmore." Pete did likewise.

Tommy looked more bewildered than ever. He turned back to Filcher. "What's going on?"

"Important meeting," Filcher said. "Me leading but need them." He waved his hand around at the others. "It was 'need to know', and I didn't." He paused then tapped the side of his nose. "But I do now."

"Pardon?"

"Please can you explain everything to Tommy, Helen?" Luke said.

"Indeed," Filcher said. "Over to you, Helen." He sat back and crossed his arms across his chest.

Helen sat in the seat next to Tommy. "When you showed me around," she began, "you mentioned the sub-contract reviews that were initiated by Oliver Knight eighteen months ago."

"Yes. What of them?"

"We were led to believe he only became Client Director a couple of months ago when Filchers' bid was successful."

"Aye, he did, but that was on the back of his two years seconded from Filchers to Supracomm to head up Procurement."

Helen and Luke exchanged a look.

"Is that important?" Tommy asked.

"Pivotal," Helen said. "So, does working on those sub-contract reviews absorb most of your time?"

Tommy laughed. "100% of my time more like. Oliver's a nice guy but he was adamant we drop everything else to concentrate on them and he can be a pretty hard task master. I get home late at least twice a week., and it's the same for my team."

"So what happened to the main contract between Supracomm and Filchers? Were you involved in drafting it?"

"Initially, yes, but after the first draft Oliver could see it was stretching us even further and he brought in an external consultant to finalise it."

"Geoff Morgan?"

Tommy looked at her in surprise. "Yes, that's him. He emailed me a few times with questions of detail but we never actually met. He worked remotely and Oliver was great, briefing Geoff and then handling everything himself. I'm really glad he did. We were overloaded as it was."

"Geoff Morgan wasn't his real name," Luke said.

Tommy looked at him in astonishment. "What do you mean?"

"His real name is Malik Habib and he works for Al Ummah."

"Who?"

"They're an international terrorist organisation."

"What?" Tommy shook his head. "Please tell me you're joking."

"This is a long way from a joke," Evan said and Tommy turned to face him, visibly shocked by what he had just heard. "Working with my colleagues in the police," Evan went on, nodding to Pete Gilmore as he said this, "we managed to trace Malik Habib from the emails that he sent you and Oliver Knight. He and Oliver were working together."

"You mean Oliver…" Tommy's voice trailed away as the enormity of what he'd just heard hit him.

Filcher's phone buzzed and he pressed the button. "He's arrived," Gloria said.

"Right," Filcher said. "Good. Ah…" He looked at Luke who nodded, walked to the door and opened it.

"Hi, Oliver," he said. "Please come in."

"Hello Luke," Oliver said. He was smiling as he walked in, but his smile faded when he saw the number of people in Filcher's office. He turned back to Luke. "I thought this was a meeting about security at Supracomm."

"In a way it is," Luke said. He gestured to the two men standing against the wall. "This is Evan Underwood from MI6 and this is Detective Inspector Pete Gilmore from Avon and Somerset Police."

Oliver looked at each of the men in turn. "MI6 and the police." He laughed. "What on earth is going on, Luke?"

"The game is up," Luke said. "We know everything."

"What do you mean?" He tried to laugh again but it was hollow this time.

"Why did you do it, Oliver?" Luke asked. "What made you work for an organisation like Al Ummah? Was it because you believe in their cause?"

Oliver snorted, and in that instant his previous bonhomie vanished, replaced by a sneer that told Luke everything.

Pete Gilmore stepped forward and Oliver turned to

face him.

"Oliver Knight," Pete said, "I am arresting you on a charge of aiding and abetting Al Ummah in the commissioning of terrorist acts. You do not have to say anything, but it may harm your defence if you do not mention when questioned something which you later rely on in court. Anything you do say may be given in evidence."

Chapter 74

Luke parked his car in the Charlotte Street car park and headed towards Queen Square. His phone rang as he reached the Frances Hotel and he looked down at the screen to see it was his brother calling.

"Hi, Mark," he said.

"Hi," Mark said. "How's work? Not too dull for you after the police?"

Luke thought back to the events of the previous few days and smiled to himself. "We keep busy," he said. "How are you?"

"I'm afraid the welcome-back-to-the-UK party is off."

Luke tried to conceal the delight in his voice as he said, "Oh dear, I'm sorry to hear that."

"Erica's changed her mind," Mark hesitated for a moment. "She's being a tad challenging."

No surprise there, Luke thought, but said, "Is it something to do with her daughter?"

"No. It's just Erica being…"

"Erica?"

"Yes, I guess so. Anyway, sorry to be the bearer of bad news."

"No problems, Mark. Speak soon."

Luke hung up, a beaming smile across his face as he walked into the Saracen's Head. It was quiet and he grabbed a table at the back of the pub. A few minutes later Maj, Helen and Sam walked in.

"Did you make it up with Chris, Sam?" Helen asked once they had all sat down.

Sam cast a fleeting glance at Luke before she answered. "Yes," she said. "It turned out he told me he was a blue belt because he didn't want to appear big-headed."

"So you're dating again?"

Sam nodded. She was aware that her cheeks were now ever so slightly pink and was keen to change the subject. To her relief she heard footsteps and turned to see Josh walking towards them. He was smiling from ear to ear.

"Why are you so pleased with yourself?" she asked.

"It's Leanne," Josh said. "She's forgiven me for what I did with Mandy."

Helen's face grew serious and she raised a questioning eyebrow. "You surprise me, Josh, you really do.," she said. "I didn't have you down as someone who plays the field."

"I don't!" he squeaked. "I didn't do anything with Mandy, but Leanne…" He looked around at the others imploringly and then back at Helen. Realisation dawned as he saw the corners of her mouth turn up.

"Sorry, Josh," she said. "I couldn't resist."

Luke decided to come to his rescue. "I've got some good news as well," he said. "They've identified and frozen an account the romance scammers were using and it looks like Eleanor and Pam are going to get most of their money back."

"That's great, guv," Josh said.

"Right," Luke said. "My throat's dry. What are you all having?"

They told him and he went to the bar to place the order.

When he returned with their drinks Maj asked, "How did it go with Oliver Knight?"

"He admitted everything," Luke said. "To be honest he had no choice and bringing him to justice is down to what Helen and Sam unearthed."

"The first clue," Helen said, "was when Luke told me how Knight had said the Comms Sector Head had given him a rough time on profit margins. I spoke to her and she was adamant she'd never done any such thing."

"So then," Sam said, "I took a fresh look at some of

the suspect invoices and I found his initials on several of them. When I went through them the first time I had assumed it was anonymous rubber-stamping by some clerk or other. It didn't occur to me that 'OK' might be someone's initials."

"And finally, we spoke to Robert Entwhistle," Helen said. "He told us he had to force Knight to instigate an investigation into the accounting anomalies. It was him that resisted not Audrey Manners and Mike Swithin."

"The police obtained a warrant on the back of what Helen and Sam found out," Luke said. "They dug into Oliver's emails, then into his bank accounts and it soon became clear what he was up to."

"Was he doing it because he believed in what Al Ummah stands for?" Maj asked.

"No. He did it for money, pure and simple."

Sam laughed. "You'll like this bit," she said. "Knight only agreed to the investigation when he found out it would be the Ethics Team looking into it. He didn't think we'd be up to the task."

"They're rubbish, that wee Ethics Team," Helen said. "Or as we say in Scotland, nithin ba Wally-Dugs."

Luke raised his pint. "To the Wally-Dugs."

"To the Wally-Dugs," the others said, and they all clinked glasses.

Thanks for reading Black Money. I would really appreciate it if you could leave a review on Amazon at:

www.amazon.co.uk/gp/product/B0C9LXLCP8

Want to read more about Luke Sackville and what shaped his career choices? 'Change of Direction', the prequel to The Luke Sackville Crime Series, can be downloaded as an ebook or audiobook free of charge by subscribing to my newsletter at:

sjrichardsauthor.com

Acknowledgements

Thanks to my wife Penny for her support and encouragement throughout my writing journey. She gave me fantastic (and constructive) feedback after my first draft.

After editing for Penny's comments, I had tremendous input from seven beta readers: Lauren Cooke, Denise Goodhand, Keith Innes, Sarah Mackenzie, Irene Paterson, Marcie Whitecotton-Carroll and my wonderful daughter Abby Davies.

Thanks also to the advance copy readers, who put faith in the book being worth reading.

Samuel James did a fantastic job narrating the audiobook and Olly Bennett came up trumps again with the excellent cover design which brought Number 42 to life exactly as I envisaged it.

Last but not least, thanks to you the reader. I love your feedback and reading your reviews, and I'm always delighted to hear from you so please feel free to get in touch.

FOG OF SILENCE

Luke Sackville is asked to investigate celebrity parties by a whistleblower at GNE, a global news and entertainment company. Two of his team go undercover and piece together a frightening picture of depravity and wickedness.

Luke is shocked to discover that celebrities are using their fame to exploit and abuse fans. He takes the evidence to GNE senior management but they refuse to take action.

Little does he know that what they have uncovered is only the tip of the iceberg. A serial killer is taking advantage of the culture of secrecy and no one is safe.

Released February 2024 - Order your copy now

www.amazon.co.uk/gp/product/B0CG4PV8S8

ABOUT THE AUTHOR

Let me start by saying that my name's Steve. I've never been called 'SJ', but Steve Richards is a well-known political writer hence the pen name.

I was born in Bath and have lived at various times on an irregular clockwise circle around England. After university in Manchester, my wife and I settled in Macclesfield before moving to Bedfordshire then a few years ago back to Somerset. We now live in Croscombe, a lovely village just outside Wells, with our 2 sprightly cocker spaniels.

I've always loved writing but have only really had the time to indulge myself since taking early retirement. My daughter is a brilliant author (I'm not biased of course) which is both an inspiration and - because she's so good - a challenge. After a few experiments, and a couple of completed but unsatisfactory and never published novels, I decided to write a crime fiction series as it's one of the genres I most enjoy.

You can find out more about me and my books at my website:
sjrichardsauthor.com